BY MARY HIGGINS CLARK
AND CAROL HIGGINS CLARK

Dashing Through the Snow *He Sees You When You're Sleeping*

Santa Cruise *Deck the Halls*

The Christmas Thief

BY MARY HIGGINS CLARK
AND ALAFAIR BURKE

You Don't Own Me *All Dressed in White*

Every Breath You Take *The Cinderella Murder*

The Sleeping Beauty Killer

BY ALAFAIR BURKE

The Better Sister *If You Were Here*

The Wife *Long Gone*

The Ex

THE ELLIE HATCHER SERIES

All Day and a Night *Angel's Tip*

Never Tell *Dead Connection*

212

THE SAMANTHA KINCAID SERIES

Close Case *Judgment Calls*

Missing Justice

MARY HIGGINS CLARK
& ALAFAIR BURKE

PIECE OF MY HEART

**SIMON &
SCHUSTER**

London · New York · Sydney · Toronto · New Delhi

First published in the United States by Simon & Schuster, Inc., 2020
First published in Great Britain by Simon & Schuster UK Ltd, 2020

Copyright © Nora Durkin Enterprises, Inc., 2020

The rights of Mary Higgins Clark and Alafair Burke to be identified as
authors of this work have been asserted in accordance with the
Copyright, Designs and Patents Act, 1988.

1 3 5 7 9 10 8 6 4 2

Simon & Schuster UK Ltd
1st Floor
222 Gray's Inn Road
London WC1X 8HB

Simon & Schuster Australia, Sydney
Simon & Schuster India, New Delhi

www.simonandschuster.co.uk
www.simonandschuster.com.au
www.simonandschuster.co.in

A CIP catalogue record for this book is available from the British Library

Hardback ISBN: 978-1-4711-9729-1
Trade Paperback ISBN: 978-1-4711-9730-7
eBook ISBN: 978-1-4711-9731-4

This book is a work of fiction. Names, characters, places and incidents are either a
product of the author's imagination or are used fictitiously. Any resemblance to actual
people living or dead, events or locales is entirely coincidental.

Printed and bound in Great Britain by CPI Group (UK) Ltd, Croydon, CR0 4YY

MIX
Paper from
responsible sources
FSC® C020471

To my dear readers, who gave me
a lifetime of encouragement.

"Approach your lives as if they were novels,
with their own heroes, villains,
red herrings, and triumphs."

—Mary Higgins Clark

PIECE OF MY HEART

Prologue

Five Years Ago

"*If I only could, I'd make a deal with God.*"

Roseanne Robinson heard that old song lyric playing at the back of her mind as she tried to do precisely that—make a deal with God. *Please, I'll be a better wife. I'll be a better person. I'll do good deeds every single day for the rest of my life. Anything if you spare my husband. Let me be with him again.*

She raised her head from her ongoing prayers when she spotted a doctor in surgical scrubs emerge through the double doors into the hospital waiting room. She held her breath expectantly, but her hopes fell when he locked eyes with an older woman in the corner who had been wiping away intermittent tears since Roseanne arrived. A sorrowful wail followed only seconds later.

That poor woman, Roseanne thought. *Please don't let that be me.*

Roseanne was only thirty-one years old but could not imagine life without her husband. They had started dating during college, and then remained serious while he launched his architectural career and she added accounts to her digital marketing agency's growing roster of clients. He had bought the motorcycle three years earlier, two weeks after their second wedding anniversary.

That stupid motorcycle. That's what brought us here.

She had made her disapproval clear. She even appealed to his older brother, Charlie, thinking a police officer would talk some sense into him. But instead, she had gotten a lecture from her brother-in-law about "letting a man be happy."

Despite the risks, part of her had been relieved at the time by the purchase. For months, her husband had seemed distracted. Inattentive. Bored. She wondered if he disapproved of her decision to go back to the agency, if only part-time. She wondered if he enjoyed being a father. Worst of all, she wondered if maybe their marriage was fundamentally broken. But once he had that motorcycle, he seemed more like his usual happy, charming, and hilarious self. Apparently whatever early midlife crisis her husband had experienced had been fixed by a shiny new two-wheeled gadget. *It could be worse,* she had told herself.

But now here she was, waiting to hear how his surgery had gone.

The police officer who called her had reported the news with icy detachment. There had been an accident, he explained. A delivery truck had blown through a red light. The motorcyclist—her thrill-seeking husband—was unconscious, even though he had been wearing a helmet, as she had implored him to do, so many times.

She looked at her watch. 11:55 A.M. Bella would be out of preschool in five minutes. Their neighbor, Sarah, would be picking her up along with Sarah's own daughter, Jenna. Bella would enjoy an afternoon playdate with her best friend, but at some point, she'd want to know where her mother and father were.

Please, God. How can I possibly explain to my daughter that Daddy won't be coming home?

Another doctor emerged through the double doors—this time

a woman, her hair still covered by a blue surgical cap. "Roseanne Robinson?" she called out.

This was it. Her and Bella's futures would turn on whatever news was about to be delivered. They'd either keep rolling down the path that was their current life, or find themselves on an entirely different route. Door Number One or Door Number Two.

She rose from her chair. "I'm Roseanne Robinson."

Or Ro-Ro, as most of her friends called her. That nickname had been the primary reason she kept her maiden name when they married. *If you live, my love, I'll even change my last name, the way you always wanted me to.*

"Please, just tell me," Roseanne pleaded. She squeezed her eyes shut, bracing for the impact of a pronouncement that would change her life forever.

"Your husband's alive."

The hug that followed was automatic, a pure display of the gratitude Roseanne felt in that moment.

The doctor outlined the treatments that would follow—additional skin grafts, physical therapy, rehabilitation. As Roseanne absorbed every last piece of data and envisioned every single medical appointment, she could not stop thinking about how lucky she felt. Her family had been spared.

But as the weeks and months passed, reality would set in. The rehab. The recovery. The resentment. Life would not go on, at least not as they had once known it. Every day would bring another domino, toppling forward.

Then one day, five years later, she'd get a phone call to learn that all the dominoes that had fallen would end with a little boy named Johnny Buckley.

Wednesday, July 15

Day One

Chapter 1

Laurie Moran flinched at the sound of yet another horn honking, this time from the pickup truck behind them.

From the driver's seat, Charlotte Pierce glanced in the rearview mirror and threw up a frustrated hand. "I don't know where he expects me to go."

Laurie held her breath momentarily while the delivery truck in front of them blasted out a dark cloud of exhaust.

It wasn't even noon yet on a Wednesday, but the Long Island Expressway was at a standstill as city dwellers lined up in search of a beach respite from the sweltering streets of Manhattan. The two-hour drive to the Hamptons would be three for them today and creep up to a four- or five-hour commute by Friday evening.

Unfazed by the surrounding snarl, Charlotte sang along blissfully to the Janis Joplin song that was playing on the radio. *"Take another little piece of my heart now, baby—"*

She flashed a grin toward her passenger. "Aaaah, the glamour of the LIE in mid-July."

Charlotte had bought this car—a new Mercedes convertible—only a month ago and was still reveling in the novelty of cruising with the top down. She wore big, dark, round sunglasses and had tucked her chin-length bob tightly behind her ears for the car ride.

Laurie could see that behind the shades, Charlotte was looking past Laurie to the car in the right lane.

"That guy next to us is checking you out, my friend. Poor dude doesn't know that you're about to be a married lady."

On instinct, Laurie turned her head. The driver of the SUV was in fact smiling in her direction. She quickly looked away.

"Please, he's staring at us because of this music. He knows we'll need hearing aids by the time we reach our destination."

The comment only made Charlotte turn up the volume even more. "*Take it!*," she sang, swaying her shoulders with the music. The deep, satisfied laugh that followed was infectious, and when traffic began to move again, Laurie found herself smiling and singing along with her friend.

She had more than her fair share of reasons to celebrate. In four days, she would marry Alex Buckley, who had spent more than two years convincing her that he could be part of her busy life as a widow and working mother. After a small ceremony at the church for their families and closest friends, then a dinner reception at one of their favorite restaurants, they would head to Italy for a ten-day honeymoon. She had not only made room for Alex in her life; they were starting an even better life together.

It had been Charlotte who had talked Laurie out of the idea of a "family honeymoon." The private trip with Alex would be the first time she had ever been away from her ten-year-old son, Timmy, for more than a couple of nights. In lieu of the post-wedding family trip, though, she and Alex had planned a three-day stay on the east end of Long Island for their immediate families to celebrate Alex's fortieth birthday in the days leading up to the actual wedding.

For the getaway, they had chosen the South Shore Resort & Spa in the Hamptons, right on the water. Joining Laurie, Alex, and Timmy would be Laurie's father, Leo; Alex's brother Andrew and his wife and three children; and of course Ramon, who insisted on calling himself Alex's butler but was more like a surrogate uncle to them all by now. To help with the children, they had also invited Timmy's favorite babysitter, Kara.

Laurie's plan had been to leave the city early that morning with Alex, Timmy, and Ramon until the world decided to interfere. She was the producer of *Under Suspicion,* a news-based reality television show that reinvestigated cold cases. She had everything ready to start filming her next case special once she returned from Italy. Eight years earlier, a journalist named Jonathan Brown had simply vanished. According to Brown's wife, Amy, he was meeting with an anonymous source about potential fraud at a pharmaceutical company. When police were unable to confirm the existence of any such meeting, public suspicion shifted toward Amy. Brown was never found, either dead or alive, and Amy was never charged.

After a year of trying to contact former employees of the pharmaceutical company, Laurie homed in on a researcher who was killed in a hit-and-run car accident only one week after Brown went missing. Even more intriguing, the researcher's widow, Carrie, told Laurie that he had been anxious about something at work in the weeks before his death. When Laurie asked Carrie whether her husband had known a reporter named Jonathan Brown, Carrie had looked confused until Laurie reminded her that Brown was a reporter who had disappeared a week before her husband's car accident.

Carrie's face had gone white.

"No," she said. "Or at least, I never thought so. But I remember him shaking like a leaf when a news report came on saying that this journalist had gone missing. I asked him why he was so upset, and he said something vague—like it was sad that someone with a family could just disappear."

Laurie was convinced that the dead researcher had been Brown's anonymous source. She had been planning to use what Carrie and

Amy knew about their husbands to pressure the pharmaceutical company to answer her other questions.

She felt a nudge on her left forearm. "Hello? Earth to Laurie." Traffic was moving again, and Charlotte turned down the radio so they could hear each other. "You look worried. Why are you worried? You have all of the logistics for Alex's birthday locked down like clockwork. The wedding and honeymoon, too. Your mind went back to work, didn't it?"

Indeed, it had. She had woken up that morning to find late-night emails from both Carrie and Amy, declaring a "change of heart" (Carrie) and a "panic attack" (Amy). Both of them, on the same night, had suddenly changed their minds about the investigation. Neither would be appearing on *Under Suspicion*.

Laurie had spent most of the morning trying to reach both women by every means possible. She had been planning to continue her efforts during the drive to the Hamptons, but just as Ramon was loading their bags into the trunk of the car, she received back-to-back emails again. This time, they were from two different lawyers, requesting that she cease all efforts to contact their respective clients, Carrie and Amy. Whether the women had been threatened or bribed, the implication was obvious. Someone had gotten to them. Laurie had no choice but to pull the plug on a production that was supposed to start as soon as she returned from her honeymoon.

At her insistence, everyone else headed to the beach while she delivered the bad news to her boss, Brett Young. Two hours later, she had gotten nowhere with him. He was insisting that she find another case in order to keep the show's current airdate. The only turn of luck she'd had all morning was that Charlotte had a summer house in East Hampton and had been planning to drive out that evening anyway. Charlotte had used Laurie's dilemma as an excuse to leave early.

"You've done everything you can," Charlotte assured her. "You can't bring two men back from the dead. You reported what you knew to the police, and that's all you can do. And if their wives took a payoff from the pharmaceutical company, that's on them. You can't set yourself on fire trying to keep other people warm, Laurie."

Laurie knew her friend was right, but she still wanted to do more. Laurie's first husband, Greg, had been shot in cold blood when Timmy was only three years old. She could not imagine any amount of money or intimidation that could have kept her from seeking answers about his death.

"You'll find another case," Charlotte said. "You always do. But you're getting married in four days, my friend. How are you feeling about *that?*"

"Honestly?" Laurie leaned her head back against the passenger seat and enjoyed the feeling of the sun on her skin. "I almost feel guilty about how happy I am with Alex. Does anyone deserve to have this much joy in their lives? It's like I'm sure the other shoe's about to drop."

Charlotte scoffed. "That's my friend, Laurie 'Gloom and Doom' Moran. You don't have to apologize for happiness. You're going to have three glorious days on the beach with your family and Alex's. And then Sunday, the two of you start a brand-new life together. You deserve to enjoy every second of it."

Laurie could imagine Greg telling her the same thing.

When they pulled into the parking lot, Laurie felt the stress of the office melt away. The South Shore Resort & Spa was bright and white and modern. It was also on the best beach in the Hamptons, almost all the way to Montauk. She smelled salt in the air and heard the roar of waves from the ocean and chirps from seagulls circling above. She spotted Alex and Timmy beside a green minivan at the front entrance to the hotel. Alex's younger brother, Andrew, and his family had apparently arrived just moments earlier from Washington, D.C.

She watched as her son, Timmy, like a perfect young gentleman, opened the front passenger door for his future aunt, Marcy. Then the sliding back door opened, and seven-year-old Johnny jumped out and hugged Timmy as Uncle Andrew helped his four-year-old twin daughters from the van. Timmy had already begun calling Andrew's three children his "little cousins."

Charlotte tapped the horn of her convertible lightly with a short *beep beep* to announce their arrival. When Alex looked up, she saw that his nose already had a touch of color from the afternoon sun, and his dark hair was windblown. He broke out into a broad smile.

Charlotte feigned an enamored swoon. "Look at your guy, Laurie. I'd say the feelings there are mutual."

Laurie returned his smile. Charlotte was right about Alex and the work that would be waiting for her in two weeks. Until then, she was going to focus on her family.

Amid the joyous greetings, no one noticed the white Chrysler that pulled into the resort parking lot as Charlotte drove away.

Chapter 2

From the back deck of the South Shore Resort, Marcy Buckley looked out at the ocean and took in a deep breath of salty air. It felt good to stand after spending more than seven hours in the minivan. They had left D.C. before dawn to try to make it to the Hamptons in time for lunch. God bless Johnny for his willingness to keep his twin sisters entertained, but she would leave this world a happy woman if she never heard another round of that "Baby Shark" song again.

Now that they were at the hotel, Emily and Chloe had shifted whatever focus two four-year-olds could muster from their big brother to Alex's fiancée, Laurie. Laurie had accompanied Marcy to take a quick look at the beach with the kids while Andrew and Alex handled the check-in process. The twins tugged at the linen of Laurie's white wide-legged pants, eager to tell her the mystery story they had made up the previous night for her benefit, about a puppy who gets left home when the family goes on vacation. The girls had always been enthralled by their Uncle Alex, a well-known criminal defense attorney who was regularly in the news and on TV. When he had agreed to become the host of a series called *Under Suspicion*, oh, how they had begged to watch.

They were even more excited once they met Laurie, who explained that she also worked on the show, not to mention her NYPD-honcho father. Marcy knew it was normal for children to think other adults were more exciting than their boring old parents, but sometimes Marcy wanted to point out that she and Andrew weren't exactly chopped liver. Andrew was a sought-after commercial litigator in D.C., and Marcy had been a successful actress for five years after she graduated from college in California. But to Johnny and the girls, she was always *Mommy*, and, after everything they had gone through to have a family, that was perfectly fine with Marcy.

While the girls were fawning over Laurie, Johnny was riveted by Laurie's ten-year-old son, Timmy. Three years younger, Johnny had been referring to Timmy as his "cool cousin" since the moment he had heard about the engagement. Now she watched as the two boys threw a Nerf football back and forth near the shoreline. Although they were about to become cousins by marriage, they could easily have passed as siblings. Like Laurie, Timmy and Johnny had straight honey-colored hair and fair skin, whereas she, Andrew, and the twins were all dark waves and olive tones. It made Marcy happy that Johnny would finally have some family members who looked more like him.

"We want to play, too," Chloe squealed. Emily looked up at Marcy with pleading dark brown eyes. The two of them had always charged ahead as a single unit, but of the twins it was easier to get Emily to calm down. Marcy scanned the beach, searching for ways her risk-taking girls could find danger. Most of the other people on the beach were couples, families, and groups. She noticed one woman alone in a billowing maxi dress, taking photographs of the water while smoking a cigarette. The only other person who appeared to be solo wore shorts, a T-shirt, and a light blue hat that reminded her of the one her mother used to wear on their boat.

She nodded her assent. "Not too close to the water, though."

She noticed Laurie smile as the girls kicked off their sandals at the edge of the deck and ran toward the boys.

"The twins are over the moon about being flower girls on Sunday," Marcy said. "They've been practicing their steps, but be warned: for all I know, Chloe will go running down the aisle screaming like a maniac with Emily not far behind."

"And all of that would be just fine," Laurie said. "You know, it's funny, I can't believe I ever got them confused. They look completely different to me now that I know them."

"That's a sign you're officially family now." And Marcy meant it. She could see that Alex was serious about Laurie when he made a point of inviting them to New York to meet her. She was the first woman Alex had ever introduced to them who seemed to have other priorities besides landing one of the most eligible bachelors in the city. Over the past two years, it had become clear how much Laurie and Alex cared about each other.

"Laurie!"

Marcy turned to see a young woman—she looked like a teenager—behind them, heading to Laurie with her arms outstretched. Her long blond hair was pulled into a ponytail and she lugged a black backpack over her white sundress. Laurie gave the girl a warm hug.

"You must be Mrs. Buckley." The girl held out her hand for a quick shake.

"Marcy," she urged. "And you must be the famous Kara. Your chocolate-chip pancakes are legendary."

Marcy knew that Kara was Timmy's favorite babysitter and a mainstay at the Moran household until she had left for college last fall at SUNY Buffalo. Their introductions were interrupted by a sand-covered ten-year-old rushing to greet Kara. Before Marcy's kids made it to the deck, Timmy was already telling Kara all about the new video game he wanted to play with her.

"Mom," Emily whined, *"Jonathan isn't throwing the ball to us."*

"Jonathan?" Laurie inquired. "Since when?"

Marcy chuckled. "A new student in his school is named Bartholomew, and he insists on being called by his full name. Now all the kids think it's cool to use proper names."

"Small world," Laurie replied. "Just last week Timmy told me he thought 'Timmy' is a little kid's name. At his request I sometimes call him 'Timothy.'"

"I'm sure for both it's a passing fad," Marcy said.

They were interrupted by the sound of male voices emerging from the breezeway. It was Alex, Andrew, and Ramon. Andrew dangled a set of hotel key cards over his head.

"We have the honeymoon suite," he boasted. "Courtesy of my big brother."

"Crossed signals with the reservations desk," Alex explained. "My betrothed and I will be keeping everything on the up and up this week. The honeymoon suite was the only one big enough for your whole brood."

"Lucky us," Marcy said, accepting one of the keys.

"So . . ." Marcy could tell that her husband was eager to say whatever would come next. "How do you ladies feel about an afternoon of golf?"

"Seriously?" She gave a playful swat in his direction. "I thought you were going to announce a spa day."

"These are Alex's last few hours of being in his thirties, and a little bird named Ramon told me golf was on the wish list."

Ramon placed a guilty palm over his heart. "It's my fault indeed. Leo won't be here until close to dinner, so this would be the best time for the four of you to hit the links."

"And what about you, Ramon?" Marcy asked. "We don't want to leave you out."

"I have a hidden agenda of my own."

"Top secret," Timmy added with a sly smile.

Marcy already knew that Ramon had promised to find a way to

take Timmy shopping alone so he could select a special present for Alex, separate from the gift Laurie had chosen for both of them.

Laurie looked to Marcy, assessing her opinion. "I'm a terrible golfer, but Alex keeps telling me that we should play together like you and Andrew do."

"Lunch at the clubhouse and then just nine holes," Andrew promised.

Marcy would be leaving her three kids with a nineteen-year-old she had met only moments earlier. On the other hand, Laurie was understandably the most protective mother she knew, and Laurie trusted Kara implicitly. *What could possibly go wrong in this ocean paradise?* she asked herself.

"Fore!" she said, acting out a full swing of the club.

The two couples entered the breezeway toward their rooms. As they walked—beneath the rim of a blue cotton hat, behind the darkened lenses of a pair of sunglasses—a stranger continued to watch the beach.

Chapter 3

Kara Sumner was having so much fun on the beach that she nearly forgot she was getting paid for the so-called work of helping to watch Timmy and his future cousins for a few days. She already knew that spending time with Timmy would be a piece of cake. She'd been babysitting him since she was in the ninth grade. But this trip involved three other, younger children she'd never met before, and Laurie had warned her that the twin girls could be "spirited." Now that she was here, she couldn't believe she had ever worried. The kids were super-sweet and managed to keep one another entertained with little effort on her part.

The biggest challenge so far had been telling the girls apart. Kara was grateful that the parents hadn't dressed them in matching swimming suits. Emily in yellow, Chloe in blue, she reminded herself. *No problem.*

To top it off, one of Kara's high school friends, Ashley Carter, was at the beach with her family and had joined the fun.

At the twins' request, they had just finished playing a practice round of "Alex and Laurie's Wedding." All of the children were included in the ceremony. While Alex's brother Andrew would serve as the traditional best man to the groom, Timmy would serve as "best man" to the bride. Johnny would be the ring bearer, and Chloe and Emily were flower girls.

In the twins' pretend rendition on the beach, Kara was the bride, Ashley the groom, and Ramon stood in for best man, while the kids all practiced their ceremony responsibilities. Emily had even retrieved plastic rings from the family's hotel room for Johnny to practice carrying down the aisle and for Timmy and Ramon to hand to the "bride" and "groom."

"Let's try it again," Emily pleaded. "Chloe walked too fast, and Johnny almost dropped the rings."

Her brother and sister protesting, Emily marched through the sand, back to the starting point of the imaginary "aisle" they had lined off with seashells for the procession.

"I'm sorry to break up the fun," Ramon said, "but Timothy and I need to make a trip into town to get your uncle Alex a birthday present."

"We got him a fancy briefcase," Johnny announced. His sisters shushed him. "What?! Ramon and Timothy can keep a secret better than you two."

Ramon looked to the babysitters with sympathy. "Do you two have this, Miss Kara?"

"I don't know, guys. Do you mind hanging out with Ashley and me for a little while longer?"

The three Buckley children all clapped and cheered. "Can we play wedding again?" Emily asked. "Pleeeeaaase!"

"If they're leaving, then I want to be one of the best men this time!" Johnny exclaimed.

"You *always* want to do everything Timmy does," Chloe said. "We're going to call you Timmy all day long now."

"His name is *Timothy*," Johnny insisted.

Kara smiled at Ramon. "I'd say we've got it all under control here."

Johnny, now pretending to be Timmy the best man, indulged his sisters in three additional dry runs of the wedding procession before declaring himself finished. "I want to ride the skim board again. I'm getting good at it."

"I'm hot." Emily's complaint was quiet but plaintive. Kara placed a hand on the top of her dark hair. The little girl's head was roasting. Chloe tilted forward, and Kara confirmed she was warm, too.

"Dark hair absorbs all the heat. Let me go see if you have hats in your room."

"Can we go inside, too?" Chloe asked.

Now that the thrill of the pretend wedding was over, the girls looked tired and overheated. "I think it's time for all of us to go catch our breath inside with the air-conditioning."

Johnny clutched the turquoise-striped skim board against his body, eagerly studying the wave patterns. It was one of the many beach toys the hotel had available for guests. He was obviously disappointed by having to go inside.

"I can stay with Johnny for a little while if you want to take them back to the room," Ashley offered.

Kara had no concerns about Ashley's dependability. Ashley was a year older than Kara and had been trusted to watch her considerably younger siblings since middle school. But this was Kara's job, and neither Marcy nor Laurie had ever met Ashley.

"I'll give him three runs on the board," Ashley vowed. "It'll be ten minutes—max. Besides, I even know the lifeguard on duty. *Jack!*" she cried out.

A good-looking guy perched on top of the lifeguard stand turned his head and then waved.

"It's really hot out here," Emily added.

"Okay, let's go in. You get three tries," Kara said to Johnny, "but that's it."

From a sand dune to the east, a stranger continued to watch— *just a little boy and a teenage girl now, all alone. It's almost time.*

•   •   •

Once Emily and Chloe were back in their hotel suite, they ran to the terrace adjacent to their parents' bedroom, marveling that they could wash the sand off of their legs with a private outdoor shower. Kara had to keep them from running around in circles when they came inside, so their wet feet didn't slip on the tile floors. Instead, they tried jumping on the sofa, to which she also put a halt. So this was what Laurie meant by "spirited," she thought.

The suite had two bedrooms. The kids would be sharing the room with two queen beds. Kara watched as the girls pulled the blankets back from both of them and began rolling around, trying them out.

In unison, they both pronounced that the bed closest to the window was where they'd sleep.

"I don't know," Kara said hopefully. "You might want to lie there for a few seconds and pretend to sleep . . . just to be sure."

After a few minutes their slow, calm breaths fell into sync. Kara wondered if all twins were so connected, as she walked out of the room, leaving the bedroom door ajar behind her.

She checked the time on her cell phone. It had been thirteen minutes since she'd left the beach. She pulled up Ashley's number and hit call.

"Hey girl."

"Did Johnny master his skim board?" Kara asked.

"Nope. He tumbled his very first try. He made it out of the waves unscathed, but I figured it was safest to keep him out of the water. We're with Jack getting ice cream at the beach shack."

Kara detected an unusual bubbliness in Ashley's voice. She suspected it was related to Jack the handsome lifeguard.

"The twins fell asleep, so would you mind bringing him back to the room as soon as he's done with his ice cream?"

"No problem. Johnny, it's about time to head— Johnny? Where'd he go?"

Kara heard shuffling sounds on the phone as if Ashley were walking.

"You *are* with him, right?" The other end of the phone was silent. "Ashley, are you there? Say something. Is Johnny with you or not?"

"He was literally just here. I don't know where he went."

Chapter 4

Laurie could not believe her eyes as her golf ball flew in a perfect arc off the head of her seven-iron, dropping only two feet from the pin.

Andrew let out a whistle. "Alex, you didn't tell me you were marrying a ringer!"

As Laurie hopped into the passenger seat of the golf cart, Alex gave her a satisfied smile. "You're a natural. We should play more often."

She had made some lucky shots around the green, but for her long game, she had taken to placing her errant fairway shots next to Alex's lest she back up the entire course trying to move her ball along.

As they were hopping out of the cart to putt, her cell phone rang. It was Leo.

"Hey Dad." She did her best to keep her voice down.

"Am I missing all the fun?" Leo asked.

"You're missing all the golf."

"Sorry, I thought I was calling my daughter. Laurie Moran, about five-six, light brown hair, hazel eyes?"

Laurie smiled. "How was your meeting?"

In addition to being Laurie's father, Leo Farley was also a former first deputy commissioner of the NYPD. Though he had accepted an invitation last year to return to the department's anti-terrorism task force on a part-time basis, his meeting in the city today was not part of a current investigation.

It was about an old murder conviction against Darren Gunther, a then twenty-one-year-old Vassar College student who stabbed a beloved bar owner who tried to break up a fight between Gunther and another bar patron. Gunther confessed the crime to Leo, but then claimed at trial that Leo fabricated the entire conversation. According to Gunther's new version, a third party had intervened in the bar fight and ended up stabbing the owner. The jury didn't buy it, and the judge handed Gunther a life sentence.

"Let's just say that the traffic on the LIE is heaven in comparison."

"Was it that bad?" Laurie asked.

His meeting had been with the District Attorney's Office, whose Conviction Integrity Unit was taking a second look at Gunther's conviction. Her father was used to defendants claiming to be innocent years after the fact, but this case had gotten under his skin. Gunther had always been charismatic, but now at forty years old, he had gone on to publish a collection of essays about prison life, earning him a group of loyal—and in Leo's opinion, naive—supporters. In Leo's mind, Gunther was using his newfound celebrity to ride a recent wave of exoneration cases and get another bite at the apple.

"They're saying another guy's DNA is on the knife handle. An ex-con with a long history of violence. It doesn't change a thing, though. The confession's the confession. I was in that room. But these young DAs don't know me from Adam."

And that was the real reason this case had struck a nerve with Leo: Gunther was calling Leo Farley a liar, and Leo wasn't going to let the accusation stand.

"My faith in you is one hundred percent, Dad."

"I appreciate that. I need someone to take my side. I mean it: maybe you can take a look at this one for your show."

Alex was waving a putter in Laurie's direction.

To "investigate" a matter involving her father would be an obvious conflict of interest. But after Greg was murdered, Leo had retired early to help her care for Timmy. He had put himself on the line over and over again for her and her son, and never asked anything in return. And she did need to find a new case in a hurry.

"Anyway, get back to your game before the marshal kicks you off the course for gabbing on the phone."

Her mind elsewhere, she missed her easy putt.

Three holes later, they were on the green when Laurie's phone buzzed again. "Hi Kara," she said, barely whispering.

"It's Kara?" Marcy asked. "What's wrong?"

Laurie could see the alarm cross Marcy's face. "I'm sure it's fine. She knows I appreciate regular updates."

Laurie could barely hear Kara over the sound of the ocean wind around her. "I'm so sorry, but you need to come back here."

"Okay, calm down. What happened?"

"I don't know. But I can't find Johnny. He's missing, Laurie. Johnny's missing."

Marcy must have seen something in Laurie's face, because she reached for her husband, her eyes wide with dread.

How am I going to tell her? Laurie asked herself.

Chapter 5

In seven years, Johnny Buckley had only been lost one other time, and Marcy could remember every millisecond of the resulting fear. He was five years old then, and Andrew wanted to take the children to see the fireworks show now that the twins were old enough not to be afraid. They knew better than to take three kids into the crowds at the National Mall, so they opted for a picnic blanket and chairs at Meridian Hill Park instead.

Unfortunately, taking in the show wasn't the only thing the girls were old enough to do as toddlers. In an early demonstration of their curious tendencies, the twins kept marching away from their picnic blanket toward every nearby gathering that seemed remotely interesting. The young couple with the two dogs. The big family with all the cousins. The teenagers playing Frisbee. It seemed Chloe and Emily wanted to be everywhere except where they were supposed to be.

Andrew and Marcy were focused so closely on Chloe and Emily that they scarcely noticed the fireworks blasting into the sky—or that Johnny was no longer perched in his little folding Nationals chair. It wasn't like Johnny to wander off. If anything, he could be a bit clingy. Andrew hurried off to look for him while Marcy stayed put with the girls. Marcy counted the seconds, holding the twins on either side of her to keep them still. Not wanting to alarm the girls, she forced herself to breathe normally. Even beneath the booming sounds above her, she could feel her blood rushing through her veins.

She had reached a count of 411 when she spotted Johnny moving toward her, his gaze bouncing between the colors on the horizon and the groups of park-goers he carefully navigated his way around. She grabbed him into the tightest hug possible. *"Where were you?!"*

He had found his way to the restrooms and back all by himself, he declared proudly. "I had to go, and you and Daddy were chasing the twins."

That was more than two years ago. She had made him promise never to wander off again without telling them, but had she reminded him enough in the interim? Did he think the rules were different when he was with a babysitter on vacation?

She flinched when she felt the touch of a hand on her shoulder. It was Andrew.

"He's going to be okay," he said. "Remember that Fourth of July?"

She wanted to scream. That was only 411 seconds. They had now been looking for him for almost twenty minutes, and that was after the fifteen-minute drive from the golf course. They had checked all the obvious places: the hotel lobby, swimming pool, gift shop, surf store—everywhere. So far, they had found a few people who remembered seeing Johnny with Kara and his sisters, as well as in the water with his skim board, but that would have been before he went to get ice cream at the beach shack.

"I can't believe Johnny was with some girl none of us had ever met before. What was she so busy doing that she couldn't keep an eye on our son?"

"Kara and Ashley both feel terrible."

"Good!"

Her tone was bitter, but in truth, the person she was angry at was herself. She never should have left the hotel.

"An employee at the beach shack says he saw Johnny collecting seashells behind the shack a little while after they ordered their ice cream cones. He may have walked farther down the beach to collect more."

"For over half an hour?"

"It's a long beach. You know how focused he can be."

"I also know he would never wander off alone this long." Marcy had felt an immediate connection to Johnny when the nun at the hospital had placed him in her arms, like energy radiating directly from his tiny body into hers. She may not have had the experience of nine months of carrying him, but in that single moment, the two of them became bonded forever.

A woman was heading toward them from the hotel. Her maxi dress blew like a sail with the wind. She was carrying a camera and a cigarette, just as she had been when Marcy spotted her earlier that day.

"Excuse me. Ma'am, pardon me," Marcy shouted. Andrew followed her as she charged through the sand toward the stranger.

Up close, Marcy could see that the woman was older than she had assumed—probably approaching sixty, with long gray-and-blond hair and skin etched by sun and smoking. She had a warm, welcoming smile.

"Well, hello." She bent down and put her cigarette out in the sand. "Not like most people here to introduce themselves to strangers, especially in the summer."

"I'm sorry. We're staying at the hotel, and we can't find our son." Marcy held up the screen of her phone. Her voice caught at the sight of the image—a photograph of Johnny, all cheeks and a toothy grin as he held up his certificate for winning second place in the first-grade puzzling contest last April. "I saw you taking photographs earlier on the beach. Did you see him playing?"

The woman's smile immediately fell. "I'm so sorry. I don't recognize him. When I'm behind the camera, I focus on the natural beauty of the topography. Human beings don't even exist in my mind when I'm looking through a lens."

"Is it possible you have pictures that might show where he went?" Andrew asked.

"I can certainly check." She switched her camera into display mode. Marcy and Andrew looked over her shoulder as she flipped through the digital images.

"There!" Marcy exclaimed. She pointed to the far-right edge of the screen. "That's Johnny on his skim board."

"Oh sure, I remember seeing a boy out there earlier today. I actually shifted my position to make sure I was getting a pure landscape." She checked the time stamp of the photograph. It was not long after they had left for the golf course, so it didn't provide any information beyond what they had gathered from Kara and Ashley.

The photographer waited patiently while they scrolled through the rest of her pictures, desperately searching for some clue of Johnny's whereabouts. Andrew was writing down her name and number just in case they needed to reach her again, when Marcy saw the photographer's facial expression shift again, this time to fear.

"What's that?" she asked, pointing toward the water. An object had washed up to shore with the waves.

Marcy felt her stomach tighten as she recognized the turquoise and white stripes from one of the photographs Kara had texted to Laurie while they were on the golf course. It was the skim board Johnny had been using. Her son was gone and he could be anywhere, even in the water.

The waves seemed to grow louder as she broke into sobs.

Chapter 6

Laurie plugged one ear with a finger as she struggled to hear her father on the other end of her cell phone over the sounds of the roaring waves.

"I reached out to the chief of the East Hampton Police Department," Leo said. "They're sending out a detective and a patrol car."

It had been almost a half hour since Andrew called 911 to report Johnny missing. He had said at the time that the dispatcher treated him like a worrywart parent who'd simply lost sight of a typically adventurous child for a moment or two. The lack of a police response in the time that had passed seemed to confirm his impression. Alex was inside trying to pull some strings, but even a federal judge could not beat Leo Farley's influence with law enforcement.

"Thanks, Dad."

"They're also going to send the marine patrol unit to your area," he added.

"Is that police?"

He hesitated before answering. "For the most part, but their beat is to patrol the water from boats."

The implication of the decision was clear and sent a chill up Laurie's spine even though it was eighty degrees outside.

As she hung up her phone, she noticed a stocky young boy with dark, wind-tossed hair walking in her direction. His swim shorts were decorated with Star Wars characters, and his tan belly popped out slightly over the waistband. He was probably nine years old or so and seemed to be looking directly, but reluctantly, at her.

"Hey there," she said, giving him a friendly wave. "Do you mind if I ask you a question?"

He squinted against the sunlight behind her.

"Sure."

She pulled up a photograph she had taken of Timmy and Johnny together two months earlier when Andrew had brought Johnny up for the Yankees-Nationals game. Before she could even ask the boy if he recognized them, he pointed at the screen. "That's Timothy and Jonathan. Are you their mom?"

"Well, I'm Timothy's mom, yes, and that's his cousin, Jonathan. You know them?"

"Just from today, but we were sharing the skim board. That's what I was going to ask you. I saw you with the lady who found the board in the water and carried it away. I was going to ask her if I could play with it, but she looked really sad."

"She *is* sad. She's Johnny's mom, and we can't find him. When was the last time you saw him?"

He looked down at the sand, struggling to remember. "I think it was when he came out of the water and was talking to that girl and the lifeguard. They walked off that way." He pointed in the direction of the beach shack.

"Have you seen him since then?"

More sand staring. "I saw him on the board in the water and he fell off."

"Okay, was that *before* or *after* he went off with the lady and the lifeguard?"

"Um . . . I think it was before?"

He was anything but certain.

"But you were using the board, too?"

He nodded.

"So you know my friend found it in the water. Did you put it in there?"

He shook his head. She pictured Johnny slipping off the board and getting pulled beneath the current. She couldn't bear the thought of it.

"But the waves keep coming up really far. Daddy had to move our umbrellas back and everything. I think the water just washed away the board when no one was looking."

At least she had one potentially positive piece of news to report back to Marcy and Andrew. It was possible that one of the kids had simply abandoned the board in the sand, and then the tide pulled it into the ocean before returning it for Marcy to find.

"Do you know where the beach shack is?" Laurie asked.

He shook his head.

She told him that if he kept walking past the lifeguard stand, there was a shack on the other side of the restrooms where the hotel stored the skim boards. "There's ice cream there, too."

His eyes lit up at the thought of it.

"But make sure you bring a grown-up with you, okay? You have to promise."

"Promise," he said, marking an X over his heart with his index finger.

"Thank you for talking to me. My name's Laurie, by the way."

"I'm Wyatt."

She was about to turn away when he stopped her. "You're really nice."

"Thank you, Wyatt. So are you."

"Was that you yelling at Timothy earlier? Was he in trouble?"

"Someone yelled at Timmy?"

Her tone was sharp, and the boy's face fell.

"I'm sorry," she said. "But I didn't yell at him, and I hate the thought that someone else did." They had decided not to call Ramon or Timmy yet, because they had left the hotel before Johnny went missing, and they didn't want to upset Timmy unnecessarily if Johnny suddenly turned up. "What happened?"

"Well, I was building a sand castle with my sister and I heard some lady yelling 'Tim! Tim!' Like maybe he was in trouble or not paying attention or something. But then when we looked around, we didn't see where the yelling was coming from, and we didn't see Timothy or Jonathan either. So maybe it was someone else named Tim."

"When was this that you heard someone yelling for Tim?"

He shrugged. "I don't know, but I don't think I've seen Timothy or Jonathan since then."

And neither had Laurie.

One ring. Two. Three.

Pick up, Ramon. Pick up the phone.

"Were your ears burning?" Ramon answered midway through the fourth ring.

"Um, what do you mean?"

"Timothy and I were just saying he has never been to Italy before, so now you and Alex will have to go back again after the honeymoon. There are worse burdens, right?"

"So Timmy's with you?"

"Yes, of course. The top-secret mission, remember?"

"Oh, thank god." There were plenty of people named some variant of Tim, she reminded herself. Some other beachgoer must have been calling out after one of them.

"Laurie, is everything all right? You sound upset."

She tried to remain calm as she gave him an abbreviated version of what they knew so far. "Please don't say anything to Timmy yet, okay? I'm still praying Johnny wandered off and will be back at any moment."

"Of course," Ramon said, his voice even.

Timmy had witnessed his father's murder at the age of three and then lived under the killer's threat to return for him and Laurie for another five years after that. He seemed drawn to Leo's police work and her research on cold cases, but she nevertheless tried to do what she could to protect him from unnecessary fear. He had seen enough darkness for six lifetimes already.

As she hung up, she registered a pang of guilt for feeling so grateful that her own son was safe. Her fear was increasing that Johnny was not.

Chapter 7

Seven-year-old Johnny Buckley felt like something was pressing down on him. No, more like *someone*. He imagined giant arms wrapped around him, but it wasn't the way his mother or father would hold him. It wasn't gentle or loving. This felt mean and scary. In his mind, Johnny imagined that the arms didn't even belong to a person. They belonged to a monster.

The monster was holding him so tight that Johnny could feel the monster's tummy rumble.

Johnny tried to sit up, but couldn't move. He was certain his eyes were open, but he couldn't see anything. He opened his mouth and tried to scream, but couldn't hear his own voice.

But he could hear . . . *something*. A growl. The sound of the monster filled his head. He imagined the monster squeezing him even tighter, and Johnny wondered if he might simply disappear, never to be seen again.

I want Mommy and Daddy.

A loud honking sound broke through the monster's snarls and pulled Johnny further out of his dreamlike state. The noise felt like it belonged to the world Johnny used to know. When he heard it again, his mind moved away from the monster. He pictured his mother behind the wheel of the minivan, saying, *Where does he think I can go? Johnny, someday you'll learn to drive. Honking your horn in traffic doesn't do any good.*

The sound was the *beep-beep* of a car horn.

Johnny's eyes darted side to side as the fog he was in began lifting more quickly. He was finally awake.

He reached for what had been the monster's arms in his dream and determined that he was wrapped in a fuzzy blanket. The rumble beneath him wasn't a monster's stomach, but the rumble of a car on the road.

Two tiny circles of light were visible from the holes for the taillights, but otherwise he was in pitch blackness. He was locked in the trunk of a car.

He had no idea how much time had passed since he'd heard the voice call out to him on the beach. Were his parents looking for him? He wondered where Chloe and Emily thought he went.

Exploring the area within his reach, he found two objects. The first felt soft, like a small pillow. He managed to hold it up against the slivers of light from the back of the car, squinting as his eyes adjusted to the darkness.

He was able to make out two big round eyes and a pair of moon-shaped ears. It was a stuffed animal. *Why is this here?* he thought. *Why am I here?* He set it aside, telling himself he didn't need a baby's toy right now.

The second item he found was made of a thin fabric. As he traced his fingers along the edges, trying to make out the shape, grains of sand fell onto his face. It was a hat—not like the baseball caps he liked to collect, but the kind with a rim that goes all the way around, like his Nana used to wear when she went on her and Pop Pop's boat. In the darkness, there was no way for him to know that it was the same light blue cotton hat that a stranger had worn while he had watched their family earlier in the day.

This wasn't a dream, but there was a monster, and he was taking Johnny away.

I want to go home.

He clutched the teddy bear to his chest as he started to cry.

Chapter 8

With ever-increasing terror, for the past two hours, Marcy had been in constant action mode—walking the beach, questioning other hotel guests, calling every business within walking distance. Now she was back in their suite, forcing herself to remain still and to focus on the information they had managed to gather so far.

She jumped at the sound of a knock on the door. Andrew opened it. It was Alex, and he was followed in by a woman about her age with long blond hair pulled back into a ponytail at the nape of her neck. "The police are here," Alex announced.

"I'm Detective Langland," the woman said. The business card she handed to Marcy gave her full name as Jennifer Langland. She was a detective with the East Hampton Police Department.

Marcy resisted the urge to say something about the police failure to respond until Laurie's father had called in a favor, but the detective appeared to sense her resentment. "I can't imagine how worried you must be right now. I'm so sorry that the dispatcher didn't prioritize the call earlier. It's no excuse, but we have a critical mass of units called out to a mess of an accident on Main Street."

The detective's tone was compassionate. She looked Marcy squarely in the eye when she apologized for the delay. *Please be good at this,* Marcy found herself pleading silently. *Please be the woman who can bring back my son.*

For the next ten minutes, Marcy listened. She willed herself to slow her thoughts as Detective Langland outlined the department's current efforts to locate Johnny.

"I already met with the hotel's general manager. He's pulling all the available surveillance tape for us. Unfortunately, they don't have much in the way of cameras on the beach itself, and only one camera in the beach shack, and it's focused on the register."

Marcy felt all hope fading away as the detective continued.

"But they'll have footage from the hotel lobby, plus the entrances and exits. Unfortunately, the only cameras in the parking lot are close to the property, but we're going to start with those. If your son left by car, hopefully we'll get a plate number and move from there."

"*Left by car?*" Andrew was clenching and unclenching his fists at his side. "We've been careful to warn Johnny. He never willingly would have gotten into—" Andrew cut himself off, considering the implication of what he was saying.

Langland nodded. "I know," she said softly.

Marcy was grateful that the detective wasn't minimizing the situation by lecturing her about the curiosity of seven-year-old boys who want to explore the beach on their own, but her heart dropped at the thought of her son in some stranger's car. She also knew that a kidnapper had probably considered the possibility of cameras at a resort. She thought about all of the paths between the sand dunes farther down the beach, paths that led to public roads where someone could park anonymously and away from the reach of surveillance.

"What about an Amber Alert?" Andrew asked. Marcy had heard the blast of her cell phone a few times over the years when police used an area alert system to notify the public about a local child's abduction.

"My supervisor is weighing the request. To restrict the notifications to the most urgent cases, the broadcast system won't allow us to trigger an alert unless we are confident there has been an abduction.

I know it's frustrating, but the fact that we haven't sent out an alarm yet is actually good news in the big scheme of things. It means we have other possibilities to explore."

"I assume you'll also be looking at the whereabouts of any natural suspects who might be on local law enforcement's radar," Alex said.

"Of course," Langland said. "I've seen you on television, Judge. So I'm aware of your expertise in criminal law. I wasn't sure how blunt to be with the rest of the family."

Marcy's brother-in-law Alex had been one of the country's most well-regarded defense attorneys before he was confirmed to the federal bench three months earlier. His stint as the host of the first three episodes of the *Under Suspicion* series of specials had only increased his public profile.

"I assure you," Marcy said, "that we want to know every piece of information you have."

"In that case, you should know that we have officers from the Suffolk County Police Department's Marine Bureau out on the water, looking for any signs that he might—"

The detective paused, and Marcy nodded that she understood the implication.

"And when Judge Buckley referred to 'natural suspects,' I've got someone running a list of high-risk registered sex offenders in the area. Also some EDPs—emotionally disturbed persons, in the parlance. We'll be looking for any matching MOs or other red flags."

"I see."

The possible explanations seemed to grow worse at every turn.

As if her mind needed a break from the darkness, Marcy found herself thinking about a trip to Anguilla ten years ago, shortly after their first anniversary. She had planned a long weekend trip for her and her best friends from college, Alicia and Liz. Alicia had gotten her MBA and was on her way to becoming a CEO, but Liz had been the one to move to Hollywood with Marcy to make their names as actresses. They were having lunch at a delicious French restaurant on Meads Bay when the sound of a small prop airplane interrupted the maître d's explanation of the daily specials.

The maître d' was bemoaning the flight's deviation from the airport's mandated path for visitors' private jets when Liz let out a loud "WHAT *did he do?!*"

The entire restaurant looked up to see a plane flying a banner above the ocean: *Liz, Be My Leading Lady. Marry Me.* Unbeknownst to any of them, Liz's boyfriend, Nic, had asked Andrew to snoop in Marcy's calendar for their itinerary. The happy couple were married on that same beach a year later.

Her mind had pulled her back to Anguilla for a reason. Like an acting coach once told her: *Pay attention to what you know, because every experience you ever had might be important right now.*

"A plane banner," Marcy called out. "Can we do that? Something that says there's a missing child. Or maybe just a message for Johnny that we're looking for him? In case he sees it?" She heard the desperation in her voice.

"Of course," Andrew said, sitting down next to her on the sofa and wrapping an arm around her shoulder. "That's a great idea."

"We'll of course put out an announcement for the public to be on the lookout for your son," Detective Langland said. "But we'll get more attention if you as the parents follow up with a press conference. It's too early to go that route now, but if we haven't found him by tomorrow, the news teams will turn up."

"*Tomorrow?*" The idea of not having her son with her by nightfall was unimaginable.

"If it even comes to that," the detective said.

She heard a fast but quiet tap on the suite door. Alex opened the door, and Emily and Chloe spilled into the room, followed by Ramon. "Sorry, even I had a hard time stopping them."

The girls jumped on the sofa on either side of her and Andrew.

"What have you been talking about? It's mean to keep secrets," Emily said.

"We haven't seen you all day," Chloe grumbled. "Where's Johnny?"

What am I going to tell them if their big brother is gone?

"I'm sorry, girls. We were just talking about what we should do for dinner. What sounds good to you?"

"Hamburgers," the girls replied.

"Hamburgers?" Marcy asked incredulously. "If you two eat one more hamburger, you're going turn into two giant hamburgers!"

Andrew spread his arms wide, as if in an unsuccessful effort to put them around his supersized daughters. The girls squealed with delight, temporarily forgetting the unanswered question about Johnny.

Chapter 9

Laurie turned the corner toward her hotel room to find Alex removing the key card from the door next to hers. She looked at him expectantly, hoping to hear good news. He shook his head.

She followed him into his room, and he pulled her into an embrace and gave her a quick kiss.

"Are you holding up okay?"

"Me? Of course. I'm sick for Marcy and Andrew, though."

"Obviously. But I know this can't be easy for you either."

Nearly three years ago, the man who had murdered Greg had made good on his lingering threat to return to kill the rest of Greg's family. In the process, he had abducted Timmy and tried to shoot Laurie before being killed by police.

"This isn't about me. I just want to help." She told him what she'd learned from Wyatt, the boy on the beach. "At least it's a possible explanation for the skim board being in the water. It sounds like the kids were all sharing it, and may have left it where the tide pulled it out."

"Better than bad news at least. Honestly, I think Marcy could use anything to give her hope right now. Can you go tell her? She's in their room. Andrew's pulling the car around for me. We're going to the copy shop to print out some fliers with Johnny's picture. The police already put us in contact with a pilot who can fly over the east end with a missing child banner."

"That's a good idea. How are the twins?"

"Ramon took them down to the lobby to get a soda."

"They don't know yet?"

He shook his head. "What are you going to tell Timmy?"

"I'm about to talk to him now. I'll make sure he knows not to say anything to the twins, but I have to tell him. You know Timmy."

"Of course. He's got your and your dad's ability to sense when something's wrong. If you don't shoot straight with him, his imagination might come up with something even worse."

Laurie was beginning to wonder if fiction could be any worse than their reality.

Marcy pulled Laurie into a quick hug when she walked into their suite.

"I'm so glad you're here," Marcy said tonelessly. "I hate to say this, but I feel like you're the only one who really understands what I'm going through right now. I'm sorry, I shouldn't have even said that."

Laurie pulled Marcy toward the sofa so they could take a seat. Laurie understood the point she was making. In one sense, Laurie had experienced a worse tragedy, losing her husband to a violent crime and living for five years under a threat of more harm to come to her and Timmy. On the other hand, Laurie's loss was in the past, while Marcy still didn't know the extent of hers.

"How are the girls?" Laurie asked.

"Too smart for what I can handle right now," Marcy said. "Ramon's watching them, but I'm not sure how long I can keep them at bay."

"I told Timmy."

"Is he all right?"

"I can't tell. But he at least knows. He's in our room and was planning to say a prayer for Johnny."

"I know this sounds crazy," Marcy said, "but I think at some level I was always expecting something like this to happen. Like he was never completely mine. We always thought of Johnny as our miracle child."

Laurie had never pried about the details surrounding Andrew and Marcy's decision to adopt their first child, but she empathized with the situation. She and Greg had tried for more than two years after they married to become pregnant with Timmy. In the back of her mind, she had been wondering if she and Alex might face similar hurdles once they began trying to add to their family.

"By the time Andrew proposed to me," Marcy said, "I had already accepted what I had been told by my doctors—that I would never be able to conceive. We simply assumed it would be just the two of us. Plenty of couples opt not to have children."

"And yet now you have three."

"Funny how that works," Marcy said. "We adopted Johnny as a newborn, and two and a half years later, he started saying he wanted a sibling. And not just any sibling. He was very specific: two baby sisters. Obviously, he was too young to understand why that was impossible, but nine weeks later, I found out I was pregnant. Then a few weeks after that, we learned we were having two twin girls. It's as if Johnny predicted the family's future."

Laurie had not only been raised by a police detective, but also had been investigating true crime cases as a journalist for years. She couldn't remember a single case where the principal suspect wasn't someone with some kind of connection to the victim. Because Johnny was only seven years old, they had been assuming that the explanation was either a tragic accident in the water or a sociopath who had targeted Johnny at random. But now that Marcy was recounting Johnny's backstory, Laurie realized there was another possible explanation.

"How is it that you ended up adopting Johnny, by the way?" she asked.

"We didn't even plan for it," Marcy said. "The priest in our parish was aware of our desire to be parents, despite the fertility issues. Out of nowhere, he asked if we were willing to take in a boy who was only days from being born. It was only seven years ago. I still remember the words he used. A young woman was 'in trouble.' The poor girl didn't even know who the father was and was trying to find a family willing to adopt the baby."

"No wonder you call him the miracle."

"Johnny still doesn't know," Marcy said, choking back a sob. Laurie could tell she was fighting to keep her composure. "When you got together with Alex, it was such an added blessing that you and Timmy sort of resemble Johnny. He never had the experience of looking like anyone in his family."

Marcy's shoulders began to shake, and this time she could not stop herself from breaking into tears. Laurie rubbed Marcy's back and did her best to comfort her.

"I'm so sorry, Marcy. I didn't mean to upset you by asking about the adoption. I brought it up for a reason."

As Marcy sniffled and slowly regained control over her breathing, Laurie could tell that she was eager to focus on what Laurie had to say.

"A random crime is every parent's nightmare," Laurie said, "but it's extremely rare. You know how I follow all the true-crime message boards looking for cases for the show?"

Marcy nodded, her tears beginning to ebb.

"Last year, a child who had been missing from Missouri for more than six years was found in Toronto. It turned out that her parents had adopted her. The birth mother had regrets years later and managed to track down the adoptive family. She lured the girl away by telling her she was adopted and that she was the 'real' mother. She even pointed out that they had the same eye and hair color."

When Marcy spoke, her voice was distant. "His light hair and eyes," she said. "He knows he doesn't look like the rest of us."

"Do you know how to get hold of the biological mother?" Laurie asked.

"No, but Father Horrigan might. I'll call him right now."

Chapter 10

For half a moment, Marcy's spirits brightened at the sound of Father Horrigan's Irish lilt. "Marcy, what a wonderful surprise to hear from you. I thought you and Andrew were hobnobbing with the rich and famous this week in the Hamptons."

She never ceased to marvel at his ability to commit to memory every last detail about the lives of his parishioners. Oh, how she wished this could just be a friendly call to fill him in on the wonderful memories they were forming on their trip.

"Father, I have to ask you something that I've never raised before. It might literally be a matter of life or death."

"I'd like to think you're pulling my leg, but you sound terribly upset."

She closed her eyes, trying not to lose control again as she had before. "We can't find Johnny. It's been hours. The police are searching for him."

She heard him suck in his breath at the other end of the line. "No. Oh, Marcy, that's terrible."

"We're looking at every possibility. One of them is that his birth mother changed her mind after all these years."

"I can't imagine that would be the case—"

"Well, I can. Because the other scenarios I've contemplated are even worse, Father. I have to think that if she took Johnny, she would at least be looking after his well-being. At this point, I'm almost praying this is the explanation, so I need to know where she is."

"It was a closed adoption, Marcy, at least from your perspective. We discussed this at the time."

The birth mother had asked that the adoption be closed with respect to her identity, meaning that Marcy and Andrew had no information about her. There was no direct contact whatsoever with her, either before or after the birth, and the adoption files were physically sealed. The birth mother had been nervous about placing Johnny with a family Father Horrigan knew directly, in case they discovered her identity from him, but Marcy and Andrew had assured Father Horrigan repeatedly that they would respect the biological mother's request for anonymity and never ask him to disclose her identity.

"Please—I just need to make sure. If we can confirm that she's nowhere near Long Island, I promise that we'll never bother her again."

The silence that followed was so long that she began to wonder whether she had lost the connection.

"Do the police believe that this woman is responsible for Johnny's being missing?" Father Horrigan asked.

"They don't believe anything yet. They're investigating every possible explanation—looking at local criminals, searching surveillance tapes. We're grasping at straws because we can't find him and have absolutely no idea where he might be."

"I'm sorry, Marcy. I gave my word, don't you see? Just as I would never break a promise I made to you, I cannot violate my obligations toward her."

"Please, Father. I'm begging you."

"I can't even begin to know how scared you are right now, Marcy, but for what it's worth, I don't think this is a straw you need to grasp. I've never gotten any indication that Johnny's birth mother regretted her decision to give him up, and why would she follow you all the way to New York when she knows exactly who you are and that you live right here in D.C. How would she even know where to find you up there? It doesn't make much sense, does it?"

Marcy took a deep breath. Father Horrigan had a good point. Laurie had been the one to suggest the possibility that Johnny's disappearance was connected to his adoption, but the theory had been total conjecture. Unlike Laurie, Father Horrigan had a connection to Johnny's birth mother and could speak from firsthand knowledge.

"I understand you made a promise to her," she said softly, "but there must be an exception if she has my son. You really don't think it's possible she came for him?"

"I don't. Honestly. She was a good young woman, despite her problems. I don't think she'd have anything to do with this. I'll say a prayer Johnny will be walking right back to you before you know it."

As she hung up the phone, Marcy found herself praying that Father Horrigan was right.

Chapter 11

By the time Leo Farley arrived at the South Shore Resort, hotel guests were gathered on the beach deck overlooking the ocean, prepared with champagne glasses and martinis to take in one of the south fork's famous summer sunsets. *That is where we should all be right now*, he thought, as a family.

It had been a long time since their family had felt complete. Of course, when Eileen was alive and they were raising Laurie together, the three of them were as close as a family could be. Eileen used to say she married the first boy she ever kissed, and Leo never questioned for a minute if she might be exaggerating. They were the kind of couple who held hands whenever they were beside each other, without even thinking about it. Leo never thought he could be any happier, and then Laurie was born. Even when he worked swing shifts, Leo joked it meant that he needed to find time to "swing" by their apartment to see his little girl before her bedtime. Then before he knew it, his little girl was a grown woman breaking into the television news business.

When he and Eileen got the call from Mount Sinai that Laurie had been hit by a cab, it felt as if their family might be gutted. But instead, what could have been a tragedy led to a new addition to the clan. Dr. Greg Moran was Laurie's physician in the emergency room. The two of them were engaged only three months later, and Eileen and Leo loved their son-in-law as if he were their own.

He still smiled sometimes at the memory of Eileen leaning into him, as Laurie and Greg exchanged vows, and whispering, "We're going to have the sweetest little grandbabies, and you are going to be the best granddaddy." She died of a heart attack a year later, before she had a chance to meet Timmy or to even know he would be born. And then, three years after Timmy was born, they lost Greg, too.

For the last seven years, "family" had been just Laurie, Timmy, and him—a widow, a widower, and a little boy who barely remembered his father.

But this weekend, that was finally going to change. Alex had opened his daughter's heart again and had proven himself worthy to be a father figure to Timmy as well. For once, their family was growing instead of shrinking.

And now Johnny was missing.

If only he had not been delayed. Leo found himself seething once again about Darren Gunther's outrageous claims of innocence. He remembered that confession like it was yesterday. It had taken hours, but Leo had finally found a way to get under Gunther's skin. When the charm of Gunther's false face fell away, he admitted that he'd stabbed that bar owner in a rage. Now he was maligning Leo's good name by claiming that the conversation never happened.

If not for Gunther, Leo would have been here at the resort all day. There would have been another set of eyes to help watch the children.

He went straight to the room number Laurie had given him and found a note on the door. *We're in 236 and have your keys there.*

Room 236 was the one next door to his. When Timmy answered the door, he wore a rare frown. "I'm really getting scared for Johnny, Grandpa."

Timmy allowed his grandfather to pull him into a hug. "It's going to be okay. You'll see."

This can't happen again, he thought. *We can't suffer another loss. We have to find him.*

Timmy led the way to the large suite at the end of the hallway. He had always been a long, lanky kid—more the shape of his father's than his mother's family—but he had filled out over the last year.

A beautiful pink sunset glowed beyond the floor-to-ceiling windows overlooking the ocean, but the weight of worry in the room was crushing. Laurie managed a small smile and welcomed Leo with a hug. "I'm so glad you finally made it."

He knew the intention behind the comment, but nevertheless felt a pang of guilt. *This might not have happened if I'd been here instead of the DA's Office.*

"I'm so grateful you called the East Hampton police," Marcy said. "The detective who was here seemed competent, but I just don't know what to do with myself right now. When I went through my phone to select photographs for Andrew and Alex to use at the print shop, it's like a switch flipped. This is really happening. Johnny's one of those kids in a 'missing child' poster."

"Timmy," Laurie said, "maybe you can go play a game while we talk."

"I want to be here with you guys," Timmy said, "trying to figure out where Johnny is. Grandpa said I'm good at police work."

Timmy waited for Laurie to decide. Her expression made it clear that she wasn't going to argue with her son about this. He wasn't a typical ten-year-old. "Any ideas, Dad?" she asked.

"Is Kara still here?"

"In the bedroom with the twins," Marcy said, nodding toward an adjacent door.

Chapter 12

Father Mike Horrigan lived in a small, brick house set back behind Blessed Sacrament Church, where he'd been assigned for nearly fourteen years. In the back of the house, he enjoyed the privacy of a brick patio and a yard with a lush garden. Out the front door, however, placed him right next to the church parking lot, which this evening was the site of a car-wash fundraiser organized by the high school's basketball team. Parker Logan, the tallest member of the team, looked like a giant next to the Prius he was sponging down at the edge of the lot.

Father Horrigan noticed Parker's mother, Betsy, speaking to Cynthia, the parish office manager, at the picnic table that sat between the church and the parking lot. He could still remember Betsy's glee when she showed off how ten-year-old Parker was already taller than she was. Betsy's husband had chimed in, "I've met Great Danes taller than you, sweetie."

He noticed that the women quickly lowered their voices when they spotted him.

Betsy threw him a friendly wave. "Hello there, Father Mike."

"You were gossiping about the *Real Housewives* again, weren't you?" he teased.

"Guilty as charged," Cynthia admitted.

"No confession required," he said. "Watching a show is one thing, living like that one is quite another."

Cynthia looked at him with compassion. "Forgive me for asking, Father, but is something on your mind?"

Father Horrigan was only twenty-six years old when he first came to Blessed Sacrament, and Cynthia, nearly twenty years his senior, had always had a maternal disposition toward him. In the years since, she had been the person he spent more time with day to day than anyone else. She knew him well. The phone call from Marcy Buckley was still weighing on him. He knew that Johnny would likely turn up any moment, the way children do, but he had heard the anguish in his mother's voice. He kept thinking about Marcy saying that she would be relieved to hear that Johnny's birth mother had taken him. At least he would be safe. He wanted to be able to ease her mind if it was at all possible.

"Betsy, would you mind if I borrowed Cynthia for a moment?" he asked. "It's about a parishioner matter."

"Not at all," Betsy said. "I've got some brownies I promised to break out once the kids hit their fundraising goal, so I'll get to work on that."

Once Father Horrigan was alone with Cynthia, he asked whether she remembered Sandra Carpenter. "She had a daughter named Michelle," he said, hoping to jog her memory.

"Yes, of course, but it's been years since she's been in contact."

Sandra had been a regular attendee at Sunday Mass during his early years at the church. Her daughter, Michelle, sixteen years old when he first met her, was one of those teenagers who only came to Mass because of her mother's pressure, but she was always sweet and polite. Once she graduated from high school, her Sunday appearances grew more sporadic over time, and she eventually stopped attending altogether. Whenever Father Horrigan asked about Michelle, Sandra reported that her daughter was doing well.

Then suddenly one day, Sandra paused before answering, and then broke down into tears. At first, Michelle had been getting good grades as a student at the University of Baltimore, but after two years, she took some time off. Michelle's plan was to live in a family's guesthouse in Rehoboth Beach and work full-time as a waitress for a few years. That way she could go back to school and graduate without a load of debt.

"When she first said she wanted to move to Rehoboth, she kept assuring me it was only two and a half hours away, and we could see each other all the time. And for the most part, that has been true. But I haven't seen her for more than three months. She kept saying she was busy, or sick, or one excuse or another. I could tell she was avoiding me, and last night, she finally told me why. She's eight months pregnant and has no idea what she's going to do. I told her I could help her if she wants to raise this child on her own, but the reality has set in. She's twenty-two years old. If she works fewer hours, she'll barely be able to support herself, let alone a baby. She knows that she'll never finish college if she becomes a single mother."

When he had asked about the father to be, Sandra had shaken her head. "Someone she met at one of the beach bars out there. A onetime thing, she said, and completely out of the ordinary for her. She doesn't even know the boy's last name or how to get in touch with him again. I'm still shocked that she did something so stupid and reckless."

Father Horrigan offered to speak to Michelle if he could be helpful, and he was surprised when she took him up on the offer. When she came to him, her face was of course fuller from her pregnancy, but she was still the same sweet, polite young woman he had met when she was a teenager. He offered the church's support and assistance if she wanted to raise the baby, but she was adamant that her first choice was to place the child with a family who would love him as if he were their own. A sonogram had confirmed she was expecting a boy.

"I don't want anything from them," she had said. "And I don't even want them to know who I am. But I want to be absolutely positive that they are good people who will give him a good life, and then I could go on with mine. But how can I be sure when so many people are not who they appear to be?"

It was one of those moments that made Father Horrigan believe that sometimes God puts people in the right place at the right time. He knew the perfect couple: Andrew and Marcy Buckley. He could still remember the relief on Michelle's face when he described the couple who would give her baby a loving home. And, of course, the joy on the adoptive parents' faces when they picked up Johnny at the hospital. He had taken a photograph so he could show it to Michelle. "I can tell they already love him," she had said.

He wanted to believe that Michelle had never regretted her decision, but she never came back to church again, nor did she return his phone calls when he tried to reach out to her a few times. Sandra made the decision to switch to another parish a few months after the adoption. Seeing the Buckleys without having a relationship with her grandchild was simply too much for her to handle, she said.

Of course, Father Horrigan assumed that, as the parish office manager, Cynthia knew none of this.

"It must have been seven years since I saw Sandra last," Cynthia said. "It's a shame that she suddenly stopped coming."

"Is it possible we still have her contact information?" he asked. "I'd like to give her a call."

Maybe he could put Marcy's mind at ease without breaking his promise to Michelle.

• • •

A few minutes later, he was back inside his house, dialing Sandra Carpenter's number. After three rings, a woman answered.

"Hello?"

The voice at the other end of the line sounded weaker and much older than the one he remembered. "This is Father Mike Horrigan from Blessed Sacrament Church. I was looking for Sandra Carpenter." It had been seven years since he'd spoken to her. She had probably changed her number since then.

"Well, you found me, Father Mike. How nice to hear from you."

Her voice brightened slightly, but still seemed frail. They spent a couple of minutes chatting about her retirement from her secretarial position with the federal government and a new priest at St. John's who was creating quite a stir incorporating what she called his "stand-up comedy routine" into his services.

"Well, I'm happy to hear you found a home there. We were sorry to lose you at Blessed Sacrament. I hope you don't mind, but I was wondering how things worked out for Michelle. Where is she these days? Is she here in D.C.?"

He had decided that there was no need to upset Sandra or Michelle by telling them that Johnny was missing. He hoped that he could get confirmation from Sandra that Michelle was nowhere near Long Island, New York, without causing unnecessary anxiety.

There was a long pause at the other end of the line. "Sandra? Are you there?"

"I guess you didn't hear the news."

He could tell from the tone of her voice that the news wasn't good. "I'm sorry. No, I didn't."

"I lost her."

"Oh, Sandra. I'm so sorry. What happened?"

"I'd say I lost her the first time not long after the baby was born. She became a completely different person. Distracted. Depressed. Defeated. She withdrew from everyone she knew, including me.

She lost any desire for happiness. Any thoughts of returning to college were out the window. She moved to Denver for a while, then to Philadelphia. She'd call me on birthdays and Christmas, but otherwise, she was practically a stranger."

He told her again he was sorry. "Is there anything I can do to help?"

"No. My daughter died six months ago."

"Oh, Sandra. No."

"It was a drug overdose. The police found my number in her cell phone, so at least someone told me. I still can't believe she's gone. At least she knew her son has a good life. Despite everything she went through afterward, she told me that she never regretted having him or giving him a chance at a happy life. How is little Johnny, by the way?"

Chapter 13

The humming sound beneath Johnny Buckley suddenly changed. The car was slowing down. His body rocked in the trunk as they drove over a series of bumps. He believed they were pulling off the highway, maybe onto a dirt road.

The car came to a halt. The engine stopped, too. He heard one of the car doors open. Maybe it was two. He couldn't tell. And then there was silence. Complete and total silence.

He began to take slow breaths—in and out—the way his mom had said they did in her yoga class. She told him doing that would make him calm. It had worked when she took him to the dentist. It was helping, but he was still so afraid.

Please, please don't leave me here, all alone.

"Hello?" he cried out. "Is anyone there?"

More silence. What if no one ever came for him? What if he was never seen again and died out here by himself?

"Can anyone hear me?" His voice was louder this time, but, still, no one answered.

He pounded his palms against the top of the car trunk. "Help! Help! Someone please help me!" He yelled as loud as he could.

The trunk popped open, and he screamed from fright. A three-inch crack of light appeared between the hood and the trunk. Someone was standing behind the car. A gray T-shirt, untucked except for the spot where it hitched up over the top of a gun tucked inside the man's waistband. That's all Johnny could make out other than the treetops and sky around them.

"See, that's why we needed to pull over in the middle of nowhere." The man's voice was deep. He sounded casual, like there was nothing weird about making Johnny ride in the trunk or the weapon only inches away from Johnny's head. "Had to see whether you were going to act up or not."

"Please, mister. Don't hurt me."

"That's the last thing I want to do, but I will if I have to. You understand? And I can go back to that hotel and find the rest of that family, too, if you don't do what I say. I can't have you yelling and screaming, do you understand?"

Johnny said nothing.

"That's better. Now . . . are you hungry?"

He shook his head, but then realized the man couldn't see him any better than he could see the man. "No, my stomach hurts."

"That's probably nausea from the chloroform. I was afraid of that. You didn't throw up in there, did you?"

Johnny couldn't tell whether the man was actually worried about him or was angry about the possibility of a mess in his car. "Uh-uh."

"Don't say 'uh-uh.' It's not polite. You're old enough to say yes or no, properly, like a young man."

"I'm sorry. No, I didn't get sick."

"That's better. Here, you're probably thirsty, and this will help your stomach." The man reached in and handed Johnny a can of ginger ale.

"I can't drink it lying down," Johnny said.

"Tell you what. I'll pop the trunk all the way open so you can sit up and get some fresh air for a bit. But you got to promise not to try to run away or yell or any of that nonsense, okay? There's no one around to hear you, and remember what I said I would do if you act up. Deal?"

"I'll be good, mister. I promise."

"Just like I knew you would be. Such a good kid."

Chapter 14

In the honeymoon suite at the South Shore Resort, Leo had asked the babysitter Kara to recount every single moment of her day on the beach in minute detail. In Leo's police experience, the exercise might lead to the discovery of an important detail that may otherwise have been overlooked.

Kara was recalling the Buckley kids continuing to practice for Laurie and Alex's wedding ceremony after Timmy and Ramon had left the hotel to shop for a birthday present for Alex. It broke Laurie's heart picturing Johnny standing in for Timmy as her best man. As she listened, it was obvious that the boy looked up to his older future cousin.

The chirp of a cell phone interrupted Kara's narration of the day. Marcy glanced at the screen with a perplexed expression and excused herself from the room.

From his spot on the sofa next to Kara, Timmy brought their attention back to the beach. "The twins were teasing Johnny before we left, saying he wanted to be so much like me that they were going to call him 'Timmy.'"

Something about Timmy's comment tugged at the back of Laurie's mind, a thought trying to come to fruition. She was about to get ahold of it, like pulling at a loose thread, but then immediately lost her grasp.

"That's right," Kara agreed. "Chloe and Emily continued like that the whole time at the beach, calling him Tim or Timothy more often than his own name. He seemed to enjoy the game. It was all in good fun."

They had been calling their brother Timmy on the beach. Laurie felt that nagging feeling again, and then pictured little Wyatt, the boy on the beach who had been sharing the skim board with Johnny and Timmy.

"Kara, did you happen to notice *anyone else* addressing Johnny by that name? Or hear someone calling out the name *Tim*, or some variant of that?" Wyatt had heard a woman yelling the name Tim, *like maybe he was in trouble or not paying attention or something.*

Kara shook her head.

"No, not that I heard. It was just the girls playing around."

Marcy re-entered the living room, her cell phone still in hand. "Do you mind if we take a break for a second? Ramon said the girls are famished. Timmy, maybe you and Kara can meet them down-stairs and make a final decision about where to go."

"They're going to ask about Johnny," Timmy muttered.

Laurie could tell that Marcy was trying to get Timmy and Kara out of the room so she could speak alone to Laurie and Leo about whatever phone call she had received. She could also tell that her son did not agree with the decision not to tell the girls directly what was going on, but he was only ten years old. This wasn't his decision to make.

"No one's asking you to tell a lie," Laurie said. "Marcy and An-drew will decide what's best as far as the twins are concerned."

He nodded his agreement, and he and Kara went to find Ramon and the girls.

"That was our priest, Father Horrigan," Marcy said, placing her phone on the coffee table. "He decided to contact Johnny's biological mother after I called him, just to be absolutely certain she had nothing to do with this."

"And?" Leo prodded.

"Her mother said she died of a drug overdose six months ago."

Silence fell over the room.

"I guess in some ways, we didn't even know her," Marcy said. "But it still feels so . . . sad. And surreal. But Father Horrigan made a point to tell me that her mother—Johnny's grandmother, I guess—said her daughter never had any regrets at all about having Johnny and making him part of our family."

Marcy wiped away a tear as Laurie patted her on the back, trying to comfort her.

The somber moment was interrupted by the sound of a rumble outside the hotel. They turned to face the windows and spotted a small-engine plane above the shoreline. *HELP FIND MISSING CHILD: FINDJOHNNY.COM. WE ♥ U, JOHNNY!*

Marcy placed a hand over her mouth. "I need to track down the twins. Now!"

Chapter 15

Marcy rushed from her suite, anxious to tell the girls about the search for their brother before they learned of it on their own. When she opened the door, Alex was standing in the hallway, his knuckles raised to knock.

He must have recognized the panic in Marcy's face. "You saw the plane, didn't you?" he asked.

"Yes, I'm just praying that somehow Chloe and Emily didn't."

"They're only four years old. They can read?"

"Their brother's name probably, plus the shape of the heart. We don't want to risk it."

Alex held up both hands to calm her. "It's okay. They were in the hotel lobby with Ramon. We saw them just now when we walked in. Andrew took them to my room so the two of you can break the news to them in private. I'm so sorry, Marcy."

"No, it's okay. I'm the one who wanted the plane banner to get the word out. I just never imagined they'd be able to do it so quickly."

"We were surprised, too. I guess custom images take longer, but they have these big red letters all ready to be strung together. When we saw they had a heart symbol, we added that, too, hoping that Johnny might see it. We told the flight company to wait an hour to give us a chance to get back here so you and Andrew could talk to the girls, but obviously the message didn't make it to the pilot."

"It's not your fault, Alex. I appreciate everything you've all been doing." Marcy turned around to face Laurie. "I have no idea how to tell the girls their brother is missing. Any advice?"

The worst day of Laurie's life was the day Greg died. It was as sudden and as violent as anything that could be imagined. She didn't even have the luxury of losing him to natural causes, or to know that his killer would be brought to justice. And the worst part of all was telling Timmy that his father was gone and their lives would never be normal again.

Laurie rose and gave Marcy a quick hug. "Kids are stronger than you think. Tell them how everyone loves Johnny and is working to find him, but don't make any promises you can't keep."

Marcy nodded her appreciation, and Laurie could see that she was strengthening her resolve. She was hopeful that this would be the worst news Marcy would ever have to deliver to her girls.

Alex wiped his face with both hands once the door closed. "I still can't believe this is happening. I feel so helpless."

"We all do," Leo said. "Missing children cases were always the hardest ones to work on the job. You feel a giant clock ticking over your head, knowing that the chances of a happy ending are decreasing with every tick. Sorry, I know that's gloomy, but I figured the two of you should know what we're dealing with."

"I keep trying to think of things I can do to help," Alex said, leading Laurie toward the living room sofa, where they took a seat beside each other. "Marcy texted Andrew earlier that she had tried calling their priest to find out the identity of Johnny's birth mother, just in case the adoption had something to do with this, but the priest said the information was confidential. I thought I could do some legal research to see if there's a way to access the records through the court system."

When he reached for Laurie's hand, she held on to it tightly. He always had a way of calming her, just with his presence.

"There's no need," she said. "The priest called Marcy back later. He did some digging on his end and found out that the mother passed away."

"So that's a dead end," Leo said dryly.

Laurie shot him a look with squinted eyes and pursed lips.

He shrugged. "My gallows humor. Sorry."

"Not in front of Marcy and Andrew, Dad. Please."

"Of course not. Only among the three of us twisted souls."

"The police are on it now, at least," Laurie said. "At this point, what else can we do?"

"Well, we got lucky and found a tech guy when we were at the print shop. He heard us writing up the text for the fliers and offered to help. He's the one who suggested setting up a website with photos of Johnny, a place to submit tips, a contact phone number—basically an informational clearinghouse. It only took him a few minutes to get a domain name and build a very basic site with the photos we gave him."

"Nice to know there are angels walking around East Hampton," Laurie said. "So now we just have to get the website shared as broadly as possible. The plane's a good start, but we can do a lot with social media."

"Well, count me out then," Leo said, holding up his hands. "I don't have any of that nonsense."

"Nor do I," Alex added.

Laurie's father believed social media was for people who needed attention, and Alex had shut down all of his accounts since becoming a federal judge. They both looked to Laurie, knowing she held a distinct advantage in this arena. The last time she checked, *Under Suspicion* had 1.8 million Facebook fans and 1.3 million Twitter followers.

"I'll post it on the show's feeds right now."

She picked up her phone to open Facebook and found a text from her assistant producer, Jerry Klein. *Brent stopped by this afternoon to make sure I knew he meant it when he told you we're still on the clock for the next episode. Crazy idea, but what about your dad's Darren Gunther case? Lots of celebrity interest, and we certainly know one of the insiders. . . . Food for thought.*

Jerry had begun working for her as an intern when he was in college, but he was now her most trusted colleague. He was also the most computer-savvy and pop culture–obsessed member of her team, so he had taken the lead on running their social media accounts.

Jerry picked up his cell phone after one ring. "I *knew* I shouldn't have texted you about work the second I hit send. Laurie, it's nearly eight P.M. on the first night of your vacation. Please tell me you're in some beautiful restaurant holding a drink with an umbrella in it."

"Far from it." He uttered a series of *oh no*'s and *I'm so sorry*'s as she laid out the reality of where things stood and the Find Johnny website they were trying to share. She heard a quick tapping of keys in the background. "You're still at the office?"

"Uh huh," he muttered, focused on his typing.

Of course he was. "And I did get your text, by the way," she said. "I was concerned about the perception of a conflict of interest, but I'll think about it." She made a point not to refer directly to Darren Gunther's wrongful conviction claim. She didn't want her father to overhear and get his hopes up.

"Please," Jerry said. "Put Brent and his ridiculous deadlines out of your mind. You have enough on your plate. Okay . . . *done!* It's on Facebook and Twitter now. Our fans are pretty fierce. They'll get it viral in no time, and I'll monitor the accounts for any comments that show potential for follow-up. Hang in there. Hopefully Johnny just got lost on the beach and will find his way back any second."

"Thank you so much, Jerry. You're the best."

When she hung up the phone, she opened Facebook to share the show's posts on her personal account. She noticed that the last entry on her own timeline was a post from Marcy three days earlier, in which she had tagged Andrew and Laurie. Two pictures were side by side. The first was a photograph from the South Shore Resort's home page of the hotel beneath a pink-and-purple sunset. The other was a picture of Marcy, Andrew, Alex, Laurie, and all four kids standing on the steps of the Lincoln Memorial, taken last fall. *Countdown: Three more days 'til a glorious family vacation in the Hamptons, followed by Judge Birthday Boy's wedding with the best sister-in-law I could ask for! #Foundfamily #blessed*

Laurie composed a post to share the Find Johnny information with her own friends and then hit enter. Her eyes drifted back to Marcy's photographs. She felt a pang in her stomach at the sight of Johnny, his arms wrapped tightly around his mother's waist. He really did look like Timmy.

She looked up from her phone with a sudden awakening.

"What's wrong?" Alex immediately asked. He could always read her emotions.

"Timmy. The twins were calling their brother Timmy. Plus there was the room mix-up. The hotel had the honeymoon suite booked under *my* name, not theirs."

"What about it?"

"What if this wasn't random? What if someone thought Johnny was *my* son?"

Chapter 16

Alex took a seat beside Laurie on the sofa and wrapped an arm around her shoulder.

"Laurie, you're literally shaking right now. It's been a long day, and I think the stress has gotten to all of us."

"Think about it. Earlier, I kept reminding myself of what we all know to be true—random crimes are the *exception*. Usually, a crime victim is targeted by someone they know. Or at the very least, they're targeted for a reason. That's what led me to ask about Johnny's birth mother. But what if the target was actually Timmy?"

"Or it might actually just be random," Alex said. "There was that horrible case last year where the defendant happened to see the little boy getting off the school bus—"

She couldn't stand the thought of Johnny suffering a similar fate as the child he mentioned. "Maybe, but we can't ignore the possibility. Your nephew looks so much like Timmy. Particularly if someone had been working from a picture of Timmy from a year ago; he's grown since then, so they'd be expecting a kid who was closer to Johnny's size. Plus his sisters were calling him Timmy, and they're all staying in a hotel room booked under my name. And Timmy and I are the ones who live two hours away from here, and I've certainly managed to make some enemies given my work on the show. Do you have any idea how many letters I get from accused murderers begging me to clear their names?"

"Of course I do," he said quietly. "I worked on the show with you, remember?"

"The numbers have tripled since then, and I don't even tell you about some of the angry follow-ups I get when we don't respond, because I don't want you to worry about me. It would only take one person to get a crazy idea in his head—"

Leo held up a tentative hand, looking for permission to interrupt the conversation. "Laurie, I hear what you're saying, but can I offer an opinion?"

"Of course, Dad."

"I watched you raise Timmy for those first five years after Greg was killed. You always put on a brave face, but that monster told your little boy in no uncertain language that he would be coming back someday to kill both him and his mother. And you lived like that for half a decade—never knowing whether *this* might be the day that Blue Eyes made good on his promise."

At the mention of Blue Eyes, Laurie had a sudden image of a younger Timmy, only eight years old. He had been even smaller than Johnny then, in his pajamas and robe, being dragged by one hand from a pool house. It all happened so quickly, during the culmination of the filming of the very first *Under Suspicion* special. The man had grabbed Timmy with one hand and pointed a gun at his head with the other. The man then laughed as he let go of Timmy and watched him run to Laurie, who was rushing to meet him. The man raised his weapon. The sound of gunfire exploded, and then a red stain blossomed across the man's shirt as he fell to the ground.

"Dad, are we absolutely positive that the man the police killed was actually Blue Eyes?"

"A hundred percent," he said. "That man spent half his life blaming me for every problem he had in life, all because of a decision I made as a young patrolman. Blue Eyes is dead, Laurie. That nightmare finally ended two years ago. He has nothing to do with this."

Alex and her father exchanged a look that was unmistakable. They were certain she was on the wrong track, but had no idea how to change her mind.

"Dad, I know I don't have your kind of police experience, but please don't look at Alex like I need to be saved from my own ideas. If you were working this case as a detective, and I was your partner, I think you'd hear my theory out. It's based on facts."

"Fair enough. But my entire reason for bringing up Blue Eyes in the first place was to suggest that maybe this whole episode has been 'triggering,' as they say these days. You were never one to put a label on what you went through, but you can't survive something like Greg's murder and the threats that followed without experiencing a bit of PTSD."

She had met so many crime victims who did in fact suffer from post-traumatic stress disorder, but she certainly didn't think of herself as having it. "Maybe someone close to Blue Eyes is still in the picture?" she said, still bouncing around ideas aloud. When she analyzed a story idea, it was always how she did her best work. "They could be trying to finish what he started."

"Laurie, there was no one close to Blue Eyes. Not a single person cared about him. That was his whole motive for going after you and Timmy—to get to me. He wanted me to lose everything and everyone I loved. He was determined to see me as isolated and lonely as he was."

Alex gave her shoulder a small squeeze. "It makes perfect sense that you would connect Johnny's disappearance to those threats against you and Timmy, but your son is safe. Blue Eyes is gone."

"Fine, so it's not Blue Eyes. I was simply saying that we should be taking a look at people who have threatened me." She was already composing a text to Jerry, asking him to pull up the file they kept of worrisome communications. With Jerry's trademark humor, he had labeled the file *Weirdos*.

"Does anyone specific come to mind?" Alex asked.

"There's a woman who has long been suspected of hurting her stepson. The boy has been missing for more than seven years, but the police are convinced that the stepmother killed him and disposed of his body so she could go on with her life without raising another woman's child. The father very much wants me to profile the case on *Under Suspicion*, but the stepmother won't agree. The last time I approached her, she said maybe I should worry more about my own son instead of someone else's. It sent a chill up my spine, and I made a vow to myself that I'd never contact her again."

"And how long ago was that?" Alex asked.

"About three months ago."

"And have you kept your vow?"

She had. Alex had a point. The woman's veiled threat had worked. There was no reason for her to target Laurie and Timmy now. "Plus, she lives on the West Coast. Okay, so she's not the most likely suspect. We do get a lot of creepy messages, though."

"An email or a tweet is one thing," Alex said. "Going from that to kidnapping a child is a big leap."

"I've never seen you push back on my ideas this way, Alex. I'm only trying to help."

He took a deep breath before answering. "You're right. I'm sorry. I just know you so well. We're all helping, but you try so hard to fix everyone else's problems, even at your own expense. This wasn't your fault, Laurie. Whatever happened, it's not because of anything you did or didn't do."

Laurie noticed that her father had been uncharacteristically silent. He appeared deep in thought, his brow wrinkled.

"You look like you're mulling something over, Dad."

He held up a tentative finger, as if he were literally trying to point to an idea he had in mind. "Alex is right, Laurie. It's not your fault. But it might be mine."

Laurie and Alex exchanged a perplexed glance before Leo continued.

"We were talking about Blue Eyes. His obsession with harming you and Timmy stemmed from his desire for revenge against *me*. When Alex asked you if someone came to mind who might want to hurt your son, you had to reach for a woman on the West Coast who made a cryptic comment about Timmy three months ago. You're not in the middle of working a case that might give someone a motive to intimidate you this very minute."

It didn't take Laurie long to follow his train of thought. She knew how important her father's meeting that morning had been with the District Attorney's Office. "But *you* are," she said, looking intently at her father.

"This could be Darren Gunther's handiwork. He won't be satisfied until I admit that I framed him for the murder of Lou Finney."

Chapter 17

Eighteen Years Earlier

Lou Finney heard the chime of jingle bells as the bar door opened, then felt a rush of cold air blow past the front booth, his favorite place to sit if he wasn't in the back office or working behind the bar. He recognized the newcomer as Rocky, one of his neighborhood regulars.

"Had a feeling I'd find you right there," Rocky said. "First snow of the year means Finn sitting right in that very spot. Only question is whether you follow the snow, or the snow follows you."

Lou's first and middle names, Louis Caron, were after his maternal grandfather, but he'd been called Finn as long as he could remember. The bar bore the same name, naturally. *Rocky's got an observant eye*, Finn thought. This was indeed one of Finn's many annual traditions. A shot of Jameson on St. Patty's Day. A good beer during the first Mets game. Watching the first snowfall from the front booth in winter.

Rocky took his time in the doorway, waiting as a group of young women made their way toward the exit from the Thursday night trivia contest at the back of the bar.

"You gonna close that door or what, Rocky?" Finn asked. "The heat don't run for free in here."

Rocky smiled, looking pleased as the line of attractive women walked past, each one thanking him for holding the door open for her on the way out.

"Such a gentleman," Finn said dryly.

As the door finally closed, Rocky threw him a wink. "Can you blame me, Finn? That's the closest thing I'm getting to a hot date any time soon at our age."

"Speak for yourself, old-timer."

Rocky grabbed one of Finn's shoulders and gave it a good, friendly shake.

"Get this geezer a drink on me," Finn said, calling out to Clarissa behind the bar.

Rocky gave him an appreciative wink. "Business must be good."

Indeed, it was, Finn thought. He'd opened this bar thirty-five years ago, when he was only twenty-seven years old, with a business loan cosigned by his parents. That was back when the denizens of the West Village were artists, rebels, hippies, and others looking for a community away from the posher, more proper areas of New York City. Finn wasn't drawn so much to the counterculture as he was to the cheap rent.

He told his folks that someday this neighborhood would take off, but never in his wildest dreams could he have imagined the hipness of downtown Manhattan in the new millennium. Now he enjoyed the best of both worlds. He still catered to regulars like Rocky, keeping the music on the jukebox about right for their era. But he also had a cocktail menu with cosmopolitans and apple martinis, trivia night Thursdays, and Sunday Bloody Mary singalongs to bring in the young people who thought it was cool to hang out at an old established joint once in a while.

As he watched Rocky settle into his usual spot at the end of the bar and take a long pull from his on-the-house beer, Finn allowed himself to enjoy a moment of pride in the business he had built.

The snow was really starting to stick by the time Clarissa appeared at his booth with a glass mug filled with dark liquid. He could tell from the way she carried it that the drink was hot.

"Is that what I think it is?" Finn asked.

"Your favorite." *Favorites*, Finn thought. Just like with his kids, Finn would never admit that he had favorite employees, but Clarissa was indeed his favorite. According to her birth certificate, she was twenty-six years old, but he was convinced that her soul was born in 1937. Plus, she made a hazelnut hot toddy that tasted like heaven in a cup.

A loud roar came from the back room, and she responded with a cross look. "We've got some numbskulls back there tonight. Angry vibes if you know what I mean. Too much testosterone. No offense, of course."

"Of course," he said with a smile.

"Some guy with a big mouth is celebrating his twenty-first birthday. He's home on winter break from Vassar, which he is quite loud and proud about. According to him, he's already got a top job lined up on Wall Street. He's going to own this town by the time he's thirty."

"So when's the wedding?" Finn asked.

"To him? Not in this lifetime! Besides, he's got his eyes set on someone else. He's trying to move in on one of the women back there, buying her drinks all night."

"Let me know if he crosses a line. If he's looking to cause trouble, I'd rather toss him out of here before he gets started."

As Clarissa turned toward the bar, the volume from the back room suddenly burst to an even higher decibel level, nearly causing Finn to spill his hot toddy. The heavy purple curtain separating the room from the rest of the bar billowed as if a heavy gust of wind had found its way inside, and two men came tumbling out, shoving each other, surrounded by a crowd. A tall guy in a sports jacket and loosened collar cried out, "Come on, Wall Street tough guy. Let's see what you've got."

They were moving so quickly that Finn could only make out the dark hair of the taller fighter, and the red hair of the shorter, squatter one. A woman screamed, "Jay, watch out!" as the dark-haired one threw a punch that landed against his opponent's jaw.

"Whoa, whoa, whoa," Finn hollered, jumping up from his booth with both palms up. Finn's was known for being a low-key hangout, but you don't own a bar for three and a half decades without learning how to break up a fight. *It's just a couple college kids*, Finn thought. *Amateur hour. I've got this.*

The men paid no attention to Finn and continued to shove and punch each other, carried by the momentum of the crowd around them. Finn jumped into the group, trying to reach the two fighters to break them apart. Before he knew it, he was being pushed through the doorway outside. The sidewalk in front of the bar was beginning to become slippery. A younger man next to him lost his footing and fell to the ground as the dark-haired fighter bent low and charged toward the redhead, letting out what sounded like a loud growl.

Finn inserted two pinkies into the corners of his mouth and gave the crowd his best attention-getting wolf whistle. "Enough of this, fellas. Break it up, break it up."

He felt a push behind him and was heading even closer to the action. *Once they can see and hear me*, he thought, *I'll be able to calm them down. I'll get right between them if I have to.*

The redhead's eyes opened wide as he registered Finn's presence in front of him. His lips parted. *He's just a kid*, Finn thought. *I can tell he's scared and wants this to be over. We're all fine here. Almost done.*

The kid's gaze lowered, and Finn allowed his eyes to follow, suddenly aware of a strange feeling in his abdomen. A sharp pain.

The glow of the corner street lantern was refracted from the top of the metal blade, two inches of it visible between Finn's sweatshirt and the knife handle. The fingers wrapped around the handle were clenched into a fist. He watched the blade get pulled out of his body, and then took a deep gasp for air, like a swimmer coming up from the water. The air turned into a scream as the knife plunged into him again.

Finn's knees buckled beneath him, and he collapsed to the sidewalk. The last thing to fall was his head against the first snow of winter on the concrete.

"Fiiiiinnnn! No, Finn, no. Please, someone call an ambulance. He's stabbed."

It was Clarissa. The last thing Finn saw was his favorite employee, futilely pressing her bar apron against his sweatshirt.

The bystanders failed to stop the bar brawl, but the sight of their beloved bar's owner, bloodied on the ground, drastically altered the mood of the crowd. No longer onlookers, they jumped into action, working together to detain the two fighters until official help arrived.

The EMTs pulled up within minutes, but Lou Finney was pronounced dead at the scene. Meanwhile, the bar regular named Rocky found an open buck knife about twelve feet from Finn's body, tossed or kicked there by either his killer or someone else, intentionally or not, during the chaos after his stabbing. As a last way to help his friend, he watched over the weapon, making sure no one touched it, until police arrived.

The earliest responding police officers learned that the dark-haired fighter was Darren Gunther, a junior at Vassar College, the one celebrating his twenty-first birthday. The redhead was Jay Pratt, a twenty-seven-year-old commercial real estate broker. Lieutenant Leo Farley, a rising NYPD star, was the detective to get the call out.

Chapter 18

Laurie noticed that her father had stood up and was pacing back and forth as he recounted the history of the case against Darren Gunther for the murder of a beloved West Village bar owner named Lou Finney. That was always a sure sign that he was feeling anxious.

"It was a bar fight that spun out of control," Leo explained. "Gunther was a good-looking, charismatic college student with the confidence of the multimillionaire he was determined to become. Jay Pratt, by comparison, was a nerdy little pipsqueak—a fancy Upper East Side kid who walked into a ready-made job at his dad's commercial real estate business. And Lou Finney? He was the nice guy who was trying to keep two hotheads from getting rowdy in his establishment. His death was a major blow to the neighborhood. Word spread fast. The entire sidewalk in front of the bar was covered with flowers and handmade sympathy cards by the following morning."

Alex leaned forward from his position on the sofa next to Laurie, his elbows against his knees, fingertips steepled. "I actually remember when that happened," Alex said. "I was in college at the time, too. A couple of my friends from Fordham went down to the village that night for drinks, but I stayed home. I had one last final exam to cram for. My friends were on their way to Finn's later that night when they saw the police and crime tape out front. The next day, they said they might have been there when the fight broke out if they hadn't been caught in traffic caused by the snow."

"I remember it, too," Laurie said. "I had just gotten home for winter break, and I remember you telling Mom about the case the next morning when you came back for a quick pit stop. By the time you returned later that evening, you had Gunther's confession."

"No," Leo said, tapping a corrective finger in the air. "It was more complicated than that. When I came home for a break, I had the *first* version of his confession, but I knew Gunther was holding back—spinning the facts to give him a shot with a sympathetic jury. It was that conversation with your mom during my break that cracked it all open. I went back to the station and questioned Gunther again. Got him to show his true colors."

The memory was coming back to Laurie more clearly. "I remember you telling Mom later that she was the one to solve the case."

Alex's gaze moved back and forth between them like a spectator at Wimbledon, trying to make sense of the conversation.

"Here's how it went down," Leo said, seeing Alex's confusion. "Finn was trying to break up the fight as it spilled out onto the sidewalk, but Gunther and Pratt were clawing at each other's throats. Plus, a bunch of people from the bar had spilled outside, too, drawing even more gawkers from the streets. It was total pandemonium. And then Finn dropped to the ground, stabbed—twice it turned out—in the abdomen." Leo's left hand touched the area just above his belt indicating the location of the wounds. "No one actually saw the stabbing, but the most likely scenario was that it was one of the two brawlers—Gunther or Pratt."

"They each blamed the other one," Laurie explained, trying to hurry the story along. She knew her father could easily spend an hour talking about the case, especially in light of the distortions Darren Gunther had made of the facts over the last several months. She understood her father's obsession with the facts, but was eager to hear how they might relate to Johnny's disappearance.

"When I first read them their rights—in separate interrogation rooms, obviously—both of them said the other guy must have been the one to pull the knife. And I had no witnesses. Gunther, Pratt, and Finn had been clustered too tightly together for anyone else to have a good view. By the time Finn fell, the knife had been dropped on the sidewalk, and from the looks of the handle, we suspected someone had done a quick wipe-down to try to get rid of any fingerprints. We found Finn's blood on both men, including their hands, but that didn't tell me much under the circumstances. So I waited a bit and told Gunther we found his prints on the knife. And, of course, I told Pratt the exact same thing."

"And whose prints did you actually find?" Alex asked.

"No one's," Leo said. "Obviously, it took the crime lab a couple of weeks to confirm that for certain. But that night, I told them both that whoever did the quickie cleanup job on the knife's handle had missed a couple spots, and that we had found two latents remaining as points of comparison. I explained how a fingerprint is made up of loops and whorls and arches. I said we had thirteen matching points on one of the latents, and twenty on the other. It was practically a forensic science seminar. I even brought in the kind of graphics an expert witness would put on a screen during a trial so they could see the similarities with their own eyes—but it was evidence from an entirely different case."

"There's nothing wrong with that," Alex noted. "Even as a defense attorney, I knew that police were allowed to use deception during an interrogation."

"Exactly," Leo said. "As long as the defendant's statements remain voluntary—which they were. Well, Pratt was absolutely defiant. He told me to bring in a Bible or a lie detector so he could swear that he never touched a knife. He insisted that the lab must have switched his print card with Gunther's. But not Gunther. I could see the wheels churning. Suddenly, he shifted his story entirely. He claimed *Finn* was the one who pulled the knife in the first place, saying he'd show the two of them for starting a fight in his bar. He claimed he was trying to take the weapon away to protect himself when someone pushed Finn toward him."

"Twice?" Alex asked with disbelief. "He accidentally stabbed the man *twice*?"

Leo shook his head. "Of course not. That's why I said this was the *first* version of his confession. I knew it was bogus. And Gunther looked so smug, almost smiling as I left the room, daring me to try to disprove his story. You've seen Gunther's interviews with those fawning TV hosts? He'll never sit down with someone with a real journalism or criminal law background. He's tapped into the celebrity showbiz market. He was the same arrogant guy, even back then."

"The profile in *Vanity Fair* called him disarmingly charming," Laurie recalled dryly.

"And he knows it," Leo said. "That charm and some smarts are what earned him scholarships to prep school and to Vassar."

"Well, it probably helped that he had lied and said he was an orphan," Laurie said.

In the lead-up to Gunther's criminal trial, Leo and the police discovered that Gunther had a dark side lurking beneath his charismatic exterior. Deeply insecure, he manipulated people to gain access to elite circles, only to steal personal items from the homes of his hosts and lie about his background. His high school teachers and college professors were under the impression that he had been orphaned during middle school after his parents died in a private plane crash, but it turned out that his single mother was alive and well and working as a housekeeper in Forest Hills.

But Leo knew none of this the night of the murder. It was Laurie's mother who had pointed Leo in a new direction of interrogation when he had come home briefly in the early morning hours after the killing.

"Eileen was always so intuitive," Leo said, his voice softening at the memory of Laurie's mother. "I saw Gunther and Pratt as two young hotheads in some booze-filled bar brawl. She was the one who wanted to know what the two men had been fighting about in the first place. Gunther never offered his side of that story, but Pratt said it started after he bought a drink for a woman he knew from boarding school. Eileen heard that and . . . *boom!*" Leo pointed a finger for emphasis. "Eileen said, 'That's it! I guarantee you, it's about Gunther trying to control that young woman. He didn't want her talking to another man.' Sure enough, I got hold of this bartender from Finn's, a woman named Clarissa DeSanto. She said Gunther had been focused all night on another customer—female, probably three years older than him, dressed down in jeans and a sweater for a night in the Village, but wearing two-karat diamond studs and a stack of Cartier bracelets."

"Out of Gunther's league?" Alex asked.

"That was Clarissa's impression, so I worked that angle. I tracked the female customer down through one of her friends' credit card charge. Her name was Jane Holloway. She and Pratt went to high school together. She said Gunther kept trying to talk to her all night. At first, she was flattered, but then she and her friends joked about him behind his back, saying he was the next Wolf of Wall Street, that kind of thing. She finally fibbed and told him she was engaged, so he'd leave her alone. Then when Pratt showed up, Gunther said something like, *You must be the lucky fiancé. Your girl's been talking to me all night.* From there, it quickly became clear there was no actual engagement. Jane had embarrassed him big time."

"So it was all about his fragile ego," Alex said.

"Exactly, or at least, that was *my* theory. I pulled him back into the interrogation room, this time making it clear I knew how insecure he was. How *rejected* he must have felt. How he had spent his entire birthday seeking attention from a woman he could never actually date. How Jane had treated him like a joke. When he realized that I knew—that I could see who he *truly* was—he finally confessed, and this time it was the truth. He called the girl and her friends names that could never be repeated in polite company, and he admitted that he stabbed Finn in a blind rage."

"All because a woman rejected him," Laurie said.

"It happens much too often, sadly," Leo said. "When the trial came around, Gunther denied ever making that confession. He told the jury I fabricated every single word of it, claiming once again that he never even saw the knife and had no idea who stabbed Lou Finney. He said someone else in the crowd must have done it."

"And you really think that Gunther might have something to do with Johnny's disappearance?" Laurie asked.

"The thing that has always made him tick was his desire to control his own narrative," Leo said. "First, he wanted to be the up-and-coming, hot-shot financial wizard. Now he wants to be the brilliant writer who was railroaded by the police. And guess who's the bad guy in this narrative—the one he needs to control if his story's going to stick?" Leo held up one hand. "*This* guy. Gunther probably hoped

I'd be six feet under by now, or living out my days playing horseshoes on a beach, not caring one way or the other about some ancient case. But that's not me. I've been fighting him every step of the way. Unless I say I fabricated that confession, the DA's not going to dump that conviction."

Laurie closed her eyes and tried to imagine Darren Gunther plotting from a prison cell to abduct a child to gain leverage over the detective who stood between him and freedom. Using an innocent little boy as a pawn would be sociopathic. But she knew Gunther was cunning and charming. He had contacts with people outside of prison who might be willing to help him obtain what they saw as justice in the long run.

But how could Gunther connect the cop he despised to a child born nearly a decade after Gunther went to prison? Her mind suddenly flashed to an image of the magazine article that was currently framed on the wall of her studio office.

"Dad, *New York* magazine did that profile last year, when you went back to the NYPD to join the counterterrorism team," she said. "The writer included that whole section about how you originally left the department to help me with Timmy after Greg was killed. Remember how upset I was when they ran that photo of the three of us from the Yankees game?"

She, Timmy, and Leo had attended as guests in the mayor's box. Laurie tried to be vigilant about protecting Timmy from the public eye, but apparently the stadium's event photographer had snapped a shot of them and uploaded it to a database of images available to the press. Rather than use the official NYPD headshot that Leo had provided for the profile, the magazine editors had somehow tracked down the old family photo online.

Alex was following the chain of her logic. "That picture from the game was a couple of years old."

Back when Timmy looked just like Johnny, Laurie thought.

"We should tell Marcy and Andrew about this before we do anything further," Laurie said.

"They're probably still in my room," Alex said. "They must have broken the news to the twins by now. Let's go find them."

Chapter 19

Johnny could tell from the slower speed of the car and the many turns the man made, one after the next, that they had left the highway. The slivers of sunlight that had found their way into the car trunk had been replaced by the back glow of taillights. It was nighttime now.

Another turn, followed by *bump, bump, bump, bump* beneath him, like they were driving on rocks or gravel or something. Then the car came to a stop.

One one-thousand, two one-thousand . . .

He began to count to himself, just as he had every single time the car had stopped before. A hundred and seventeen was the furthest he'd gotten so far. That was the one time the man actually got out of the car and talked to him and gave him a ginger ale.

Ever since then, the stops had all been false alarms. Probably stop signs or red lights, Johnny guessed. Were they finally stopping, and was the man going to come for him again?

Eight one-thousand, nine one-thousand . . .

He heard a low humming sound somewhere outside the car. Not like a bird or other animal, he thought. Like a machine of some kind.

The sound stopped at the count of fifteen, and the car began to move again. He felt a small bump, and then the surface beneath the tires seemed to go back to a smooth road. No more rocks and gravel.

Another stop.

One one-thousand, two one—

The man cut the engine. This was the first time that had happened since the ginger ale. He held his breath, terrified of what might happen next.

The mechanical humming sound started again. This time it was louder.

As soon as the noise ended, he heard the man's voice. "Not one little peep, you hear me?"

Johnny opened his mouth to tell the man he wasn't going to say a word, but then stopped himself. That would be saying something, and he didn't want to make the man angry.

He heard the quiet pop of the trunk. The man looked directly at him through the crack.

"Sssssssshhhhh, little boy. Not a word."

The voice was a whisper, but it was the scariest sound Johnny had ever heard. He needed to get out of the car before he wet his pants. He didn't want to think about what the man would do to him if that happened.

As the top of the trunk slowly rose, Johnny saw that they were inside a two-car garage. There was enough room for the car they had traveled in, but the rest of the garage was filled with all kinds of things sticking out everywhere. A bike on top of an old sofa next to a lawn mower. Boxes stacked all over the place. A huge mess.

"You can sit up now," the man said. "It's okay."

Johnny followed the instructions but moved slowly, not wanting to upset the man. He couldn't take his eyes away from the gun in the man's waistband.

"You're probably ready to get out of that little compartment, aren't you?"

Is he trying to trick me? Johnny wondered. He didn't want to sound like a complainer. The man looked at him expectantly. Johnny nodded slowly, hoping he had guessed the right answer.

"We're going to go inside this house now," the man stated. "But you have to follow my rules."

Johnny nodded again.

"First one we already talked about before. No yelling or making a fuss or trying to run off."

Johnny nodded, even though he didn't want to go to a strange house. He had never, ever been inside someone else's house unless his parents took him there. He tried to imagine what they were all doing now at Uncle Alex's birthday party, but it didn't even seem real that they were still out there in the world while he was here, alone with this man.

"And I'm going to have to give you a little haircut." The man made a snipping gesture above his own head.

The thought of this man holding scissors near his head made Johnny shake, but he forced himself to swallow and nod again.

"And you're going to need another name, too. You're Danny now. Don't forget that. It's Danny from here on out. You'd better get used to it."

Get used to it? Johnny thought, frightened. *How long is he going to keep me here? I want to go home.*

Chapter 20

The waiter in the hotel restaurant had just finished clearing the table when Marcy's cell phone buzzed. *Please let it be good news.* She wanted to believe that any moment, the message would be delivered: Johnny had simply gotten lost on the beach and was waiting for them to come pick him up from the warm, comforting home of whatever nice family he had approached for help.

Instead, it was a new message from Laurie: *We looked for you in Alex's room. Where are you?*

Marcy hit reply and typed, *Getting dinner at the hotel restaurant.*

The letters looked up at her from the screen, judging her. How can you go out to dinner when your son is missing? What kind of woman responds that way?

Her husband, Andrew, had made the decision. He had been the one to pull her aside and force her to read the booklet that Detective Langland had given them. It was a publication from the National Center for Missing and Exploited Children. The title alone— A *Child Is Missing*—had brought on yet another wave of nausea. She kept reminding herself that this was really happening. Johnny was . . . missing.

But Johnny wasn't their only child. They had Emily and Chloe to take care of, too. Marcy was not going to let them find out about Johnny from anyone other than her. That's where the pamphlet came in, with a section devoted specifically to the needs of the missing child's siblings. After reading the materials, Marcy and Andrew decided that the best thing they could do for their daughters was to tell them everything they knew, and then make them feel as safe as possible by maintaining their usual routines and structures.

And so here the four of them were, finishing up a meal she had forced herself to eat, because the manual said that it was important for the children to see that their parents were taking care of themselves. She set aside her guilt and finally hit enter on her text reply to Laurie. Laurie was a mother, too. She'd understand that Marcy and Andrew needed to look after the twins, despite the terror that Johnny's disappearance instilled.

Marcy feigned a small smile as Emily and Chloe debated what menu item Johnny would want when he got back to the hotel. She told herself that it was a sign that the girls were accepting their brother's "temporary absence," in the words of the manual.

Please, God, let it be temporary.

Her phone buzzed again as the check was arriving. Laurie again: *My father has a theory he wants to share with you and Andrew. I think I might be able to help if you want to pursue it. Alex can watch the girls while we talk.*

Marcy had always been the kind of person who read the instructions for any project from start to finish before touching even a single part. Andrew, on the other hand, would unpack all the pieces and start putting them together, pausing for a passing glance at the directions only if he hit a snag.

Their different styles were on apparent display in their hotel suite as Leo laid out his theory that a convicted killer named Darren Gunther had orchestrated the kidnapping of their son out of a mistaken belief that he was actually Laurie's son, Timmy. According to Leo, it was nearly certain that Gunther would have read a recent magazine profile about Leo, which had highlighted Leo's close relationship with his grandson. It was Leo's belief that Gunther planned on using the child as leverage to force Leo to admit—falsely—to fabricating the confession that had landed Gunther in prison for life.

As Leo spelled out all the facts, Andrew interrupted with follow-up questions.

"How could he take our son if he's behind bars?"

"Gunther has become a bit of a celebrity," Leo explained. "It's not uncommon for prisoners to attract supporters—in some instances, even what you might call groupies. And Gunther is extremely charismatic. I could imagine him persuading someone with a vulnerable mind to help him from the outside."

"If he plans on manipulating you, why haven't you heard anything yet?"

"He's behind bars. If he's the one calling the shots, it might take a while for the actual kidnapper to communicate with Gunther and plan the next steps."

Marcy sat quietly next to Andrew on the sofa in their suite, saying nothing, absorbing every last bit of information. True to form, she would listen first and ask questions later.

"If you're right," Andrew continued, "what's going to happen when they realize they have the wrong boy? It's possible they might panic and—"

The thought had sent a chill down Marcy's spine, and still, she said nothing.

When Leo was finished spelling out his theory, and her husband was done with all of his questions, she finally spoke. "How or when will we know if you're on the right track?"

Leo shook his head sadly. "I wish I could tell you, Marcy. If somebody connected with Gunther reaches out to us regarding Johnny, we'll be certain. Darren Gunther has had eighteen years to blame me for the fact that he's in prison, and he's not the kind of man who has ever played by the rules. I keep trying to figure out when and where he's working a con, stacking the deck in his favor. And now your son is missing. Could it be a coincidence? Maybe. But right now, this is more of a theory than anything else we've got."

Marcy found no comfort in the words.

"Laurie, you said you were in a position to help if we wanted to pursue this."

"Maybe. The way I see it, Gunther distrusts police, yet craves attention. Media. Fame. And I have my show. Dad has been pitching Gunther's case for *Under Suspicion* for weeks, but I was worried about the potential conflict of interest."

Leo started to interrupt, but Laurie stopped him. "The *perception* of a conflict of interest," she emphasized. "If there's any chance that Gunther has something to do with Johnny's disappearance, I'll use my show to get access, both to him and to the people he knows outside of prison. And I don't have to deal with Miranda warnings, court orders, or any of that. There's a reason we've been able to unearth evidence that police missed for years in some cases."

Marcy felt Andrew's hand squeeze hers. "What do you think, babe?" he asked.

Marcy opened her mouth to speak, but nothing came out.

Laurie offered her a small smile. "We just gave you a lot of information at once."

"If we say yes, what would you do first?" she asked.

"The very first thing would be to run it by my boss at the studio, but I know he'll say yes. Then I'd contact Gunther's attorney to invite Gunther to sit down with my show for an interview."

Marcy nodded, letting the information sit with the other facts. "And is that something you could do right now, or . . ."

"No," Laurie said. "I'd call the attorney first thing in the morning, and then of course it would take however long to get an answer. But from there, we'd go in for the questioning as quickly as we could possibly do it."

"So we can think it over for a little bit, is what you're saying." Marcy found herself rising from her spot on the sofa, unsure of where she wanted to go from there.

"Absolutely," Laurie said. "It's just that—"

"Johnny's missing," Marcy said flatly. "Trust me, I don't need a reminder." Looking at Andrew, she said, "We'll let you know for sure early tomorrow morning."

Andrew reached for her hand. "Are you okay?" he whispered.

She looked blankly at him. *Am I okay?* Her own voice sounded distant when she finally answered. "Remember how it said in that manual that the consumption of a parent's consciousness and awareness by a child's disappearance can lead to physical shock?"

The last thing Marcy heard before she hit the floor was her husband crying out her name.

When Marcy woke, she was in bed. The room was pitch-black, but she just knew that the hand holding hers was Andrew's.

Where am I?

She felt like she had been asleep for years. She had been dreaming about helping Johnny with his school science project. He had made a battery out of pennies and nickels, tinfoil, a paper towel, and some salt and vinegar. Johnny's smile beamed from ear to ear when he was able to light a 100-watt bulb with his concoction. "Mom, if we make enough of these, we can light up the whole house!"

Johnny!

She jolted upright in the bed, fully awake now, her heart racing. She was tucked into bed in her pajamas, but next to her, Andrew was on top of the duvet, still dressed.

He reached for her and hugged her, making shushing sounds to console her.

She looked at the digital clock on the nightstand. 12:10 A.M.

"What happened?" she asked.

"You collapsed. You don't remember?"

Do I?

She remembered Alex bringing a woman into the suite's living room. She was a doctor who happened to be staying at the hotel. Marcy answered all of her questions: her name, the year, the name of the current president. She remembered putting on these pajamas, in fact, and tucking the clothing she had worn that day neatly back into her suitcase, as she always did to speed the ever-dreaded task of repacking at the end of a trip.

"I remember every bit of it, actually," she said. "But it feels like each step was taken by some other person, not me. That sounds crazy, doesn't it?"

Andrew kissed her gently on the forehead. "Not at all. I've felt numb all day. That manual says that people process the stress differently. Try to get more sleep—"

"The girls—"

"Already dozing away. I don't think the reality has sunk in yet."

One of the many benefits of youth. "We should all be so lucky." She let herself recline again, her head sinking into the down pillow.

They stayed there like that, in bed in the dark, breathing into the silence and holding hands.

"Andrew?"

"Yeah?"

"That manual . . . it said that some parents grow apart when a child's missing. That they—"

He turned on his side and placed a hand gently on one of her cheeks. She could make out enough of his face to see that he was crying. "That is *never* going to happen to us. Do you hear me? *Never.*"

She reached over and wiped the tears from his face. A few minutes later, his breaths slowed and deepened. He was asleep.

She fumbled for her cell phone on the nightstand. No new messages.

She pulled up the phone number she had saved for Detective Langland and composed a text message. *Please call me as soon as you can. There's something I need to discuss with you.*

She set down her phone and then picked it back up again, realizing she was much less important to the police than they were to her. *P.S. This is Marcy Buckley. It's about a man named Darren Gunther.*

She closed her eyes and tried futilely to find sleep again.

Wherever you are, Johnny, try to sleep and don't be afraid. We're going to find you. I promise.

Chapter 21

As the man walked out of the bedroom, he flipped the light switch next to the door, enveloping the room in blackness.

"Sorry," Johnny said, just as the man was about to close the door behind him. "But I'm afraid of the dark. My parents always leave a light on for me when I go to sleep."

Johnny felt like the man was searching his face for more information. Did he know that Johnny was telling a fib?

Johnny had stopped using a night-light at the very beginning of the first grade, but that was when he was at home—his *real* home, with Mom and Dad and Chloe and Emily and their two cats, Salt and Pepper. Home, where he felt safe. He didn't want to be in a dark room in a house with the man who'd brought him here. He didn't want to be in this house at all.

He was afraid the man would yell at him after his fib. That he'd somehow know it was a lie and punish him. Or he'd scold him again, the way he had when Johnny said, "Uh-uh," earlier in the car. If the man thought he was *old enough to say yes or no, properly,* he probably thought he was too old to be afraid of the dark, too.

But the man surprised him by flipping the switch again, and then leaving the room and returning with one of those dim little lights that was a plug that went right into the wall. Johnny noticed that the cover on the bulb was the shape of an angel.

"Is that enough light, Danny?" the man asked, hitting the same wall switch again to turn off the lights on the ceiling. "I don't want these overheads on full blast all night or you won't get any sleep. You probably need some rest after that car ride."

Johnny said nothing, and the man's voice softened. "Not very comfortable, was it, Danny?"

Johnny wanted to scream, *Stop calling me Danny! That's not my name!!* Instead, he simply shrugged. The man kept looking at him, waiting for a different response.

"That's enough light," Johnny said.

The man was still staring, waiting.

"Thank you."

The man smiled slightly, appearing pleased. "There's no bathroom in here, as you may have noticed. Do you need to go again before you go to sleep?"

"No, thank you."

"Can you make it through the night?"

"I don't have accidents anymore."

Another pleased smile. "Of course not. Such a good boy, Danny."

Then he left. The clicking sounds from the door sounded like locks tumbling into place, confirming what Johnny had suspected.

Now Johnny was locked in the room all by himself, and he could use the dim light to try to figure out where he might be and why he was here.

He pulled his knees to his chest and wrapped his arms around them. The white wooden rails of the headboard of the bed pressed into his back. That's how hard he was leaning away from the bedroom door, as if he might just disappear into the wall itself. He tugged at the front of his hair. It was so short. He shivered at the memory of the man standing so close to him, clipping away with those shiny scissors.

He hadn't seen much of the rest of the house—just the kitchen during the haircut, and then the bathroom across the hall. But what he'd been able to take in as the man marched him from one spot to the next was almost as messy as the garage.

Not this room, though. This room was clean, he thought. No, it was more than "clean," at least by his parents' rules for stars on the chores chart. At home, a tidy room meant making his bed and picking up his toys and returning everything back to the drawers and shelves and cubes where it belonged.

This room was . . . empty. And lonely. It contained this bed he was sitting on and a dresser over by the window, and that was all.

He let go of his knees and allowed his feet to swing over the edge of the bed. As he stepped to the floor, he tried to make himself as light as possible. He made his way over to the sole piece of furniture other than the bed. The dresser was lightly stained wood, and the handles were all in different colors—red, yellow, blue, green. He couldn't imagine the mean man who brought him here owning such a thing.

He tugged the top drawer ever so gently. It slid open easily. Inside were stacks of neatly folded T-shirts. He was afraid to touch them, but they looked like clothes for his size. A little boy. Him.

BAM!

Johnny flinched and automatically slid the dresser drawer shut at the sound of the loud noise coming from somewhere else in the house. Upstairs? Down the hall? He couldn't tell. It was loud, though. So very, very loud. Something crashing to the ground.

He heard the man's voice yell one of the bad words Mr. Norton who lived next door wasn't supposed to say in front of Johnny and his sisters. The man's voice sounded angry and ugly.

Johnny scurried back to the bed, climbed beneath the blankets, and pressed his eyes shut tightly. *I didn't do it.* He never said the words out loud, but in his head, Johnny was screaming. *Please don't blame me. I'm here, trying to sleep, just like you told me to.*

He lay in silence, praying that the man wouldn't return to his room in such a furious mood. Minutes passed, and then Johnny heard what sounded like footsteps on the floorboards above him. He also heard the man's voice again, but this time it was lower and calmer. Whatever had made that *BAM* sound was over. The moment had passed.

Johnny let himself wonder what his parents and Chloe and Emily were doing right now. *Try to go to sleep, Mama and Daddy.* Maybe they would all dream about each other and it would feel like they were really together.

Johnny thought maybe he had actually fallen asleep and was having a dream when he suddenly heard a new and different sound above him. A voice, but gentler. Higher pitched.

Mama?

No, he was still in this stupid house. He was fully awake, and the voice was real, and it did not sound at all like the man who had brought him here.

There's another person upstairs, he thought. *And it's a lady.*

Thursday, July 16

Day Two

Chapter 22

Laurie smiled as Alex tucked a loose strand of hair behind her ear and left a small kiss on her cheek. "Maybe we should get married right here on the beach while the sun rises, just like this," she said.

It was the crack of dawn, only five-thirty in the morning, and they had the ocean view all to themselves. Timothy wouldn't wake for another two hours, so Laurie and Alex had snuck off to the beach to enjoy a quiet moment together.

"I was the one who said I would marry you anytime and any-place. Say the word and we'll cancel the plans for Sunday."

"We're canceling them anyway, don't you think?" She felt guilty for even thinking about their wedding while Johnny was missing, but at some point, they needed to notify the church and the guests and the restaurant and the florist and the band . . . and she was sure she was forgetting a few others. Even their small reception would take some work to erase.

"If we start making those phone calls, it's going to crush Andrew and Marcy," Alex said.

She remembered that first night after Greg was killed, lying in bed alone, realizing she would never sleep under the same roof with him again. If they called off the wedding now, it would be an admission that they didn't believe Johnny would be coming back by Sunday, which might mean he was never coming home at all.

"You're right. We've got to keep faith. With luck he'll be found by the time Marcy and Andrew even wake up."

"The rest of the world does continue to move, though," he said. "Anthony texted me at four in the morning. I swear, the man works twenty-four hours a day. He says the contractor installed the master bathroom backsplash in the kitchen, and the kitchen backsplash in the bathroom. He says he thinks it works, but will tell the contractor to do it all over again if that's what we want."

Anthony was the interior designer overseeing the remodeling work on the Upper East Side apartment they had purchased two months earlier. In theory, it was in mint condition, "turn-key ready," as the Realtors liked to say. But after Laurie was followed there and threatened by a gun-wielding assailant when she first viewed the property, they had joked that a few aesthetic changes might be justified to purge the apartment of any evil spirits.

"If Anthony says it's fine, I'm sure it's beyond beautiful. He's a perfectionist."

Anthony had come to them by way of an enthusiastic recommendation from Ramon, who had been friends with Anthony's parents in the Philippines before they all came to the United States thirty years ago. Ramon had known Anthony since he was a baby, but these days, Anthony Abad San Juan was one of the most sought-after designers in the New York City area.

"Ramon hinted that Kara was a little uneasy about whether she should stay given how drastically the situation has changed," Alex said. "She, Ashley, and that lifeguard are all completely distraught. They feel terrible. They were out all last night, walking the beaches and handing out fliers."

"I know Marcy and Andrew don't actually blame them for what happened, but I understand why Kara's uncomfortable being here under the circumstances." Even Laurie's friend Charlotte was distraught and helpless about Johnny's disappearance, offering to help however she could. But Kara and her friend felt personally responsible.

"So I was thinking that Ramon could rent a car to drive her back home today and then stay in the city to help with anything that comes up while we're still here. He can take a look at the tile, too."

"God knows he'll use that kitchen more than either of us," she said with a weak laugh. "And you know I trust Ramon implicitly."

In another sign that the new apartment was meant to be their next home, they had been able to purchase a one-bedroom apartment two floors beneath them where Ramon would be able to live separately.

Alex suddenly pulled her close and wrapped his arms around her. It felt good and safe.

When he loosened his embrace, she was surprised to see that he had tears forming in his eyes. She reached up and wiped them away. "Not exactly the way we thought we'd be celebrating your fortieth, is it, birthday boy?"

He shook his head. "I'm sorry, it's so selfish, but all I've wanted for so long is to start a life with you. I kept dreading that your show or my court docket or something somewhere would blow up and get in the way of the wedding or the honeymoon, but now it's poor little Johnny. Is it possible some cosmic force is plotting against us?"

"Are you kidding? What are the odds that the two of us were ever going to meet, let alone adore each other's families or like the same food or finish each other's sentences? Or fall absolutely head over heels in love where I can't even imagine a tomorrow without you?"

His face broke out into a small grin that took her breath away. "Okay, you just managed to make this a happy birthday after all. The happiest, in fact."

"Until the next one and all the ones after that."

He kissed her, and for just one second, she stopped worrying about anything at all.

Chapter 23

Marcy could count on one hand, with four digits to spare, the number of times she had ever lied to Andrew.

It was on their fifth date, when the conversation ventured into past relationships. Had any of them gotten serious? Ever talk of marriage? Why hadn't they worked out in the end? As far as Marcy was concerned, nothing in Andrew's past could possibly matter. She knew on their very first date—a setup by a mutual friend—that she was going to spend the rest of her life with him. And when he proposed to her exactly one year later, he said he had felt the same way.

But nevertheless, they had that inevitable, awkward conversation the way people do. As it turned out, Andrew had dated a bit in college, but was never serious with anyone until law school. Her name was Christina. They stayed together through their judicial clerkships and had even talked about marriage, but then she accepted a job in London, and the long-distance relationship eventually played itself out. It all sounded very cordial.

Marcy, like Andrew, had also had only one serious prior romance: Brian Lassiter. They went to college together in Northern California and then took their dreams to Los Angeles, hers to be an actress, his to be a screenwriter. There was no ring because he couldn't afford one, but they vowed to get married as soon as they both had their feet planted in their future professions. It happened for Marcy first.

She wasn't a star by any definition, but within a year, she had her Screen Actors Guild card, two national advertisements, and a recurring role in a network TV drama. Marcy would have been perfectly content to head to city hall, but Brian wanted to wait a little longer, until he sold his first screenplay. She agreed, because she supported him unconditionally.

A "little longer" turned out to be three more years, but the wait had paid off—at least for Brian's screenplay. One week before the big splashy premiere of what would become one of the year's top-grossing films, Brian broke the news. He loved her—he would always love her—but he was no longer *in love* with her. It was over, and Marcy was devastated. She couldn't get out of bed, but she couldn't sleep either. She couldn't eat. And she certainly couldn't act. For the first time in her young life, she was a complete and total mess.

But all of that was in the past by the time she was on her fifth date with Andrew and he was asking her, "So why didn't it work out?"

She knew in her heart that she was going to spend the rest of her life with this wonderful man.

So she lied. "We were so young. We just grew apart, is all."

She immediately felt guilty about the fib, but she assured herself it was harmless. She never wanted Andrew to look at her and wonder if he had been her rebound guy, or a second choice that she had settled for. The truth was, Marcy had always thought the idea of a "soul mate" was preposterous, until she met Andrew.

But then, this morning, for the first time since that fifth date, she found herself lying when Andrew asked where she was going as she reached for the car keys on her hotel nightstand. "To get more of the flyers copied."

Technically, that was true, but the copy shop would be Marcy's second stop in town. Her first was to see Detective Langland on her own.

•   •   •

Three minutes after her own arrival, Marcy spotted Detective Langland through the front window at Babette's and rose to greet her at
the corner table she had requested for their visit.

"I took the liberty of ordering you a coffee," Marcy said.

"Bless you. How are you holding up?"

"I'm not. I feel . . . numb. Like I'm forcing myself to put one foot
in front of the other, even though I don't know what direction I'm
supposed to be moving."

"I'm so sorry we haven't found your son yet. The good news is we
finally got permission for the Amber Alert to go out. It should blast
all over phones and highway alert signs any second now. And we've
got hundreds of volunteers forming search parties, and officers vol-
unteering to knock on doors, house to house, working off-duty."

Marcy mustered a smile. "We're very appreciative."

"So I looked into the Darren Gunther matter, as you requested,"
Langland said. The detective had called Marcy at precisely six this
morning, probably when she woke up to her alarm and saw the text
message Marcy had sent the previous night. Marcy told her about
Leo Farley's theory that a convicted murderer named Darren Gunther may have kidnapped Johnny under the mistaken belief that he
was Leo's grandson, Timmy. He and Laurie wanted to use Laurie's
television show as a way to approach Gunther outside the formal
legal process. "With all due respect to the esteemed former deputy
commissioner, I'm afraid it's a little more complicated than Leo and
his daughter may have described it."

This was precisely why Marcy had wanted to speak to the detective privately. Leo and Laurie were Alex's family now, and by
extension, they were Andrew's and therefore hers. But how well
did she really know them? Johnny, on the other hand, was a part of
her. He was her heart. Laurie had already gotten Marcy all worked

up about the possibility of Johnny's birth mother going after him. Now she was convinced some person Marcy had never heard of had somehow managed to mastermind the abduction of her son from a prison cell. Laurie was a brilliant woman, but part of her talent in her job was having a colorful imagination for alternative story possibilities. On the other hand, Laurie had good reason to believe her father.

"My brother-in-law, a very experienced defense lawyer and now a federal judge, says he's never seen a law enforcement officer with the natural instincts of Leo Farley," Marcy said. "He seems to think that if Leo believes Gunther is planning some way to cheat the system in this wrongful conviction claim he made, then he must be right."

"Have you ever heard of tunnel vision?" Langland asked.

"Sure, like when you can only focus on one thing. Like right now, all I can think about is my son."

"Yes, it's that, but it means something else when we talk about police having tunnel vision in an investigation. If a detective is convinced a suspect is guilty, they focus only on that suspect to the exclusion of other possibilities. It's not that they intentionally *try* to frame anyone, but they see what they want to see, hear what they want to hear. They stop being objective, and view all of the evidence through the lens of the theory they already believe."

"And you're saying Leo Farley's not objective when it comes to Darren Gunther?" Marcy asked.

Langland shrugged and took another sip of her coffee. "I'm saying it's possible. It takes more than a book of essays written in a jail cell to gin up the kind of support Gunther has for his release." She reset her coffee cup in its saucer and leaned forward across the table, preparing to explain. "During his trial, Gunther claimed that a third person became involved in the fight between him and another bar patron after they spilled out onto the sidewalk, and that this stranger was the one to pull out a knife and stab the bar owner. Obviously, the jury didn't believe him, but Gunther has stuck to that same story all these years in prison."

"Don't all convicts say they're innocent?"

"A lot of them. But not many of them have DNA evidence on their side. Any chance you know what touch DNA is?" Langland asked.

Marcy shook her head.

"It's the ability to get DNA evidence off of skin cells left behind on an item. That kind of technology didn't exist eighteen years ago, but we do it all the time now. It's not quite like *CSI* where the bad guy walks into a room and leaves his DNA on every single surface, but it's much more sensitive testing than was available even ten years ago. Well, last year, Gunther asked a court to order the state to test the knife that was used to stab Lou Finney. He got lucky, and the court actually agreed. Sure enough, the lab was able to get a testable sample from a spot on the very end of the knife's handle, near the blade, and it didn't match either Gunther or the other man in the original bar fight. At that point, the case was assigned to the District Attorney's Conviction Integrity Unit."

"And what is that?" Marcy asked. She suddenly imagined Johnny sitting in the empty seat next to her, crying. He was everywhere and nowhere.

"Basically, what it sounds like. They reinvestigate closed cases where there's a reasonable claim of innocence. New York maintains a DNA database that contains samples from certain categories of convicted felons. Through the DNA database, the DA's Office matched the skin cells on the knife to a man named Mason Rollins.

"At the time, Rollins was just a twenty-year-old with a misdemeanor assault arrest and one conviction for a low-level drug offense. But now he's got a rap sheet taller than I am, including four years upstate. Guess what for?"

"No idea."

"Stabbing someone in a bar fight ten years ago."

"Leo didn't explain all of this," Marcy said.

"That's what I meant about tunnel vision. He probably has some theory as to why Rollins and the DNA don't matter, because he's convinced his guy's guilty."

"Leo said Gunther confessed."

"And Gunther says he didn't. No one else witnessed the confession, and this was before they started routinely videotaping interrogations."

Marcy didn't know Leo Farley well, but she knew him to be a good and honest man. She couldn't imagine him fabricating a statement that hadn't been made. She told Langland as much now.

"I'm not saying he made it up. He questioned Gunther multiple times over the course of several hours, alone and without a lawyer. Some cops don't want to believe it, but it's a proven fact that innocent people can be made to give false confessions under the right circumstances—or the wrong ones, as the case may be."

"With all due respect, Detective, you don't sound like a typical police officer. In fact, you sound more like my brother-in-law, Alex, and he was a defense attorney."

Langland held up her palms. "I'm not saying that's what happened. But I made a call to someone I know in the DA's Office in the city, and she said Farley's got his heels dug in on this case. He sees it as a personal attack on his integrity. She told me that if it were any ordinary detective who had handled the case, Gunther would probably have been released by now."

"Based on skin cells?"

"They've got a hardened criminal's DNA on the murder weapon, and no explanation for how it got there. I don't want to get into the middle here, but Leo might not be objective when it comes to this.

My focus is on finding your son, Marcy, not something that happened in the West Village eighteen years ago. Think about it: Leo Farley thinks Gunther's behind Johnny's disappearance because he's convinced the man's the type of sociopath who would kidnap a child to help his case. But if he's *actually innocent* and his case is legit?"

Marcy now saw the connection between the new information Langland was providing and her belief that Gunther had nothing to do with Johnny's disappearance. "Then the last thing he'd do is go out and commit a major new crime when a court is about to exonerate him."

Langland leaned back in her chair, her point made.

"So you think I should ask Laurie not to pursue this," Marcy said.

"Laurie and Leo can do whatever they would like. I just don't think it's going to help us find Johnny, I'm sorry to say. I don't want you to have false hopes. And on that note, it's now tomorrow. I think it's time to set up the press conference we talked about yesterday."

When Marcy returned to her hotel suite, she held three hundred fresh copies of the FindJohnny.com fliers. Her husband immediately rose from the sofa when she entered. Alex and Laurie were there as well.

"Thank God," Andrew said, greeting her with a long hug. "We were getting worried about you."

"The print shop took forever." Another lie.

"I was texting you."

"I'm not getting a signal out here," she said. That was not a lie. According to Laurie, cell phone service in the Hamptons was notoriously glitchy. "I'm sorry I scared you. Where are the girls?"

"Leo volunteered to take them out to the lighthouse in Montauk. Giving them the appearance of normalcy like the experts say. I hope that's okay with you. That's why I was texting. Also, I don't want to push, but I was thinking about that press conference. I think we should do it."

"You read my mind," she said, feeling guilty that she had already asked Detective Langland to set it up.

Chapter 24

Fifteen minutes later, Laurie hung up the phone on the desk in Alex's hotel room. She was working from his room because Timmy was still sleeping in their room next door. From a chair in the corner, Alex looked at her expectantly.

"Well, that was the easiest 'yes' I've ever gotten from Brett Young," she announced.

"It sounded like it was going well from this end." Alex's blue-green eyes sparkled with approval, and she realized how much she still missed working with him on the show. "He's on board?"

"More than on board. He told me he's behind me a hundred percent and to use the studio resources however I can to get the answers we need."

"Maybe your stubborn, self-centered grump of a boss has a heart after all."

"Or maybe he wants this wrapped up in time to spike our ratings before the next fiscal quarter. He was nearly panting at the thought of budding cultural icon Darren Gunther on camera, investigated by the daughter of the cop who landed him behind bars. Regardless of his intentions, what matters is that he's giving me the green light."

"But you're still worried about the perception of a conflict of interest."

"Not really. If there's any chance Gunther's involved in Johnny's disappearance, I've got to try to find that out. It's just a hunch for now, but I'm in a better position to act on that than the police. I can always pull the plug on the show if I have to. Brett will be furious, but Johnny's the top priority. Now I have to pray that Gunther's narcissistic enough to take the bait."

"Only one way to find out." Alex handed her his iPad. The browser on the screen was pulled up to the website of Tracy Mahoney, Esq., the criminal defense attorney who had recently agreed to represent Darren Gunther free of charge in his wrongful conviction claim. "Her number's right there at the bottom. If I recall correctly, it forwards directly to her cell if she's not in the office."

As it turned out, Mahoney was in her office, and her secretary put Laurie's call through when she explained who she was and that she was calling regarding Darren Gunther.

"Ms. Moran, what a surprising call! Or is your name Mrs. Buckley by now?"

Even though Laurie tried to keep her private life private, she wasn't surprised that news of her engagement to Alex had spread like wildfire in the local attorney circles where Alex was a well-known fixture.

"First of all, call me Laurie. And we're not quite to the altar yet, but I'll be keeping my name in any case." It was a decision she had finally made after weeks of uncharacteristic vacillation. She was young when she married Greg, less established in her career. She had taken Greg's name because she wanted the entire family to share a surname, and it wasn't a bad idea as a journalist for her to have a separate name from her well-known law enforcement father. Plus, she thought Laurie Moran had a nice ring to it. Now that was her name, and one she shared with Timmy and his father. When she broke the news to Alex, he told her he was surprised she had even considered the alternative.

"Good for you," Mahoney said. "I did the same, but my husband's last name is Macy, so that was an easy decision. Tracy Macy, can you even imagine? Besides, at this point, shouldn't the men be taking our names? Women, we get the job done, right?"

Alex had already filled Laurie in on what he knew about Tracy. According to him, she had an easygoing manner and a sharp sense of humor. But beneath the breezy demeanor, she was also one of what he called the "true believers" of the defense bar, who fundamentally believed that the criminal justice system was broken at its core. Whereas Laurie recognized that even the best police departments had room for improvement, Tracy Mahoney was once quoted as comparing the NYPD to the Mafia. Alex said she was a skilled trial attorney, enough so that she could have earned a small fortune defending corporations and white-collar criminals. Instead, she took a few high-paying cases a year so she could afford to represent the rest of her clients pro bono to correct what she viewed as injustices. Gunther's case was supposedly one of her passion projects, but Laurie knew that he could be looking at a huge payout if he succeeded in his wrongful conviction case, and his lawyer would be entitled to take a healthy percentage of the award.

"Well, I'm hoping you'll be able to help me get *my* job done, Tracy. I'm calling about Darren Gunther."

"If I'm not mistaken, you've got a direct personal connection to the case."

Laurie wasn't entirely surprised that the attorney already knew she was Leo's daughter. "I'm calling in my professional capacity, however. We'd like to give your client a chance to tell his side of the story to a national audience on our next *Under Suspicion* special. Are you familiar with our show?"

"Absolutely. I'm probably one of your top fans. I'm all for any show that points a spotlight on the failures of our *so-called* justice system."

"That's not exactly how I think of our program."

"Why not? You've shown time and again that you and your team are able to get to the truth years after the police dropped the ball. You've not only caught more than your fair share of murderers, but also in the process, you've exonerated innocent people who for years lived under a cloud of suspicion. If you ask me, that makes you one of the good guys."

"Then I'll take the compliment, I suppose." Laurie reminded herself that she did *not* want to like the woman accusing her father of wrongdoing.

"Well, I'm glad, because I'm afraid that's all you're going to get from me," Tracy said glibly. "No way am I letting my client go on national television to be questioned by Leo Farley's daughter."

"As a fan of the show, I'm sure you're aware that I don't do the actual questioning. That would be done by the show's host, Ryan Nichols."

"Oh, even better: a blow-dried, blowhard former federal prosecutor. No thanks."

A year ago, Laurie actually would have agreed with Tracy's dismissive description of Ryan Nichols. Her boss Brett had chosen him over Laurie's reservations, not because of his Harvard degree, Supreme Court clerkship, short stint at the U.S. Attorney's Office, or even his sandy-blond hair, bright green eyes, and perfect teeth—but because he happened to be the nephew of Brett's college roommate from Northwestern. After a rough start, however, Ryan had managed to ease into his role at the studio. He'd never fill Alex's shoes or be her BFF, but he had proven to be an excellent on-camera questioner, deserving of at least half of the praise he enjoyed lavishing upon himself.

"Right now, your client has a handful of fawning celebrities who make a hobby of his case to burnish their own public images as justice crusaders. Sure, he's gotten a couple of sidebar write-ups in national magazines, but I can offer him a prime-time national television viewing audience."

"Again, courtesy of a biased producer."

"You don't think I'm aware of the potential perception of a conflict of interest?" From the corner, Alex flashed her a thumbs-up. She had run this argument past him in advance. "If anything, I'll be the one to bend over backward to give Darren a fair shake. The last thing I want is for people to question my professionalism and say I was covering up for my father."

"Giving him a 'fair shake,' as you say, might not be so easy when it involves some very serious accusations of wrongdoing against the beloved Leo Farley."

Laurie closed her eyes and took a deep breath. In her heart, she knew that no set of facts could ever convince her that her father would perjure himself to send an innocent man to prison. She pictured Johnny, alone in a dark room, crying. *One step at a time*, she reminded herself. *Johnny first, worry about the show later.*

"I wouldn't make the offer if I didn't think I could handle it," Laurie said. "And if I'm not mistaken, it's not your decision to make, Counselor. You have a duty to extend the offer to your client, do you not?"

She heard Tracy sigh on the other end of the line. "Guess you can't be engaged to Alex Buckley without learning a thing or two about this job of mine."

"Guess not." She smiled in Alex's direction.

"I'll get back to you." She did not say good-bye before disconnecting the call.

Laurie heard a knock on the door connecting Alex's room to hers and Timmy's. "Mom, is that you?"

She opened the door, and Timmy entered, wearing his Star Wars pajamas, his expressive eyes still sleepy behind the sandy-blond bangs that hung over his brow.

"Sorry, I didn't realize it was locked," she said. "You mean you could hear me through the walls?" She brushed his hair back away from his face and planted a kiss on his forehead. "I didn't think I was that loud."

"Nah, but I could sort of hear a woman's voice and I thought, *Well, that* better *be my mom*." He flashed a toothy grin at Alex. "Happy Birthday, Alex!"

"Why, thank you very much, kind sir."

It was so much like her sweet boy to have someone else's birthday at the top of his mind first thing in the morning.

"Is Johnny back yet?"

She saw the disappointment in his eyes as he read her expression. He looked down at his toes, and she pulled him into a hug. "Everyone's still looking. Try not to worry."

"But it was supposed to be surf lesson day. And then opening presents at lunchtime. We can't do any of that without Johnny. We have to wait for him to come home."

"I know, sweetie. And you're right. We're going to save all the fun stuff for him. And your grandpa has an idea about where Johnny might be, and I'm helping him figure it out."

"Really?" Timmy's eyes brightened with cautious optimism. She felt a pang in her heart. How long would this little man believe that his mother could fix the world's problems?

"We're going to try. Depending on how things play out, we may need to go back to the city early."

An hour later, she and Alex were in Marcy and Andrew's suite, helping them prepare for their press conference while Timmy played a video game. She stepped to the corner of the room to answer an incoming phone call. It was Tracy Mahoney.

"I spoke to my client. Against advice of counsel, he insists on sitting for the interview. But he wants it all on camera. I'll be in the room, but won't interfere, absent something beyond the pale, and I get a copy of the unedited footage in case you're tempted to doctor it. I leave it to you to make arrangements."

All eyes were on her when she ended the call. "Gunther took the bait. He'll do the interview."

They had already agreed that she'd be going back to the city to get her team ready in the event Gunther agreed. Marcy nodded stoically. "Thank you so much."

"I'll stay through the press conference."

"No," Marcy said. "I don't want to waste a single minute. We'll be fine here. Please, go do everything you can from the city."

"Okay. I'll be in constant touch."

She was almost done packing when Alex arrived in her room, his own roller bag in tow. She had assumed she and Timmy would be driving his car home alone.

"Are you sure?" she asked.

"Marcy and Andrew insisted. I go where you go."

Chapter 25

Marcy felt an involuntary smile break out across her face as Chloe and Emily spoke over each other with breathless delight on the other end of the telephone line.

It had taken her four tries before she was able to reach them. It turned out that Leo had lost his cell phone signal during the drive out to Montauk, but she had spent the intervening minutes in a panic, terrified that her girls had fallen into danger, too. She wondered if she would ever spend another moment unworried about her children again if they were out of her sight.

Now that she heard the girls' happy voices, she realized they couldn't be any safer than with Leo—always vigilant and always armed.

Even though most people would say the twins were as identical in sound as they were in appearance, Marcy had no difficulty differentiating their voices as they yelled into Leo's cell phone.

"We went to a diner, Mama, and Grandpa Leo let us order chocolate-chip pancakes with blueberry syrup and whipped cream on top!" That was Chloe, always so excited about her food. "And we had bacon, too—the real kind. Don't tell Aunt Laurie because she tells Grandpa he's supposed to eat the turkey kind."

"And now we're driving to see the lighthouse," Emily squealed.

"Grandpa Leo says we'll be able to go to the very tip top and look out over the entire ocean."

They had started referring to Laurie's father as Grandpa Leo the previous evening after dinner, and Leo seemed happy enough to accept the honorary role.

She was on the sofa in their hotel suite. In a chair across from her, Andrew used his laptop to check the Find Johnny website for any tips that might have come in overnight. She placed her hand over her heart, letting him know how relieved she was that the girls were safe and sound after all of the redialing she had been doing in her search for them.

"Okay," she said, "I'll let Leo hang up the phone before you two give him an earache with all that yelling."

In addition to wanting to hear their voices, Marcy had called to make sure that Leo knew they were about to go live with the press conference, not to mention the various search groups that the police department had already organized around the area. On Marcy's drive back from the print shop, she had noticed a group of upper-middle-aged women slowly walking through a nature preserve at the edge of the village. Wondering if they might be some of the volunteers Detective Langland had mentioned, she pulled over. It turned out they were a group that usually did a morning water aerobics class together at the YMCA pool, but had decided to spend their time helping with the search for that "cute little boy" instead.

As Marcy had driven away from the scene, all she could think about was the fact that the women had been looking down on the ground and behind the bushes as they walked. They weren't looking for a boy who was playing or running or looking for his way back to the hotel. They were looking for a body.

She didn't want the girls to overhear their brother's name out in public, and couldn't exactly warn Leo while his phone was on speaker with the girls in the car. She told the girls she loved them and thanked Leo again for entertaining them. Once she'd hung up, she sent a quick follow-up text to Leo that he would see once he was out from behind the wheel.

As she set her phone down, she saw her husband through fresh eyes. They'd known each other ten years, but in her mind, it had whizzed by in a flash, and he hadn't changed one bit. Same wavy head of dark hair and steely blue-gray eyes. He had a fuller face than his more famous older brother, but to her, he was even more hand-some. She suspected that if she and Andrew were lucky enough to turn one hundred together, she'd still see him as a young man.

But in this single moment, she saw the strands of gray peering out from his temples, and the lines that had formed around his eyes and lips. And, more than anything, he looked exhausted. Of course he did. So did she.

And in ten minutes, they were expected to step in front of the camera crews assembling in the parking lot outside the hotel. They would lay their pain bare for public consumption—for strangers to suspect them of harming their own son, to judge them for losing sight of him, to feel grateful they weren't the ones begging to see their child again—all in the hopes that maybe, just maybe, one person would recognize Johnny from a picture and help bring him home.

Her phone buzzed with a new text from Detective Langland. *We're all set up outside. Let me know when you're ready. I'll walk you from your room. There's quite a crowd gathered.*

She thought again about the booklet's mention of the number of parents who divorced after a child went missing. Those irreparable fractures had to start somewhere, maybe with the tiny little crack of one parent speaking to the police without the other.

"I have to tell you something before the press conference," she said.

Andrew immediately closed his laptop and looked up at her with his full attention.

"This morning, I didn't only go to the print shop. I met Detective Langland at the coffee shop."

"Okay," he said tentatively.

She explained to him that she had wanted Langland's unvarnished views of the case, including Leo and Laurie's theory about Darren Gunther. "And maybe because she was a woman, I thought it would somehow help if I met with her, one-on-one—to make sure Johnny wasn't just a case number to her. But I'm sorry. I should have told you."

He rose and made his way toward her, setting his laptop down on the coffee table. "You don't have to apologize, babe. I would *literally* do anything—*anything*—if I could take this pain away from you and carry it for both of us."

"But that's why I owe you an apology. All I've been thinking about is my own pain—my special bond with Johnny, the way my body somehow felt different once we brought him home, as if nature was telling me that he was mine, just as if I had carried him myself. But I'm not his only parent."

"No, but you're his only mother."

"You were the one who could always sense if he was fussing in his crib, even if we couldn't hear it over the baby monitor."

He smiled sadly at the memory. Johnny was the only baby they'd ever seen who could be red in the face from fretting, his little hands balled into fists, without making the slightest sound.

"Well, I don't know if this helps, Marcy, but you're right: I *have* always felt that kind of psychic connection to Johnny. And, somehow, I just know that he's out there, waiting for us, alive and alert and trying to get home."

"But how much longer can he wait?"

She sent a text to Detective Langland to say they were ready. They were about to be those poor parents you see on the news.

Chapter 26

Laurie felt the heavy weight of her assignment as she stepped out of the elevator into the offices of Fisher Blake Studios. If everything had gone according to plan, she would not have set foot in 15 Rockefeller Center for another two and a half weeks, the longest she had ever been away from work other than after Greg's murder. Now here she was, trying to launch a new investigation in the hopes that the trail would somehow lead to Johnny.

When she arrived at the entry to her office, she saw that Grace Garcia was away from her desk, but then quickly heard her assistant's distinctively throaty but upbeat voice emerge from Jerry's office next door.

"I'm telling you, Jerry, you would *love* it. I've seen you at your dance parties. Come with me next week and try it out."

"Me? Absolutely not." The tone of Jerry's voice suggested less resistance to the idea than his words did. "Goofing off at a party with friends is one thing. A public workout class based totally on Beyoncé's dance moves? I'd land flat on my face before a room full of strangers by the second chorus."

A smile broke out across Laurie's face and she had to stifle a giggle. She was about to interrupt, but gave herself a moment to enjoy another brief bit of workplace banter before she'd have to pull Grace and Jerry into the darkness with her.

Grace suddenly broke out into song, bending her knees and swaying low to the floor. "Six-inch heels," she crooned. "She walked in the club like . . ."

"Are you kidding me?" Jerry balked. "My knees would quit in protest if I tried to make them do that!"

Laurie stepped into the office and gave Grace a short round of applause. "Nice moves. But you're probably the only person in the class who wears six-inch heels when it's snowing outside, so I imagine you have a leg up on everyone. Pun definitely intended."

Grace suddenly stood upright. "Sorry, Laurie. I didn't expect you to get back to the city so fast."

She had called them as she was leaving the Hamptons so they could prepare for a brainstorming session about Darren Gunther.

Grace pulled Laurie into a hug that was followed by another from Jerry.

"I've been praying for little Johnny all day long," Grace said. "We watched the press conference. Poor Marcy and Andrew. They must be absolutely beside themselves."

"Are you okay?" Jerry asked. "How are you holding up?"

How am I feeling? she thought. *Anxious. Overwhelmed. Terrified that violence may have struck Alex's family—my family, once again.*

Jumping into Darren Gunther's case as a way to find Johnny felt like such a shot in the dark, but she reminded herself of her father's reasoning. He had been absolutely certain that Gunther wouldn't use his one chance at a court's exoneration without somehow trying to cheat during the process. So far, Leo had been unable to figure out what Gunther might have done to try to stack the deck in his favor. Now that Johnny was missing, Leo believed he had found the answer to his question.

"Honestly?" Laurie said. "Nothing would be more comforting right now than to get straight to work."

Chapter 27

Once they were clustered around the conference table in Laurie's office, Laurie asked Jerry to begin by laying out what he knew about Darren Gunther from publicly available reports. Most of what she knew so far was from her father, who obviously had his own opinions about Gunther and the evidence against him. Now Laurie wanted to hear the other side of the story, even if she'd never believe it.

Jerry began with a description of the fight that had spilled onto the sidewalk in front of Finn's Bar eighteen years earlier, followed by the arrests of both men involved, Darren Gunther and Jay Pratt. "I pulled up the original news articles about the case from the archives. Even before the police made an official announcement about which of the men would be charged with murder, the early reports found ways of painting Gunther as a bad guy, out by himself on his twenty-first birthday, getting drunk all alone. I mean, that's sort of weird in itself, right? Plus there's a quote from an unnamed customer at Finn's that night, saying that Gunther had been aggressive to a couple of the women at the bar."

"And Pratt?" Laurie asked.

"A twenty-seven-year-old commercial real estate broker who went to boarding school and Yale. It's not evidence, mind you, but the news has a way of planting subtle messages. Pratt came across looking better."

"Not in *all* the ways," Grace said. "That Darren Gunther is *fine*."

Jerry threw Grace an icy stare, while Laurie shook her head.

"Sorry," Grace said. "Inappropriate."

"No, it's relevant," Laurie said. "Public opinion isn't always driven by evidence or even personal biographies."

"Apparently so," Jerry said, "especially if we fast-forward to now."

"I haven't kept up with all of it, but my father makes it sound like the press fawns over Gunther as if he's a modern-day Hemingway with the face of a young Paul Newman."

"You've got it, Laurie." Jerry flipped through the pages in front of him, reading a few quotes he had highlighted in advance. "'Gunther's green eyes twinkle with the same spark of quiet intelligence that saturate the pages of his searing essays.' 'Gunther's bright smile and slim, youthful face belie the years he has spent in prison, captured so poignantly in this impressive debut.' Oh, and this one's my favorite: 'That's the hottest felon I've ever seen.'"

"Stop it," Laurie said. "That can't be real."

"Okay, it was a reader comment on that little piece that *Vanity Fair* ran, but it was funny."

For a minute, it felt like a regular workday, preparing for a regular production. "So he's managed to work the public relations angle in his favor. What about the actual evidence? Dad says that even the DA's Office has been backing away from the original conviction, even though Gunther confessed. What am I missing?"

"Well, it's just—um . . ." Jerry looked down at his notes again, but said nothing.

Laurie had not seen Jerry this nervous since he was a shy college intern. She noticed that Grace was looking down at her hands, avoiding her gaze.

"You guys, you're not going to offend me. I know Gunther claims my dad fabricated that confession. If we're going to do this, I need to make sure I've got the complete picture."

Seeing her resolve, Jerry took a deep breath and tried again. "So, after he got a couple of small but favorable press pieces about his book, Gunther filed a petition claiming that he was wrongfully convicted. He wrote it himself, using the prison law library as a resource. He used the advancement in DNA technology as a reason to request DNA testing of the murder weapon. Once the court ordered the state to conduct the testing, Tracy Mahoney agreed to begin representing Gunther as his lawyer."

Laurie knew that so-called touch DNA found on the edge of the knife's handle, closest to the blade, had been matched to a felon named Mason Rollins. Leo had been trying to find an alternative explanation for Rollins's DNA on the murder weapon, but had so far come up short. Now that she heard the facts from Jerry instead of her father, she was starting to understand why the court was giving serious consideration to Gunther's innocence claim. Mason Rollins's convictions included multiple assaults against strangers when he perceived insults against him, ranging from bumping into him on the street to pushing past him to a subway turnstile. He clearly was a violent man.

"To be fair," Jerry said, a hint of hesitation returning to his voice, "it would be one thing if some other random person's DNA was on the knife—maybe a retail clerk who handled the sale. But the DNA just happens to match someone who stabbed a person in a bar fight eight years after Lou Finney was killed? Plus, your father emailed me copies of everything he had on Rollins for me to print out. Rollins pled guilty to a misdemeanor assault when he was nineteen years old, two years before Lou Finney was killed. The charge was for throwing punches, but Rollins attacked the victim at a party when the victim told Rollins to knock off this little party trick that involved throwing his knife in the air and catching it. So that proves Mason Rollins was already in the habit of carrying knives."

"I agree it's intriguing," Laurie said. "The problem for Gunther, of course, is that he actually confessed."

"Which is why he's claiming that Leo made it up," Jerry said.

"That's a ludicrous position," Laurie said, "but I guess someone who doesn't know my father personally might look at the DNA evidence and wonder. Besides, my understanding is that Gunther initially claimed that Lou Finney was the one who originally pulled the knife on him and Pratt, and that he was struggling to get control over it when Finney was pushed toward him. Only after my father went back to the station to question him again did he admit that he was in a blind rage because that woman in the bar rejected him."

"Jane Holloway," Jerry added. Laurie was always impressed by Jerry's ability to quickly commit to memory the names of everyone involved in one of their cases.

"Yes. But here's my point: if a detective were going to fabricate a confession, why would he make up two versions of the admission? My father could have simply said that Gunther fessed up during the initial interrogation. It makes no sense."

"It's more complicated than that," Jerry said. "Gunther concedes that he made the first statement—about Finney falling on his own knife. He claims he only said it because he was exhausted and half-drunk, and both of the interrogating investigators refused to believe that he was innocent. So he offered them a story that he thought might get them to back off."

"Both?" Laurie asked. "I thought it was just Gunther and my father, alone in the room."

"Not at that point. It was Leo and another detective named Mike Lipsky."

Laurie remembered the man her father referred to as Hot Lips well. "My dad's former partner. Salt of the earth. He passed away about six years ago."

"Well, Gunther says they didn't seem to buy his story about the stabbing being an accident, but eventually they left the interrogation room and had him booked for murder. Then your dad came back alone a couple hours later, badgering him to take more blame for the homicide. Gunther insists that he stuck to the same story, and then suddenly your father stood up and began claiming he'd confessed to intentional murder instead."

Laurie realized that in her rush to move quickly in the hopes of finding Johnny, she had not been careful enough in gathering the specifics of the interrogation from her father. When she asked Leo why he was alone with Gunther during the confession, he explained that Lipsky had gone home by then. She now realized that both detectives had left after the initial round of questioning, and only Leo had returned to pursue the "spurned Casanova" angle. "My father warned me that Gunther is cunning. Pretty convenient that he only denies the part of the conversation when he and my father were alone in the room together. It's easier to accuse one detective of perjury than two."

Grace was nodding along. "He may not have known that one of the detectives had passed."

"He probably also had no idea just how hard it would be to malign someone with Leo Farley's reputation," she said. "Dad thinks Gunther would have been released by now, except the DA's Office knows it will have a major problem with the NYPD if they essentially concede that the former first deputy commissioner framed an innocent man."

"Not to mention the defendants who would come out of the woodwork claiming they were set up, too," Jerry added.

"But if my father were to admit it? Gunther would walk out of prison tonight, a free man."

Jerry shook his head. "I'm starting to understand why your father's so convinced Gunther may have been trying to kidnap Timmy. Your father would do anything for that boy."

"Okay." Grace held up both of her hands dramatically. "But how does a man in prison manage to pull this off from a jail cell?"

"He would need to have outside help," Laurie said. "Gunther's only family is his mother, and according to my father, she's in assisted living in Staten Island. But Gunther has attracted some pretty die-hard supporters. There is a Facebook page called *Darren Gunther Is Innocent*. It promotes his book, but also pushes his claims of innocence. We should make a list of the most active posters on the page and see if any of them sets off alarms."

"Will do," Jerry said. "I know our focus is on finding Johnny, but I went ahead and put in a request for the trial transcripts. And I started a list of the people we'll eventually be wanting to interview. So far I've got Jay Pratt, of course. And we'll need to contact the victim's family."

"His wife passed away a few years ago," Laurie said. "They had three children, but only one who still lives in New York—their daughter Samantha. She owns a hair salon in midtown. I already left a message." Laurie knew from her father that Finney's daughter was distraught over the possibility of Gunther's release. Laurie wanted to be certain that she heard about *Under Suspicion*'s involvement directly from her.

Jerry added Samantha's name to his running list and placed a checkmark next to it. "We'll also want to track down the woman Gunther was hitting on that night, Jane Holloway. And Clarissa De-Santo, a bartender who was working that night."

Laurie nodded along, finding it hard to focus on the aspects of the case that did not relate to her immediate concern for Johnny. "My father mentioned that Clarissa didn't testify at Gunther's trial. It struck him as odd at the time. She was a critical witness to prove

Gunther's aggressive demeanor that night, and she had been very close to Finn. They got the conviction even without her testimony, but it would be nice if we could get her side of the story on screen."

Laurie turned at the sound of knuckles rapping against her open office door. Ryan Nichols flashed the perfect smile that had helped to land him on *People*'s most recent list of "sexiest men alive," an accomplishment he touted even more brazenly than the Harvard degree hung just inside his office door. His sandy-blond hair appeared slightly damp.

"I thought I heard voices in here," he said. "Aren't you supposed to be in the Hamptons?"

The Hamptons. Alex's birthday party. The wedding and honeymoon. It all felt like a dream now. "You didn't hear?" Laurie asked.

Ryan's smile suddenly fell with the tone of Laurie's voice. "You broke up?"

Jerry groaned at the rudeness of the comment.

"No, thank you very much. It's Alex's nephew, Johnny. He's— missing. We think he's been kidnapped. I assumed you knew." Laurie also assumed that Brett would have spoken to Ryan about it already. From Ryan's first day at Fisher Blake Studios, he had enjoyed a closer relationship with the boss than she ever would. Even without the many perks of nepotism, she would have thought Ryan followed the news closely enough to hear about a missing child on Long Island, whether or not the story penetrated the city's new cycle.

Ryan's shock appeared genuine. "I'm so sorry, Laurie. What can we do to help? You don't need to be in the office. We can take care of everything here."

It took her a few minutes to spell out Leo's theory that Darren Gunther might have mistakenly abducted Johnny in an attempt to grab Timmy instead, and her plans to use the show as a way to confront Gunther directly. "His lawyer's Tracy Mahoney. He agreed to be interviewed against her advice."

"*That's* his lawyer?" Ryan's green eyes widened with concern.

"Alex warned me she can be a challenge. A true believer, he called her."

"Oh, she's far more sinister than that. If you're trying to figure out how Gunther could get help from the outside world, Tracy Mahoney is the answer."

Chapter 28

Johnny sat on the hardwood floor, his legs folded criss-cross-applesauce. Scattered on the floor in front of him were two hundred and fifty pieces of a jigsaw puzzle the man had brought this morning after Johnny had eaten a breakfast of fried eggs and white toast. Johnny liked eggs to be scrambled, and his mom always used wheat bread at home, but he made himself eat all of it anyway. He didn't want the man to be mad, which was also the reason why he was trying so hard to put the puzzle together. It wasn't the largest one he'd ever seen. He had worked on a giant one with a thousand pieces before, but that was with his whole family, where his dad was nicknamed the Puzzle Master. That's how good he was.

When the man gave him the puzzle, he said, "This should keep you from getting too bored. Plus puzzles are good for the mind, Danny." He had tapped his temple with his index finger for emphasis. It felt to Johnny like some kind of test—one he didn't want to fail.

Following his dad's strategy, Johnny had located all four corner pieces and had separated out all the edges. Now he was studying the image on the puzzle box, trying to figure out which pieces belonged on which edge.

The picture was of two children, a boy and a girl, sitting in the grass with a big brown dog on a red, white, and blue plaid quilt, looking up at a sky filled with fireworks.

He suddenly pictured himself walking on the grass at Meridian Hill Park on the Fourth of July when he was only five years old. He remembered the way his mom had grabbed him and pulled him into a hug that was so tight, it almost scared him. *Where were you?!* He remembered how worried she sounded. He had only left to find the park bathroom, but she made him promise never to go off alone again. Then, the next day, they had a longer talk about staying safe and not talking to strangers.

I didn't wander off, Mommy. Not this time. Not really. I was with Kara's friend, Ashley, and the lifeguard named Jack. We went to the beach shack for ice cream cones. They were talking about music I've never heard of, so I went looking for seashells. I was going to pick the best ones and have them waiting for you in the hotel room when you got back from golf. I went behind the beach shack, but only for a second, and I could still hear Ashley laughing, so that's not really wandering off. And I saw the ice cream truck man get out of the truck and go inside the store, saying he needed more Fudgesicles before heading back out on his route. And then I heard a car. It pulled in behind the ice cream truck. I turned around to go back to Ashley and Jack, then a man's voice behind me said I missed a pretty shell by the truck. I remembered what you told me, Mommy. I didn't talk to the stranger. I tried to run when he walked toward me, but he was too fast. He grabbed me, and I woke up in the trunk of his car.

Johnny could hear the man walking around upstairs now, and he was talking again. Johnny crept to the corner of his room and crouched down on the floor, placing his ear in front of the air vent. He could only make out a few words. *The boy . . . Changing everything.* The more the man spoke, the more upset he sounded.

Then he heard a second voice. It was the woman he had heard last night. *How are we going to take care of him?* That part, Johnny heard loud and clear. It was easier to make out the higher voice.

The man said something about having plenty of money from the insurance. Then he said something about a *court order*.

When his mom warned him about stranger danger, she told him that if he ever did find himself alone and lost and in need of help, he should look for a police officer or a teacher. And if he couldn't find one, then he should find a woman or a group of women. He always assumed it was because they'd be more like a mommy.

But Johnny couldn't imagine what kind of woman would be here in this house with that man. *Is it possible she might help me?*

The man was speaking again. "It's all going to be fine. Trust me, Diane."

At least, that's what it sounded like he said. *Diane? Roseanne? Lee Ann?* Something like that. Maybe she would be nicer than the man. Maybe she would find a way to take him home to his family.

Johnny heard footsteps on the staircase and scrambled back to the puzzle. It seemed hopeless. There were too many pieces. But he had a terrible feeling he would have a very, very long time alone with it.

Chapter 29

Ryan Nichols was pacing the length of Laurie's office, like a litigator making a closing argument to a jury.

"Tracy Mahoney isn't your typical defense lawyer—someone like Alex, for example."

"I certainly don't consider anything about Alex Buckley typical," Jerry quipped. "He did become a federal judge after all."

Laurie knew that Jerry took a certain amount of satisfaction comparing Ryan to his beloved predecessor. Last year, a rabid fan of the show had posted a "Which Host Is Most" poll on the *Under Suspicion* Facebook page, asking viewers to vote between Ryan and Alex as their favorite TV host. Jerry had taken it upon himself to share the poll on the show's official feed, touting it as a "fun survey!" When the votes favored Alex by nearly fifteen points, Ryan didn't seem to revel in the "fun" results.

"What I mean," Ryan clarified, "is that even as a former prosecutor, I value the role that defense attorneys play in our criminal justice system. They make certain that the government is put to a fair test. They protect all of us by ensuring that every defendant is treated fairly and that there's sufficient evidence for a conviction."

"We all agree on that," Laurie said. "As the old saying goes, 'Better that ten guilty people go free, than for one innocent to suffer.' So how does Tracy Mahoney fit in?"

"She doesn't simply believe in doing her job *within* the system. She believes it is justified for defense attorneys to take actions *outside* the system. She calls herself a 'movement lawyer,'" Ryan explained. "She says that she advocates for the broader political interests of her clients, rather than simply the specific legal issues they may face in an individual case."

"So give me an example," Laurie said.

"About four years ago, she represented a defendant in a robbery case. It was a home invasion in Southampton. The police had him dead to rights on one specific incident, but they believed he was part of a larger group that pulled off a series of robberies targeting millionaires and billionaires who donated to political causes they opposed. They would divert the stolen money to their own favored special interests. The defendant immediately invoked his rights when the police tried to question him. He didn't even need to ask for the public defender's number like most suspects. He had Tracy Mahoney's number already loaded into his cell phone. She showed up, saying her client was interested in an early cooperation deal but insisted on seeing the evidence against him before finalizing the agreement. The discovery package included some evidence that came from an active wiretap monitoring the entire crew. The prosecutors deleted any mention of the wiretap itself, but she'd be smart enough to wonder how police learned about some of those conversations. All of a sudden, the phone calls stopped. Radio silence. And Mahoney's client never took the deal."

"You think she tipped them off," Laurie said.

"Well, the DA's Office certainly did. They thought about bringing charges or reporting her to the State Bar, but they had no way of proving their suspicions."

"How do you know so much about this?" Laurie asked. Ryan had worked at the U.S. Attorney's Office, which was for federal prosecutions. The District Attorney's Office was separate, for state-level offenses.

"Because she pulled a similar stunt when I was at the U.S. Attorney's Office. The federal prison system had in place what were called Special Administrative Measures, or SAMs, to regulate conversations between high-risk federal defendants and their lawyers. Basically, anything the lawyers learned from a client couldn't be passed on to others."

"And Mahoney violated the orders?" Laurie asked.

"The client was part of a ring of ecoterrorists. They vandalized companies that abuse natural resources and experiment on animals. Tracy Mahoney would take mission statements from her client and repeat them verbatim to cable news stations. She wasn't acting as a lawyer so much as a public relations rep."

"So how is she still getting away with all this?"

"Because she's a darn good lawyer," Ryan said. "She cherry-picks her cases wisely. At least half are run-of-the-mill cases. Another quarter are highly paid white-collar trials that fund her entire practice. And the rest are her passion projects, and that's where she skirts the line."

Laurie's thoughts were interrupted by her cell phone.

"This is Laurie," she said.

"This is Samantha Finney. You called about my father?"

Laurie had begun to explain that *Under Suspicion* would be investigating Darren Gunther's wrongful conviction claim, when Samantha interrupted. "I don't conduct any business that matters over the telephone. I need to see a face in person and look them in the eye to form an opinion. I learned that from my father."

"Just name the time and place," Laurie said.

Chapter 30

The smell of ammonia tinged with a faint whiff of lilies greeted Laurie as she walked into Organique, the hair salon owned by Samantha Finney. The decor was naturalism meets minimalism, all white with bleached wood accents and flourishing potted plants for pops of green.

"Oooh, great color," the receptionist gushed as Laurie approached the check-in desk. Her name tag identified her as Rachel. Her own tresses were streaked with pink and piled in a loose bun at the nape of her neck. The hoop in her left nostril was gold. "You're clearly in no need of a touch-up. It's just perfect with your stunning hazel eyes."

Laurie had read once that businesses that cater to a woman's physical appearance make a point to comment on their customers' attractiveness. The idea was to build a customer's self-esteem while also reinforcing the importance of aesthetic beauty. Or perhaps Rachel was simply paying her a compliment. Indeed, Laurie had been to her own hairdresser only three days earlier. Charlotte had convinced Laurie to add a few blond highlights to her natural honey color for the wedding. According to her friend, the blond would shine more in photographs, without looking fake. A time when her hair color was the pressing matter of the day felt like a different lifetime.

"I'm here to see Samantha," Laurie said, raising her voice to be heard over a hairdryer blowing on the other side of the reception desk. Rachel began to flip through the appointment book. "Laurie Moran, but I'm probably not in the schedule. Samantha's expecting me, though. I spoke to her on the phone this afternoon."

Laurie noticed that the hairdresser at the back station of the busy salon was looking in their direction. Rachel turned and caught the woman's eye. The woman managed to expertly wrap a section of her client's hair in tinfoil while simultaneously pointing to herself, as if to say, *Is that for me?*

Rachel nodded, and Samantha flashed a peace sign with her fingers.

"She'll just be a couple of minutes," Rachel said.

As promised, two minutes later, Samantha snapped off a pair of latex gloves and dropped them in a wastebasket on her way to the salon's waiting area. She gave her palms a quick wipe on her black smock before greeting Laurie with a handshake.

"Samantha Finney. Thanks for coming." Samantha had bright blue eyes, alabaster skin, and dark wavy hair that framed her round face. Laurie guessed Samantha was at most a few years older than she was. "Sorry, I know I told you I had a hole in my schedule, but my five o'clock got here half an hour late. No apology, of course, and she never tips more than five percent, but hey, the customer's always right." She flashed an obviously forced smile. "Anyway, I assume your show wants to highlight that lying lowlife who killed my dad, so, yeah, I brought you all the way downtown to tell you to your face you're being suckered. You can produce whatever story you want, but I'm not going to help you turn that man—"

"Darren Gunther."

Samantha winced at the sound of his name. "I refuse to say it out loud. My father, he was a hero. He was *my* hero. And that piece of garbage took him away from me. To me, he doesn't even deserve to be thought of as a human being, let alone . . . some kind of oppressed artist?" She shook her head. "You can't understand. You just know he'll help your ratings."

"I know a little something about having a hero for a father. I'm Leo Farley's daughter."

Samantha's eyes widened. "Wow." As she processed the information, Laurie could see Samantha's expression soften. "We can talk in my break room."

Samantha took a deep breath and exhaled once the break room door was closed. "Most draft-proof door the contractor could find, plus I run an air purifier back here 24/7. Those chemicals are no joke."

"But they're . . . Organique?"

"Rebranded last year. Everybody wants to sound so green and natural these days. But guess what? If you want your curly hair straight, or your straight hair curly, there are chemicals involved." Samantha took a seat at the small dining table at the center of the room, and Laurie did the same. "Anyway, you've definitely got my attention. Your father was such a rock for me all through the investigation and trial. I'm surprised he didn't call me himself. I'd do anything for Leo Farley."

Aware of the clock literally ticking on their meeting, Laurie did her best to explain the separation she was trying to preserve between her father's role as a witness and the decisions she was making as a journalist and television producer. She saw no reason at this point to mention Johnny's kidnapping or its possible connection to Samantha's father's killer.

"I've got to assume you're not the number one fan of the man accusing your father of perjury," Samantha said.

Laurie held up her palms. "I'm keeping an open mind."

"Gotcha. Well, despite everything I said out there, you no longer need to convince me. I'm all aboard, whatever you need. But I can't imagine he's going to go along with it. Not if he finds out who you are."

Laurie knew that the *he* was Darren Gunther, the man whose name Samantha refused to speak. "*He* already agreed, against the advice of his lawyer. I just need to work out the logistics with the prison."

Samantha nodded slowly. "It's his ego. What better way to hurt a fine man like your father than to turn his own daughter against him? So, what exactly do you need from me?"

Laurie slipped a copy of the show's participant consent agreement from her briefcase and handed it to Samantha. "We can go over the schedule and details later, but this lays it all out."

Samantha rose from her seat to pick up a pen stashed next to a single-cup coffeemaker on the countertop.

"That's all right. Take your time and read it. I can pick it up tomorrow—"

Samantha was already handing her the signed document. "No need. The trust I have for your father's big enough to extend to you."

Laurie smiled at the sentiment. Tucking away the completed contract in her bag, she pulled out a second copy and placed it on the table. "Okay, but I'm leaving this here. If you have second thoughts, call me anytime."

Samantha was leading the way out of the break room when she stopped and turned. "Finn's."

"Your dad's bar."

"Right, yes. But Finn's. That's what I should have renamed the salon. As a tribute. Man, I loved that bar. Dad used to let me draw beers from the tap for the regulars, even as a little rug rat. Blatant liquor commission violations, but who was going to say anything? That place was like my second home."

Laurie could see that Samantha's eyes had drifted to an invisible screen playing scenes from her past.

"You didn't want to keep it open after your dad passed?"

"I sure did. Clarissa and I were going to keep it going together."

Laurie recognized the name. "Clarissa DeSanto," she said.

"Yep. She was practically Dad's second daughter. Salt of the earth, that girl. But commercial Realtors don't see a couple of young women as family. The landlords knew the neighborhood would rebel if they tried to hike the rent on my dad, but the loyalty didn't extend to the next generation. They said it was because we didn't have a track record and they didn't want to gamble on two novice businesswomen, but they saw an opportunity to make more money and they took it."

"What's there now?"

"Yet another bank. My heart hurts every time I pass it."

"I'm sorry."

"Me too," she said sadly. "Shoot, I better go. If that timer goes off while I'm back here with you, my client will act like she was stranded for hours on a desert highway."

"One more thing, if I may? Did you remain in contact with Clarissa?"

"Sure did," she said, beaming at the mention of her name. "The best friend I ever had. She always wondered what would have happened that night if Darren Gunther's loser friend hadn't left the bar. Maybe he wouldn't have been in such a vengeful mood. My father would have lived, all because that vile punk didn't feel alone on his birthday."

"Gunther was there with someone else? I was under the impression he was alone."

"No, Clarissa said he arrived with someone else, but then the other guy moved on without him, and he continued to pester one of the female customers."

"I'd love to talk to Clarissa directly. If you have a number for her, or could give her my information—"

Sadness fell across Samantha's face. "Clarissa passed away three months ago."

"Oh no. Samantha, I'm so sorry. I didn't know—"

"It was a car accident. She was on her way to Boston to visit her aunt, and it was pouring rain. She ran off the side of the road into a ravine. No one saw it happen, but the police think she took a curve too fast and lost control. All I know is that I lost my best friend, and the only other person who understood how much that bar meant to my dad."

As Laurie left, she looked up at the sign on the facade above the storefront and wondered how long Samantha would wait to rename it again. A hair salon called Finn's would be a nice tribute indeed.

Sunday, July 19

Day Five

Chapter 31

On the television screen in the living room of Laurie's Upper East Side apartment, the chief of the LAPD was dressing down a city politician for using a homicide case as campaign fodder. Laurie glanced over at her father, sitting in his favorite lounge chair next to the sofa. These were usually the types of scenes in a police procedural that could send him on a rant about the lack of realism. Instead, she saw him nodding along.

On her other side, Timmy was similarly enrapt from his spot on the couch. The three of them were catching up on the newest season of *Bosch*. Timmy had had a nightmare last night, as he had every night since Johnny was missing. She was trying to find ways to take his mind from his worries. A detective show might not be the typical ten-year-old's comfort fare, but Timmy was not a typical child. This was his favorite program, and they only watched it together as a family. She hoped that watching justice in a fictional setting might somehow comfort him at a subconscious level.

Leo had dark circles under his eyes, and she knew she had a matching set. They both knew the gruesome statistics. More than 90 percent of abducted children survived and were eventually found, but with each passing day, the odds worsened. More than a third were recovered in the first twenty-four hours, another third within the next forty-eight. Those who were missing for more than a week were more likely to be dead than alive. It had been five days of volunteer searches, chasing down reported sightings of fair-haired boys, and the Coast Guard's search of the ocean with boats and helicopters, and Johnny was still missing.

Perhaps the roughest moment since Johnny's disappearance had come this morning, when Marcy and Andrew made the painful decision to return to Washington, D.C., with Johnny's sisters. The mysterious vanishing of their son had become the hottest chatter on the east end of Long Island. Over margaritas and rosé wine, vacationers would speculate that the boy had drowned, or been killed by a predator, or been taken hostage because of some imagined wrongdoing of his parents. He had become a topic of conversation rather than a real person.

And every time Marcy and Andrew left their hotel room, they had to protect their daughters from the relentless gossip and the glare of the public eye. Finally, a family friend who was a therapist pleaded with them to go home and stay in touch with law enforcement from there. Laurie couldn't imagine how gut-wrenching it must have been to drive away without Johnny.

So, for now, for just a little while, their favorite television show was a way to escape. The scene on the screen hit its climax just as her cell phone buzzed on the coffee table in front of her. The area code was 518, Upstate New York. She hit the pause button.

"Mo-oooom." Timmy was not happy about the interruption.

"I'm sorry," she called out as she ran to the kitchen. "I have to get this."

She wasn't surprised when Leo trailed behind her, listening to her side of the conversation expectantly.

"Absolutely, Warden . . . I understand. . . . We will definitely abide by all of those conditions. Thank you again for accommodating us. I know these are unusual circumstances."

Arranging for media access to a prisoner was always tricky, but what Laurie had sought for Darren Gunther was probably unprecedented. This was going to be an in-custody interview of a convicted murderer, in the presence of his lawyer, conducted by a television show produced by the daughter of the detective in charge of the original investigation. She had needed the consent of not only Gunther and his lawyer, Tracy Mahoney, but also the NYPD, the District Attorney's Office, and the Department of Corrections. Now that the prison warden was signing off, she finally had all of the pieces in place.

So far, only the NYPD commissioner and Detective Langland knew they suspected Gunther's involvement in Johnny's abduction. They didn't want to run the risk of anyone tipping off Tracy Mahoney to their suspicions and depriving them of the element of surprise.

She flashed a thumbs-up to Leo as she hung up. "The warden is on board. We can do it tomorrow. We're scheduled for two o'clock." Gunther was serving his sentence at the Clinton Correctional Facility in Dannemora. It was a five-hour drive from the city. "It's rushed, but I've got the whole team ready. As I suspected, the warden's only letting us bring one camera, so it will be a pretty basic setup."

She and the entire team had been at the office all weekend.

"It'll be fine," Leo assured her. "I know you're the one calling the shots — but Ryan knows the case cold now, as well as I do, in fact."

They had been walking a fine line to keep her production's decision-making separate from her father's role in law enforcement. Laurie knew from past experience that if her show did manage to obtain any incriminating evidence against Gunther, his lawyer would argue that the show had been acting as a "stalking horse" for the police. That said, she and Ryan had already conducted a thorough informational interview with Leo as the investigating detective. Laurie made certain they could show a pattern of following the same procedures in other cases they had featured. In short, it was permissible for them to communicate with Leo as a witness to the story they were covering, but they could not let him dictate the course of their investigation or reporting.

She glanced at her watch. It was already 6:45. "Shoot. I better change before Alex picks me up." She was wearing the jeans and Coldplay concert T-shirt she'd donned only a couple of hours ago to watch TV. "Maybe I should cancel—"

"Don't you dare," Leo scolded. "At the very least, you two deserve to have a little time alone tonight. I'll stay here with Timmy as planned and then come back whenever you need me tomorrow so you can take off bright and early in the morning."

Alex had called earlier, announcing that he had a surprise and would be picking her up at seven o'clock "for a date."

"Okay, but you have to promise that you're going to make time to see Maureen soon." Her father had met Chief Judge Maureen Russell at Alex's induction three months earlier. He had been tight-lipped about their ongoing interactions, but she could tell from the way he smiled as he read his texts on occasion that he enjoyed her company. "I'm not the only one with a love life."

"And I have no plans to discuss any of that with my daughter. Now, really, there's nothing more you can do before you get in the room with Gunther—for either your show or for Johnny. Get out of here."

Knowing her father was right, Laurie made her way to her bedroom closet and selected a black cap-sleeved A-line dress for the evening. She'd dress it up with strappy sandals and a statement necklace. She tried not to look at the white garment bag consuming a good percentage of her hanging space as she closed the closet doors.

In it was her wedding gown. In another world—one where Johnny had stayed safely on the beach with the rest of the family— today was the day she was supposed to have worn it. As she tinkered with the clasp of her necklace in the mirror, she realized that the cap sleeves, V-neckline, and princess waist of her outfit all matched the unworn dress left hanging in the closet and wondered if that was why she had opted for it. Her necklace in place, she took one last look in the mirror and wiped away a tear.

When she stepped outside, Ramon was waiting and opened the back door of Alex's black Mercedes. Alex was seated inside, wearing a tuxedo.

"You look amazing," he said.

"Seriously? I changed out of a T-shirt, but I had no idea this was black tie. I have such an early morning, Alex."

He grabbed her hand and clasped it. "For a few minutes, let's pretend the world is normal."

Normal. It had only been five days, but she couldn't remember what normal felt like. The unimaginable had happened, and now, day after day, they were left to wonder how to go on.

Ramon took a left turn on 86th Street, then continued past Third Avenue and took a right turn on Second, heading south again.

"Ramon, I hate to be that typical New Yorker to question the route, but where are we heading?"

Alex gave her knee a gentle squeeze. "Surely you must realize where we are."

It became obvious to her as Ramon took the next turn on 85th Street. They were right around the corner from their new apartment. Ramon pulled in front of the building and stopped.

Seeing her confused expression, Alex said, "We just need to approve a couple of final touches with the designer. It will only take a second, then we'll have our date."

She recognized the doorman on duty as Luis. She already knew that he was from Puerto Rico and had a daughter who was Timmy's age. He gave them a friendly wave as they made their way to the elevator. "You're certainly upping the wardrobe game around here. When are you officially moving in?"

"Ask the contractors," Alex said. Most of the new furniture they had ordered for the apartment had already been delivered, but the bathrooms and kitchen still needed some finishing work.

"Maybe we'll see you next year then," Luis said dryly.

Laurie felt a tiny ripple in her stomach as Alex slipped a key into the front lock. For so many years, it had been just her and Timmy. Now they were adding Alex to their family, and their move to this apartment was a big part of that. They were so close to the finish line.

When the door opened, she was struck by the smell of something fresh and natural, a mix of sweet fruit and musk. Alex hit a light switch in the front hall. The entire apartment was filled with flowers. Roses, lilies, orchids, tulips, daffodils. White, yellow, red, pink, purple.

She spun in a circle in the living room, taking in the sight of what had to be at least fifteen flower arrangements. "Are we running a floral shop on the side now?"

Alex's shoulders shook with his chuckle. "Remember how we split up all the phone calls we needed to make?"

"How could I forget?" The choice to call off the wedding had been obvious, but every phone call had been a reminder of how excited they had been to start a new life together and how dire Johnny's situation was to require them to cancel the ceremony.

"So . . . I was the one who called the Four Seasons to cancel our suite." After their wedding and a small reception, they had planned to spend the night in the penthouse suite. "But I sort of forgot that I had made a separate florist order to surprise you in the room. So . . . here they are, in our new home instead."

"Alex, this is crazy. How many flowers are here?"

"One for every single day since I first met you."

She wrapped her arms around his neck. "You're a crazy person, but you're my crazy person."

"Have I told you how lucky I am to have you?" he asked.

She looked up at the ceiling, feigning a search for the answer. "Not for at least an hour. Seriously, I can't believe you did all this."

He tucked her hair behind one ear and dropped a kiss on the nape of her neck. "Will you, Laurie Moran, take me to be your completely charmed and enchanted husband?"

"I will. A hundred thousand percent."

Monday, July 20

Day Six

Chapter 32

Six days.

There was a time when six days rushed past in a minute, filled with PTA meetings, playdates, music lessons, and the general rhythm of keeping up with a busy family's daily life.

But now Marcy had lived six days without speaking to her son. Every second felt like an hour. Every hour felt like a year. Every night felt like another eternity. She pressed her hands against her face, trying to remain calm.

It had been too many days since she had seen Johnny, and now she was also obsessed with the physical distance between her and the beach where she had last seen him.

"Maybe we should have stayed in New York." She had uttered the same sentence at least a hundred times in the last twenty-four hours, after she and Andrew had driven the girls back to D.C. from the Hamptons.

They had consulted with both a crime victims advocate and two child psychologists before making the decision to go home. Detective Langland was keeping them up-to-date on the state of the investigation, but there was no quick ending in sight. Meanwhile, they had Chloe and Emily to think about. According to the experts, children were remarkably resilient. The absence of a routine, however, was a constant reminder that something was wrong with the world. In a hotel in the Hamptons, waiting each day for news about Johnny, they were suspended in limbo. And every time they left their room, they had to worry about a stranger offering awkward condolences or, worse, someone sneaking a clandestine photograph of the grieving family to post on the internet.

At home, they supposedly would feel more secure about their own safety. They'd be able to rely upon the familiar setting and old patterns of behavior to move through the days—or weeks or months—lying ahead.

And so back to D.C. they had gone.

At least it was summer. A few months from now, the girls would begin half days at school for pre-K. Marcy couldn't imagine sending them out of her sight right now.

She was sitting at the outdoor table on their back deck, reading through the comments on the Find Johnny website, hoping that whoever had him might try to make contact online. *Whatever you want*, she thought. *I will give you everything we own. I'll trade my life for his. Please, just send him home.*

But instead, she found the usual posts from well-intentioned strangers expressing their thoughts and prayers for Johnny and their family. She tried to ignore the negative ones. A small group of true-crime buffs had developed a conspiracy theory that Johnny must have been taken as revenge for some kind of criminal activity his parents were involved in. Then there were the cranks who believed the entire case was a "hoax" to drum up publicity for some unknown reason. But the comments that really stung were the ones blaming Andrew and Marcy for placing their son in danger: *What kind of parents leave their kids with a sitter on a family vacation?* Sometimes she thought she might die from the guilt.

Marcy's stomach felt hot when she read the next comments:

I wonder if they would have watched him closer if he weren't adopted.

Wait: The boy was adopted? How do you know that?

I'm obsessed with this case and have been reading everything I can find about it online. The adoption hasn't been mentioned by any of the big outlets yet, but I read it <u>here</u>. Very interesting.

Marcy clicked on the link. It was to a website called New York Crime Beat. She'd never heard of it. There was no byline on the article. She skimmed through a basic summary of facts that had already been widely reported, until her eyes landed on the eight-letter word she'd been searching for: *adoption.*

According to a law enforcement source, the missing boy was adopted by the Buckleys as a newborn. When asked whether his disappearance might be connected to the adoption, the source stated that police had eliminated that theory and were working on the assumption of an abduction by a stranger.

When Detective Langland answered her cell phone, Marcy did not bother with an introduction. "How does some website know that Johnny is adopted?" she demanded.

"What are you talking about?" The detective's voice was gentle, even though Marcy had lashed out at her. "What website?"

Marcy could tell that this was the first Langland had heard of the report. She waited while Langland pulled up the article herself.

"Marcy, I'm so, so sorry. I promise you, it wasn't me. Both fortunately and unfortunately, this case has been a huge news story, at least locally. The downside is that it's brought out the vultures.

No responsible journalist would invade your privacy that way. Plus it sounds like they only had one anonymous source, which would never be enough for reputable media outlets."

"Johnny doesn't know. Neither do our girls. We were going to tell him when he was a little older." Marcy heard a heavy sigh on the other end of the line.

"Look, I can't tell you how sorry I am, Marcy. But this website? I've never even heard of it, and I'm a cop. I'll make sure all my people know how completely unacceptable this kind of leak is, and hopefully this crummy little site is the end of the story."

"Mommy, look!" Chloe was stomping her feet in the water of the kiddie pool Andrew had set up for them in the backyard.

"You'll let me know if any reporters contact you trying to follow up on this?" Marcy asked.

"Absolutely. I promise."

As she hung up, Chloe was still trying to get her attention, sloshing around in the water. "Look how much I can make it splash!"

Emily crossed her arms in protest. "Stop it, Chloe. You're making a mess, and the pool's going to be empty."

"Then we'll fill it up again from the hose."

"Well . . ." Emily struggled for a retort. "Then you're taking water away from fish that need it."

Chloe was telling her sister that wasn't how it worked when the doorbell chimed. Marcy jumped up from the table. *Please be good news. Please.*

Through the living room window, she caught sight of a light gray Buick parked in their driveway.

"Andrew," she cried out. His home office was down the hall. "Someone's here!"

She ran to the front door and peered through one of the side panels of glass. She didn't recognize the woman standing there alone, nervously looking down at her tapping foot. Marcy guessed she was around sixty years old. She had a soft, round face framed by a blond-ish gray bob, parted in the middle. She wore a short-sleeved navy-blue cotton dress with a simple chain holding a small cross pendant.

"Can I help you?" Marcy asked from behind the door.

"Mrs. Buckley?"

"How can I help you?" she asked again.

"My name is Sandra Carpenter. My daughter was your son's . . . She gave him to you for adoption."

Chapter 33

Marcy poured a glass of iced tea for their unexpected guest and then took a seat next to Andrew, who had emerged from his office just as Marcy opened the front door. Now they were seated at the kitchen table, where she was able to keep an eye on the girls through the sliding glass doors.

She felt Andrew's hand squeeze her knee beneath the table. With that small touch, she felt so connected to him. He was the only person on the face of the planet who truly shared her pain.

She patted his hand and kept it there. Sandra had already explained her reason for coming over. She was offering to help however she could.

According to her, she had found the Buckleys' address but no phone number on the papers that she'd been able to locate in her old files from the time of the adoption. Marcy wondered why she wouldn't have simply called Father Horrigan to reach out to them on her behalf, but then recalled the priest mentioning that Sandra had switched to another parish after Johnny was born. Perhaps she was reluctant to involve Father Horrigan any further into matters involving her daughter and the adoption. Whatever her reasons, Marcy was starting to wish she had never opened the front door to their surprise visitor.

"We appreciate your keeping us in your thoughts, Sandra," Marcy mustered. "I know this must be very hard on you, as well."

"I haven't been able to sleep," Sandra said. "It didn't seem right not to reach out to you. I know my daughter gave her baby up, but I still think of Johnny as the last living piece of my little girl, even though I have never been a part of his life. To know that he's in danger—and to realize how scared you must be—makes me miss Michelle all over again. Does that make any sense at all?"

"Of course."

"When Michelle was young, we were so close. She used to tell me I was her best friend, all the way up until she was in high school. When she decided to go to the University of Baltimore, she chose it over a more prestigious college in Colorado because she didn't want to be so far away from home. She was always a top student, even though she was waiting tables part-time along with her classes. I trusted her when she told me she wanted to take time off from college for a little while. The couple that owned the restaurant she worked at in Baltimore was opening a sister restaurant near their vacation house in Rehoboth Beach, Delaware, and wanted her to manage it for them. It sounded like a sensible move. They were offering her a nice place to live in their guest cottage. She'd make a lot of money during the summer, and then they would basically match that during the off-season for her to stay on their property and look after it. I understood why she saw it as a good opportunity. She was a short walk's distance to the beach, and only two and a half hours from me, so we visited each other regularly. She even had room for me in the guesthouse, so it was like I had a little vacation spot of my own. She thought after three years, she'd have enough saved up to go back to college without any debt or even a part-time job, so she could commit herself a hundred percent. She wanted to be valedictorian. I remember her saying, *Top of your class from a public*

school is better than the middle of the pack from Harvard. She had
big dreams. She wanted to be a journalist."

Marcy had no doubt this woman believed she had come here to
help another family, but it was clear that Sandra's thoughts and heart
were still focused on her own loss.

Andrew, as if reading Marcy's mind, began to rise from his chair.
"Thank you so much for coming, and, again, we are so grateful that
Michelle—"

It wasn't enough to stop Sandra from reminiscing, and Andrew
retook his seat. "My biggest regret is how I handled the news of
the pregnancy. My views are very . . . traditional. *Very.* When she
couldn't even tell me who the father was, that she met him at a bar, I
could have been more supportive. I did my best to focus on the matter at hand—how to take care of the baby—but I'm sure I left her
feeling judged. I think that's the moment everything began to spiral
downward for her. After she gave up Johnny for the adoption, she
pushed me away. I think she felt ashamed. I thought it was temporary, but weeks became months, and months became years. When
the Philadelphia police called me about her overdose, it was so cold,
as if I were a stranger."

Marcy could see that this woman—a mother, just like her—was
in pain, still mourning the loss of her own daughter. But to Marcy,
she *was* a stranger, and her unannounced appearance at their front
door ultimately did nothing to help them find Johnny.

Next to her, Andrew stood again, and this time, he did not let
Sandra's storytelling deter him. "Mrs. Carpenter, thank you so much
for reaching out, and we're sorry for your loss. We need to be alone
as a family right now. Let me walk you out."

Alone at the kitchen table, Marcy felt her shoulders begin to
shake as she envisioned herself getting a phone call like the one
Sandra had gotten about Michelle. Perhaps it would be from Detective Langland in East Hampton. Or a cop in New York City or

Cleveland or New Orleans or Phoenix, whatever place someone had taken Johnny off to. How long would she need to wait for an answer? And just as Sandra could trace the beginnings of her daughter's demise to her own conduct, Marcy would forever blame herself for leaving Johnny on that beach with a babysitter she didn't even know.

Her thoughts were interrupted by the buzz of her cell phone on the table. It was a text from Laurie.

We just got to the prison.

Chapter 34

Laurie silenced her cell phone after sending a quick text update to Marcy. She couldn't imagine the anguish she and Andrew were feeling. She hadn't slept more than a few hours at a time since Johnny went missing. The idea of being away from Timmy for nearly a week and having no idea where he was? It would be more than Laurie could bear.

Tucking her cell phone in her blazer pocket, she turned her attention to her cameraman, who was studying his digital screen. "How's it looking, Nick?"

The space provided by the prison was small, one of the rooms typically used by defense attorneys to meet with their clients. Laurie had planned accordingly, keeping the team small—just her, Ryan, and her head cameraman with a single field camera in tow. Tracy Mahoney, Gunther's lawyer, had already introduced herself to them and said she was amenable to any seating arrangement as long as she did not appear on camera.

"Check it for yourself," Nick said, stepping back to give her a look. "This is as good as I can get it."

The only furniture in view was a small round table and the two chairs they had positioned at it. Ryan was seated closest to the entrance, with his back to the door, reviewing notes he had scribbled on a legal pad.

The challenge was to get both Ryan and Gunther in the same frame from such a close perspective. Nick had managed to do it by positioning the camera in the farthest corner from the table.

"As you can see," Nick explained, "you get a slightly better view of where Ryan's sitting than of the other chair."

Ryan flashed a smile and a quick wave to the camera. The result was far from the film quality they'd usually have, but it would suffice.

"So we'll put Gunther there, and, Ryan, we'll shoot you more in profile. And then we've got this chair in the corner out of camera view for the defense lawyer."

"Works for me," Ryan said. "It creeps me out having my back to the door anyway."

Laurie flashed Nick a thumbs-up. "You're a miracle worker, always a pro."

"You're just saying that because I got up at the crack of dawn to make the trip up here."

"Hey, at least the drive came with a little care package from the Doughnut Project."

Laurie had learned that Nick was a sucker for the pastry shop's bacon maple bar, which was exactly what it sounded like.

Nick patted the front of his shirt with a smile. "My arteries say no, but my belly says 'please and thank you.' By the way," he added, lowering his voice, "I just wanted to let you know that the missus and I have been including Johnny in our prayers. Anything we can do to help, we're there for you."

Johnny's presumed abduction had been prominent in the local news, including his family connection to federal judge Alex Buckley.

"I appreciate that," Laurie said. "Being here, doing the work . . . that's the help I need right now."

Nick nodded knowingly. "Gotcha. Well, I'm ready to go here whenever you are."

Laurie had a feeling that Nick suspected a connection between Johnny's disappearance and the sudden urgency with which Laurie was tackling the show's latest case, but he wasn't the type to ask questions beyond camera angles and lighting choices.

She looked to Ryan, who had repositioned himself on the opposite side of the table.

"Let's rock and roll," he said.

She knocked on the narrow glass pane in the security door, and a guard opened the door. "We're all set here," she said.

"Let me get your prisoner. His lawyer's on-site, too."

When the door was closed again, she felt a wave of panic wash over her. This might be their one shot to save Johnny. They couldn't blow it.

If it weren't for the forest-green prison jumpsuit, Darren Gunther could have passed for a Hollywood actor strutting into an audition room, full of cool confidence and a laser-beamed focus.

"Ah, a nice sojourn to the luxurious legal team suite. Much more refined than the riffraff common area."

He politely thanked the guard who unlocked his shackles and replaced them with a single set of handcuffs to connect one of his wrists to a bracket at the edge of the tabletop.

Tracy Mahoney, Gunther's lawyer, was tall with broad shoulders and an untamed mop of curly gray-blond hair. Her Brooklyn accent was hard to miss. "Is all that really necessary? We're on camera. The locks on the door are Fort Knox–worthy."

The guard shook his head. "You know the drill."

Once the guard left, Gunther used his free hand to offer a self-assured shake to Ryan.

"You must be Ryan Nichols," he said. "I recognize you from your television show. I looked up your pedigree, too. Impressive. I look forward to the opportunity to tell you the truth about my case."

"I'm sure we'll have an enlightening conversation," Ryan responded.

"And you must be Ms. Moran," he said, nodding toward Laurie.

"I am." Usually, she would have had a thorough preproduction interview with any subject by now, but these weren't usual circumstances. "I'm looking forward to hearing your side of the story."

He held up the index finger of his free hand. "Be careful what you wish for, Ms. Moran. You know that saying about never try to meet your heroes? Your dad's considered to be quite a hero, and you may not like what I have to say about him. There's a side of him I doubt he displays for his admiring daughter and adorable little grandson. His name's Timmy, is that right?"

His feigned smile appeared kind, but a white-hot burn filled her throat at the sound of her son's name on Gunther's lips. She was reminded again of the tricky challenge that lay ahead of them. If Gunther had orchestrated the abduction of a boy he thought was Leo's grandchild in order to gain leverage over Leo, he certainly couldn't admit it to them on camera. He would have to drop veiled clues to confirm an implicit trade: the kidnapped child's freedom in exchange for his. Gunther had immediately mentioned Laurie's son. Was that the type of hint they were looking for, or simply his way of trying to get to the TV producer whose show he wanted to manipulate?

"Why don't we get started," she said.

Chapter 35

As Ryan walked Gunther through his version of the story behind Lou Finney's death, Laurie realized how badly she wanted to vindicate her father, even if it turned out Gunther had nothing to do with Johnny's abduction.

The interview covered all of the events on the night of the murder, and the supposedly exonerating DNA evidence, without a single interjection from Gunther's lawyer. So far, Gunther had not strayed from either his trial testimony or the motions filed in his wrongful conviction case. He was also nice-looking, articulate, and even charming at times. The average TV viewer would look at him and think it impossible for him to be a killer. Laurie knew from experience, though, that a murderer could reside inside the most unlikely people. There had to be some other explanation for the presence of Mason Rollins's DNA on the murder weapon. Laurie would never believe that her father had fabricated a confession to frame an innocent man.

As if reading her thoughts, Gunther suddenly shifted away from the DNA evidence, looked directly into the camera, and said, "I know what people are thinking: even if I sound like a reasonable person to you; even though I've been a model prisoner for all these eighteen years, insisting on my innocence; even though I can *prove*, beyond any doubt, that it's not *my* DNA on that murder weapon, but that of a *known* felon with a penchant for attacking people with knives"—he ticked each point off on his fingertips—"at the end of the day, many of you are going to think, *But a decorated cop says he confessed*, and for you, that will be enough. Because the cop I'm up against isn't just any old man in blue, it's former first deputy commissioner Leo Farley, who soared through the ranks like a rocket after my conviction. For people who don't know what that means, he's literally one step down from the commissioner himself. Farley was considered a shoo-in for the next commissioner if he hadn't retired, but he's still treated like a rock star. He gets profiled in *New York* magazine and hangs out with the mayor in a private suite at sports events."

A jolt of electricity shot through Laurie's brain at the mention of that magazine profile. That was the publication that had run the photograph of them in the mayor's suite at Yankee Stadium. Timmy had looked then so much like Johnny did now. They now at least had confirmation that Gunther had seen that picture. She forced herself to focus as Gunther continued to list Leo's many accolades.

"He marches beside the cardinal at the front of the St. Patrick's Day Parade, with the grand marshal's float. My goodness, the man has so many commendations that the medals on his dress uniform flicker like a disco ball."

"I think your point about First Deputy Commissioner Farley's reputation has been made," Ryan said. "You're saying that in a swearing match between you and him, you suspect most people will simply defer to the decorated police veteran."

"Precisely. But here's the thing." Gunther aimed his penetrating gaze directly into the camera again. "How did Leo Farley climb up to such rarified air? What made him so different from all the other beat cops and detectives whose names no one knows? What made Farley so special that he's practically law enforcement royalty?"

Ryan seized his opening. "One explanation is that he's the kind of dedicated investigator who, for example, goes back to the station house after his shift because he still hasn't gotten to the truth. And then he's so good at his job that he manages to get someone as smart and controlled as you to confess to stabbing a man in a fit of rage after being rejected by a woman at a bar."

Gunther smiled quietly. "You sound like a man who works for Leo Farley's daughter. I assume this production will disclose the blatant conflict of interest so viewers can take that into account when forming an opinion."

"We always give our viewers the straight facts."

"Well, did you know the *straight fact* that Leo Farley was under consideration for the job of deputy commissioner of public information at the time of my arrest? Until then, he was an ambitious cop, but hadn't had the kind of high-profile cases that would put him in the spotlight. But Lou Finney's case had all the hallmarks of a front-page story. The beloved owner of a popular bar in one of the hottest neighborhoods in Manhattan. A private college student and a rich-kid real estate heir were the suspects. A tale of old New York City meets new. A clash of the classes. And Leo supposedly getting the goods on me made him the star of the story. Then guess what? He got the big promotion, making him the chief public spokesperson for the entire NYPD, able to command as much media attention as a mayor."

Laurie did not like what she was hearing. Gunther was wielding her father's stellar reputation as a weapon against him. On Nick's digital screen, Laurie could see Gunther's gaze shift off camera. He was looking at her, but then he directed his attention back to Ryan.

"I suggest you check into the timing of Leo Farley's trajectory in the department. You'll see that I'm right. Did you know I'm not the first prisoner to have accused Farley of fabricating evidence?"

Even in profile, Laurie thought she saw a flicker of doubt in Ryan's reaction. He was probably thinking that in any other case—with a different police investigator, with a normal timeline for production—Laurie would have researched any possible pattern of complaints prior to conducting on-screen interviews. He recovered quickly, though.

"You've been in prison eighteen years," Ryan said. "I assume you know how common wrongful conviction complaints are. Any police officer with thirty years of service will have multiple defendants accuse them of misconduct over the course of a career. It doesn't make the allegations true."

"The newly discovered DNA matches a man with a demonstrated pattern of threatening people with knives, including at least one known stabbing in a bar fight, the exact conduct at issue in my case. Did you know that the District Attorney's Office's Conviction Integrity Unit has confirmed that Mason Rollins was living in Greenwich Village at the time Lou Finney was stabbed? His apartment was only a ten-minute walk from that bar. Rollins slammed the door in my lawyer's face when she tried to talk to him, and my understanding is that he refused to speak to the DA's investigator as well."

"So what is your theory about why Rollins would stab a bar owner with whom he had no known grievance?"

"Because we all spilled out onto the sidewalk. I was trying to disengage, but the other guy from the bar, Jay Pratt, kept punching me and grabbing my shirt. We bumped into some other guy—hard—and he was the one who pulled the knife. The next thing I knew, Mr. Finney was falling. There was so much blood. And the other guy . . . He was long gone. There's no doubt in my mind that man was Mason Rollins, and I have the DNA to prove it. You're an excellent lawyer, Mr. Nichols. You tell me: If my case isn't good enough to raise doubts about my guilt, whose is?"

Chapter 36

Gunther held Ryan's gaze, as if daring him to suggest any weaknesses in his arguments. *If my case isn't good enough to raise doubts about my guilt, whose is?*

It was a made-for-the-camera moment, striking just the right tone for the end of the interview. Ryan hadn't managed to shake Gunther away from any part of his side of the story. If anything, Gunther had strengthened his case, maximizing his use of the DNA evidence while calling into question Leo's credibility.

Ryan looked to Laurie. She understood it was a sign that he was coming to a close. She nodded.

"Just a few more questions before we wrap up, Mr. Gunther. I'm going to read you a list of names of people who were at Finn's Bar the night of the murder and ask whether you had any contact with them either before that night, or since."

"Very well, but I don't see the point of it."

"According to your version of the story, you were at the bar alone and didn't know anyone there, so we'd like to confirm that. And then we'd like to make sure you didn't make any attempt after the fact to contact potential witnesses against you, either at your original trial or in your wrongful conviction case."

For the first time since the cameras started filming, Tracy Mahoney spoke up. "Don't answer that, Darren. It's too vague."

He used his free hand to wave off her concerns. "Please, I've got nothing to worry about. Let's hear it."

One by one, Ryan read from the list that Laurie had created: Lou Finney, of course; Jane Holloway, the woman Gunther had been hitting on that night; Jay Pratt, the man Gunther had fought with in the bar; Clarissa DeSanto, the waitress who'd surprised Leo by not testifying at Gunther's trial; and, finally, Mason Rollins. According to Gunther, he had no preexisting connection to any of them, and no contact with them since.

"What about the friend you were celebrating with earlier that night, before the confrontation with Mr. Pratt? Perhaps he could shed some light about your demeanor that evening."

Gunther squinted, as if confused by the question. "I was at the bar alone. I had been planning to meet some other Vassar students who were in the city for break, but never linked up with them. I headed down to the Village to find some fun on my own. Little did I know that the decision would ruin my life."

According to Samantha Finney, Clarissa the waitress had said Gunther arrived with another man, but there was no way to know the truth at this point. This checklist of names was actually only a lead-in to the next question—the one that mattered the most.

"And finally," Ryan asked, "we'd like to know who might serve as character references on your behalf."

"Meaning what?"

"People who could say what type of person you were eighteen years ago, but also anyone close to you now. You say you've been a model prisoner. We think our viewers would like to hear from the people who know you best, to get a better sense of who you are as a person."

If Gunther was involved in kidnapping Johnny, this was his opportunity to put them in touch with a third party who might continue a potential trade for his freedom, outside the confines of the prison.

"My mother went into a nursing home four years ago with dementia," he said, shoulders slumping. "They wouldn't even let me out to say good-bye to her while she still recognized her son. I'd probably say my lawyer is the person who knows me best at this point." He nodded in Tracy's direction. Laurie knew that a lawyer could not serve as a formal witness on behalf of her own client.

"No one else?" Ryan asked. "Maybe an old friend from the neighborhood, or even a former prisoner you've stayed in touch with whom we could interview?"

Come on, Laurie thought, *take the bait. Point us in the right direction.*

"Sorry," Gunther said with a shrug, "it's not exactly easy to keep or make friends from behind bars."

Ryan's face fell as he looked to Laurie to make the call. He knew it, too. They hadn't gotten what they needed.

"I think that's all we have for today," she said.

"You sure?" he asked. "Not like I've got big plans for the rest of my day." Those twinkling eyes and dry smile again. She could see why so many media types had fallen for him.

"All good." She felt a chill as she walked behind his chair to rap her knuckles on the door, indicating to the guard that they were finished.

As she heard a key enter the lock, Gunther spoke again. "By the way, Ms. Moran, my thoughts and prayers are with your fiancé's nephew and your entire family."

She nearly jumped at the direct mention of Johnny's disappearance. "What did you say?"

"I'm a bit of a news junkie. Five different newspapers, a mix of local and national, every single day. The *Post* and the *Daily News* have certainly done a good job getting his picture out everywhere. He looks like a sweet boy. I hope he's found safely, and soon."

Laurie's mind raced, silently shuffling through the press coverage she had been monitoring. Several of the stories noted that Johnny had been in the Hamptons for the birthday party of his uncle, newly confirmed federal judge Alex Buckley, but so far they had mentioned neither Laurie nor her father. At the very least, Gunther's comment revealed that he had made the connection. But was this his way of letting her know he could lead them to Johnny?

She felt no closer to the truth.

"Let's just say that the entire family is eager to get him home—no matter what."

She searched Gunther's face for some glimmer of a reaction as the prison guard re-shackled him. He did not turn to look at her again as he was escorted from the room.

Nick led the way toward the prison exit, lugging his field camera in a cross-slung leather bag.

Laurie found herself moving slowly, not wanting to climb into the studio van without a better lead.

She stopped walking as they approached the check-in window and turned toward Ryan at her side. "Is it just me, or did that not go well?"

"Not just you," Ryan said. "It's everything we already knew, but in his own words, which, frankly, sounded pretty good. And you know I like your father, but Gunther put some points on the board. We're going to need to look at the timing between Gunther's case and your dad's promotion to the Public Information Office."

Laurie pressed her hand to her forehead. There had to be something else they could do before leaving. She suddenly looked up. "The common folk digs," she said.

Ryan's expression was confused.

"Gunther remarked that he was on a sojourn to the luxury legal team suites, nicer than the meeting areas for the *riffraff*."

It only took Ryan a beat to catch up to her train of thought. "Meaning, he has other visitors."

Ten minutes later, they had a name: Summer Carver. She first showed up in the guest log about a year earlier, but over the last six months, she had only rarely missed the twice-a-week visitation hours that Gunther was allowed.

"So much for not having any friends except his lawyer," Ryan said dryly.

As they waited for a corrections official to print out a computer scan of the woman's New York driver's license, they saw Tracy Mahoney standing in the alcove just inside the prison entrance. She turned away and held up her phone as if making a call, but Laurie was certain the lawyer had been watching them.

Tuesday, July 21

Day Seven

Chapter 37

The next morning, Laurie stood in her office, before three white-boards containing everything they knew so far about Johnny's disap-pearance, Darren Gunther and the murder of Lou Finney, and the possible connections between the two. Jerry, Grace, and Ryan sat at the white oval conference table, taking notes as she summarized key points.

She drew a circle in red ink around Summer Carver's name. "If Gunther has someone acting as his eyes, ears, and legs on the ground while he's in prison, we think Summer Carver is the most likely candidate. She is his only visitor at the prison other than his lawyer and, on occasion, his editor."

She drew a second, smaller circle around Tracy Mahoney's name. "There's some possibility that his defense lawyer plays a com-plicit role in facilitating communications, but we think it's unlikely she does any dirty work herself." Tracy had seen them speaking to the prison guard at the check-in counter. It was certainly possible that the lawyer would have notified Summer by now that their pro-duction team was aware of her contacts with Gunther. The purpose of this meeting was to prepare before making any attempt to contact Summer directly.

"Jerry and I got an early start this morning looking into Summer's social media, and hit pay dirt. Jerry, I'm going to let you spell out what we found."

With only the four of them, Laurie would have simply had them huddle around her computer. Jerry, however, had been eager to connect his laptop to a projector so he could present what they had found on a larger screen.

As Laurie took a seat, a Facebook profile for Summer Carver appeared on a pull-down screen at the head of the conference table. In the profile image, a lanky young woman with long black wavy hair and pale skin held a fluffy white kitten up to her strawberry-freckled nose. "So Summer's only social media presence is on Facebook. The first thing we noticed is that her only public posts—meaning we can see them even though we aren't her online 'friends'—are shared posts from the *Darren Gunther Is Innocent* page. We also know that she is active on Darren Gunther's advocacy page, which isn't surprising given that she visits him in prison."

Jerry moved the cursor to the place on Summer's profile where you could link to the profiles of any family members. Two family members were listed: her mother, Julie Carver, and a brother, Toby Carver. Jerry moved the cursor to Toby's name and clicked.

"Her brother hasn't posted anything for four years, so . . . dead end." The profile picture wasn't even of a person. It was a scenic shot of some woods near a creek. Jerry then pulled up the profile of Summer's mother. "Mama Julie, however, is quite the active Facebook user."

Julie's profile photo depicted two women, smiling in close-up. One was Summer Carver, and the other wore a blue T-shirt that said *60 Is the New 40* in bold white letters. Julie was shorter and heavier than her daughter, with shorter, lighter hair, but they shared the strawberry freckles. Jerry double-clicked on the profile photo to reveal the date and caption. "This is from about three years ago. As you can see from the caption, they were celebrating Julie's sixtieth

birthday." The caption read, "Best birthday gift possible. My beautiful daughter is back with me. So happy to have her home again!"

Grace raised her hand, but didn't wait to be called on. "Would it
be a spoiler to ask where Summer was before that?"

"If we knew, I would tell you. So, that's mystery number one. On-
ward." Jerry speed-scrolled through hundreds of typical social media
posts: pausing to point out Julie's regular mentions of her daughter,
including a few pictures of the two of them together at the meal-
delivery nonprofit called God's Love We Deliver.

"I brought an extra sous-chef with me for my regular Tuesday
shift in the kitchen," Julie had captioned one of the photos. "Click
here to donate to an important cause!"

Jerry continued scrolling before stopping suddenly on a post
from four months earlier. "Now *this* is where things get interesting."

Instead of a personal photograph, the post was of white cursive
text against a dark blue background. *Mothers Don't Sleep*, it read.
They Just Worry with Their Eyes Closed. It was posted with the caption, "SO TRUE!"

Laurie noticed Ryan drop his pen to the table, taking a break
from the notes he was scribbling intensely, as if he had been assuming that nothing promising could come from a so-called mommy-
meme. He was wrong. The key was to read the replies from Julie's
friends.

Katie Lundt: *Julie, I want to think you're kidding, but this doesn't
sound good?*

Beth Trainor: *LOL, honey, but I agree with Katie. You're worrying
us. Is Summer okay?*

Julie then replied: *She has made some choices that are . . . well, I
don't understand them.*

Katie Lundt: *But is everything OK?!*

Julie: *I couldn't hold my tongue any longer, so now she left the
house to stay with Toby (half brother). Long story, but, honestly, I'm*

concerned. Pray for me and my daughter, please. I can guide her but I can no longer control her. Why do they have to grow up so fast?

Laurie would never understand people who engaged in intimate conversations on the internet. If she had to guess, Julie Carver never imagined that a total stranger would end up scouring her social media for a glimpse into the most private details of her family.

Ryan's pen was back in hand, furiously at work on his legal pad. "It sounds like there was a falling-out," he said. "And the timing is right. Starting around six months ago, Summer ramped up her prison visits to Gunther to twice a week. Her mother may not have been happy about her daughter's newest friend."

"That's exactly what we think," Jerry said. "Since this post four months ago, there's no indication that Julie has seen her daughter even once. In fact, there's no direct mention of Summer at all. On Mother's Day, a few people posted notes to Julie that they were thinking of her and wishing her better days with her children, so it would appear that they're still on the outs. And Summer's profile says she has a brother named Toby. It seems he's a half brother, and not Julie's son."

Ryan squeezed the bridge of his nose. "It's still really thin. All we really know is that Summer supports Gunther and has had some falling-out with her mom. A big leap from that to kidnapping. Do we have any reason to believe Summer's capable of that?"

Jerry clicked off the overhead projection as Laurie explained that she had called Jennifer Langland, the Long Island detective in charge of Johnny's case, the previous night.

Grace shook her head, not trying to veil her displeasure. Her long red fingernails gleamed as she raised an adamant hand. "I'm sorry, I know I've never met the woman, but from everything I've heard, she is convinced we're on a wild-goose chase with Gunther. Just have your father do his thing. The NYPD can run Summer through every database known to man. Done!"

Grace wasn't wrong. Langland was clearly skeptical of Gunther's involvement in Johnny's abduction, but she was also the investigator in charge. She was Laurie's first stop unless it became clear they needed a Plan B.

"I think I caught Langland at a good time," Laurie said. "Apparently they spent nearly two days trailing a guy who had been seen watching children on the beach the day Johnny was abducted. They finally pulled him over for failing to signal. They thought they might actually have him when they found a receipt in the car from that day, from one of the food trucks that works the beaches. But then they tracked down the food truck and learned it was in Southhampton when Johnny disappeared. Anyway, whether she thinks we're on the right track, or was just embarrassed about hitting a dead end, she promised me she'd run Summer and get back to me."

"Her brother, too?" Grace asked.

"All known associates."

"It's a start," Grace said begrudgingly, "but I have a feeling that Mama Carver could tell us a whole lot about what Summer's been up to. It's just a few Facebook posts, but I know the sound of a mother who thinks her kid is up to no good. I mean, not that I was ever that kid," she added.

"Of course not," Laurie said. "Funny you should say that, Grace, because if I wanted to find Mrs. Carver today for a preliminary background interview, where would we look?"

Grace's heart-shaped face broke out into a broad smile as she realized she knew the answer. "Tuesday afternoon. Her regular volunteer shift in the kitchen. Can I come? Please? Moms who Facebook love me!"

Laurie had been looking for ways to give Grace more responsibility, and she did have a natural talent for bringing out a person's chatty side. "Sounds good."

Laurie took a quick look at today's outfit: an ocean-blue, above-the-knee sheath dress that was practically a nun's habit compared to Grace's normal attire, paired with glossy five-inch, nude-colored stiletto heels. "Don't worry. I keep flats in my desk drawer for when I need to look less . . ."

"Spectacular?" Laurie said.

"Exactly."

Chapter 38

Grace looked up at the gleaming six-story building on the SoHo corner of Spring Street and Sixth Avenue. From the sidewalk, she and Laurie could see the action unfolding inside a state-of-the-art commercial kitchen. Chefs in white aprons and black caps chopped carrots and onions, peeled potatoes, and rolled meatballs.

"*This* is the soup kitchen?" Grace marveled. She glanced at the plain black ballet flats she had slipped on for their trip downtown. "My Louboutins would have fit right in here, though mine are knockoffs, to be clear."

Laurie shot off a quick text, *We just arrived*, and then held open the front door for Grace. "Not what you expected, huh? They built new headquarters a few years ago to expand operations. And it's not a soup kitchen. They deliver close to two million at-home meals a year to clients who are too sick to shop or cook for themselves."

Laurie had attended the annual gala for God's Love We Deliver multiple times and was a regular donor. Last year for the fundraising auction, she had donated a tour of Fisher Blake Studios, culminating in a lunch with both the host and the producer of *Under Suspicion*.

That connection had come in handy when she wanted to meet with Summer Carver's mother, Julie. Laurie had culled her old emails for the contact information of the staff member who had solicited the auction donation.

"Caroline," Laurie called out, now recognizing the face of the young woman making her way to the reception desk to meet them. As Laurie rounded out the introductions, she noticed Grace eyeing Caroline's high heels with a knowing smile. "Thank you so much for helping us out, especially on such short notice."

"I was happy to do it," Caroline said. "Julie Carver's one of our best volunteers. She and her husband used to run their own restaurant in Queens. When he passed away, she decided to sell, but, turns out, she missed the work. Her retirement was very much to our benefit."

Rather than bombard Summer Carver's mother without notice during her weekly volunteer shift in the kitchen, Laurie had called Caroline and asked her to act as intermediary. According to Caroline, Julie had said she was a regular viewer of *Under Suspicion* and seemed eager to speak to someone about concerns she had regarding her daughter's connection to a convicted killer.

Caroline's eyes brightened at the appearance of a woman emerging from the first-floor commercial-style kitchen, drying her hands on her apron. Laurie recognized her from her Facebook photographs. "There's Julie now. I held one of our conference rooms for you to meet in private."

It only took a few minutes for Laurie to explain that they were conducting research for a special covering Lou Finney's murder and Darren Gunther's claim that he was wrongfully convicted. "As Caroline probably mentioned, your daughter's name arose in our investigation because she frequently visits Gunther at the prison. We looked at her social media accounts to see how the two of them might be connected and happened to come across your posts, suggesting you had some concerns about your daughter. We were wondering if they related to Darren Gunther."

"Those prison visits are what really put me over the edge with her," Julie said wistfully. "At first, I was heartened by her interest in his criminal case. After a couple of very rocky years, Summer was back in New York, living with me, trying to figure out what she wanted to do next. She finished some course work she needed for her bachelor's degree and started studying for the LSATs to go to law school. She has always been interested in the criminal justice system. In fact, she's the one who got me hooked on your show. We watch it together."

Laurie allowed the comment about Summer's "rocky years" to lie for now, but she recalled Julie's Facebook post from three years ago, mentioning that her daughter had moved home.

Julie continued. "You have to understand, my daughter has one of the best hearts in the world. You couldn't ask for a more loyal or compassionate friend. But sometimes her feelings are almost *too* much. She'll go to the end of the earth for someone she cares about, but to the detriment of herself—or anyone else for that matter."

"My sister's like that," Grace said. "She's willing to burn up her own life to help someone she loves."

Julie smiled sadly. "So you understand. Let me ask you something: Does the person your sister is trying to help always deserve it?"

"Heck no," Grace said. "One man ended up dumping her by text message—on her birthday no less. When she called and asked him why, he put his *new* girlfriend on the phone to talk to her. If some fool did that to me, the police wouldn't find the body."

Laurie was starting to wonder if it had been a mistake to bring Grace along, until Grace followed up with "I take it Darren Gunther isn't the first person you've had to worry about in Summer's life."

"Definitely not," Julie said. "She would have been the high school valedictorian except a boy who was a smidgen behind her in the class convinced her to flub a test so he could have it instead.

He told her he needed it to get a scholarship, and then he broke up with her as soon as grades came out. But nothing beats the guy she met the summer before her senior year at Stony Brook. He wanted to be an actor. Convinced her to quit college at the start of her last semester to move to LA with him and be his manager. For two years, she lived her entire life around him, to the point that she stopped calling me because we couldn't even talk without fighting. When she ran out of money to spend on him, he found another woman and moved on. The only bright side is that she finally came home."

Because of Grace's comment about her sister, they now had an answer to where Summer had been before returning to New York. Laurie was also starting to understand the value that someone with Summer's personality could provide to a man like Darren Gunther. If she truly believed Gunther had lost eighteen years of his life for a crime he didn't commit, could she justify taking a child's freedom for a few days to balance the scales of justice?

"How have things been between you and your daughter since then?" Laurie asked.

"We were good at first. She wanted to pursue a career in criminal law and started reading more and more about the innocence movement, which led her to Darren Gunther's case. At first, she made it sound like she was working as an intern for his defense lawyer or something. I was overjoyed, thinking that would give her a leg up on her law school applications."

"By his lawyer, do you mean Tracy Mahoney?" Laurie asked.

Julie apologized and said she did not know the attorney's name. "In fact, I have no idea whether Summer even had contact with the lawyers. The next thing I know, she's driving up to Dannemora as often as the prison will let her in. At that point, I knew this wasn't any normal office volunteer situation and confronted her about it. Turns out, she'd written that man a letter in prison. She had been working on her admission essay about wrongful convictions and was hoping to collect personal stories. It went from a pen pal situation to her meeting him in person, to what seemed to me to be practically an obsession. Suddenly, there were no more LSAT books on the dining room table, there was no more talk about applying to schools. Just Darren this, Darren that. I honestly got so worried that I called the prison to try to bar her from seeing him, but I couldn't give them grounds for doing so."

Laurie heard the obvious anguish in Julie's voice. "You said the prison visits were what 'put you over the edge' with Summer. Exactly what did you mean by that?"

"I felt like I was enabling her, letting her live here, paying her bills, all so she could give her time and energy to this murderer. And honestly, even if he's innocent, he's taking advantage of her goodwill. I didn't want my daughter falling prey to some prisoner she barely knows instead of figuring out how to live her own life. So I put my foot down. I told her she had to stop visiting him and focus on her future if she was going to continue to live under my roof. That was four months ago. She hasn't spoken to me since."

"I'm sorry," Laurie said. "That must be terribly painful."

Julie nodded, accepting the concern. "Sometimes I wonder if I made a mistake giving her an ultimatum. I thought she'd have no choice but to respect my wishes. Or at the very least, she'd have to get a job to support herself, which might keep her from spending so much time upstate."

"What did she do instead?" Laurie asked.

"To my complete dismay, she moved in with her *brother* of all people."

"Why was that so surprising?" Laurie asked.

"They've never been particularly close—he's older and is actually her half brother from my husband's first marriage. They were more . . . *different* than any sort of conflict between them. Where I always expected Summer to finish school and be a success, my husband had to ride Toby just to get him through high school. And while Summer will give someone the coat off her back in a storm — let's just say Toby's not like that. When Summer packed her stuff and said she was going to Toby's, I tried to get him to send her back to me, or at least make her get a job. But from what I can tell, he's been supporting her this whole time, when I don't even know how he supports himself."

"You don't know what your stepson does for a living?" Laurie asked.

"See, that's the thing: Toby doesn't really *do* anything. When my husband died, they each got a bit of money. Not a fortune, mind you, but a good financial head start for a young adult. Summer squandered it all on that wannabe actor, and Toby bought a small, modest house upstate. He works as a property caretaker for some of the vacation owners. Does seasonal work selling firewood, shoveling snow, that kind of thing. Honestly, sometimes I wonder how the math adds up. I know he had some kind of interaction with the court system a few years ago, but he told me it was nothing to worry about. Then he supposedly went camping for a few months."

"You sound skeptical," Laurie said.

"I thought it was possible he was sent to *jail.*" She whispered the word as if someone might overhear. "He laughed when I raised the theory, but it left me unsettled. It's a horrible feeling to doubt the word of my husband's only son. But now I wonder if Toby might have some connection to Darren Gunther, too — like the man is stealing my family from me. Does that sound crazy?"

Laurie thought about Gunther's flair for charm. He wanted — no, *needed* — people to love him. Was it possible he had managed to win over not only Summer and her overly big heart, but her brother as well?

"No, it doesn't sound crazy at all."

"Good, because I know with a mother's gut, with every fiber of my being, that my daughter is in big trouble. Somehow, some way, this man is going to get her to do something that could ruin her life forever. Please, Ms. Moran. Please try to stop that."

If Laurie's suspicions were right, it might be too late to save Summer Carver. The question was whether they even had time to save Johnny.

Grace looked glum as they climbed into the back of their Uber.

"You okay?" Laurie asked, waiting for her cell phone to power up again.

"I feel bad for her is all."

"She's definitely worried about her daughter."

Something else seemed to tug at Grace. "If I had a mom who loved me that much, I'd tell her everything—the good, the bad, and the boring. Someday, Summer's going to regret shutting her mother out."

It dawned on Laurie that Grace often spoke about her sister and occasionally referred to a monthly dinner with her godmother, but rarely mentioned her parents. She was trying to figure out how to follow up on Grace's comment when her phone finally came back to life. A text message from Jennifer Langland was waiting for her. *Sounds like your phone is off. Please call me as soon as you get this.*

Laurie hit a button to call Langland.

"I looked into Summer Carver and her known associates like you asked."

Laurie braced herself for disappointing news. Langland was convinced that Gunther had nothing to do with Johnny's abduction. "I had an interesting meeting with her mother, Julie, just now. She described Summer as extremely vulnerable to influence. She said her daughter was, quote, 'obsessed' with Gunther. Summer's apparently living with her half brother, and it sounds like the mom thinks he may be a bit shady. She thought he might have some kind of agenda for helping his sister right now."

Langland's response was immediate. "Tobias Anderson Carver, six years older than his baby sister. Current address in Brewster, New York. He was accused of fraud about four years ago, for raising money for a nonexistent condo project. Served three months and got his record expunged after two years for keeping his nose clean."

"He told Julie he was camping during those months. Is it possible Toby met Gunther while he was in jail?"

"No. The brother's charges were federal. Two completely different systems. But if Toby's involved with Gunther, too, maybe he has more of a financial incentive. If Gunther wins his wrongful conviction case, he could get millions as compensation. Summer may be helping out of love, while the brother sees a pot of gold at the end of the rainbow."

Laurie was surprised to hear how open Detective Langland was to the possibility that the Carvers might be behind Johnny's disappearance. "You found something," Laurie said.

"I did. According to the E-ZPass electronic toll records, last Wednesday, at 1:02 P.M., a Toyota Camry registered to one Tobias Anderson Carver crossed the George Washington Bridge into Manhattan, then onto the Throgs Neck Bridge at 1:37. At 7:52 P.M., it returned to the Throgs Neck again in the other direction, then back to the GWB."

As Langland spoke, Laurie's thoughts raced, calculating the timing and the route from Brewster, New York, to the Hamptons. The route meant only one thing: a one-day trip onto Long Island and back. "It lines up," Laurie said.

"Like clockwork. And it's the only time Toby Carver's account shows any travel east of New York City in the past twelve months. It looks like your father may have been right, Laurie. Now we need to figure out how to bring Johnny home."

Chapter 39

Sitting at her office conference table, Laurie took a deep breath before dialing Summer Carver's cell phone number. She thought she heard her own blood pulse through her veins as she waited for an answer. With each ring, she pictured the rustic cottage that Toby Carver owned on four acres of land in Brewster. She imagined little Johnny, locked away in a basement or an attic or a tool shed.

In cooperation with Detective Langland, local police had sent an unmarked car to drive by the property, but they saw no obvious signs of foul play. The investigative team had decided against knocking on the door. Until they had a search warrant to authorize entry into the house, which a judge had declined without further evidence, they didn't want to tip off Summer and her brother that they were suspects.

The voice that answered was perky and peppy. Laurie reminded herself that Summer's own mother said that she had been acting like a different person under the influence of Darren Gunther.

Summer let out a high-pitched squeal at the mention of *Under Suspicion*. "Oh my goodness, you have no idea how much I love your show. I've seen every one of them. I read all the comments on the fan pages and message boards. I have to admit, I thought maybe you were on the wrong track with the runaway bride case, but I eventually came around once all the facts were revealed. Your show is better at crime solving than even the FBI."

Laurie explained that she was calling because she had learned from the prison that Summer was a frequent visitor of Darren Gunther. "Mr. Gunther is the focus of our next program. We interviewed him yesterday, in fact. Perhaps he mentioned that to you."

"That's great news. I've followed his case for over a year and am convinced he's innocent. He's such a gentle soul, plus a brilliant writer. Every day he's behind bars is a tragedy."

"So, did he mention that we interviewed him?" Laurie prodded.

After a long pause, Summer finally answered. "I consider myself part of his legal team. I don't think I should repeat any communications I've had with him."

Laurie was no lawyer, but she was pretty sure that wasn't how attorney-client privilege worked. "As a fan of *Under Suspicion*, you may have read that the nephew of our former host, Alex Buckley, recently went missing from a beach in the Hamptons."

This time, Summer didn't pause. "I saw that! I'm so sorry. I should have expressed my thoughts and prayers as soon as you called. I can't imagine how terrified his parents are."

Laurie felt like she was floundering. She needed to get Summer to initiate the idea of trading Johnny for Gunther's freedom. "His family—which is *my* family, as you may know—would do absolutely anything to rescue Johnny. Maybe that's how you feel about Darren," she added. She had come as close as possible to saying directly that they were willing to strike a deal.

"Darren's not a little boy," Summer said, "but he was barely an adult when he was sent to prison. And he's just as innocent as Johnny."

"Can you and I meet tomorrow?" Laurie asked. "You could provide valuable insight that our show is missing. And anything you want to say to me, I'm open to hearing it—completely off the record if you want it that way."

The pause returned. "Let me call you back."

Laurie turned off the recorder attached to her phone.

Chapter 40

Johnny tried not to cringe as the man's fingers tousled his hair. Johnny could feel the man's breath on his cheek as he leaned over Johnny's shoulder to inspect his artwork. "You're doing an excellent job. I knew you'd be happier once you were able to leave that little bedroom and roam around the house a bit more. It's a comfortable place to be, right?"

Johnny started to say "uh-huh" as he continued to color, but quickly corrected himself. "Yes, sir. It's a very nice place. Thank you again for the drawing table," he added.

Two mornings ago, the man had unlocked Johnny's bedroom door and then walked away with no comment, leaving the door ajar behind him. Johnny sat and stared at the open door for what felt like hours. Eventually, he heard the clanging of pots and pans from the kitchen, followed by the smell of bacon. Still, he stayed put until the man returned, saying, "Breakfast is ready if you'd like to join me in the dining room."

Since then, he had allowed Johnny to watch an hour of television a day in the living room and to eat all of his meals in the dining room. They had even sat on the screened-in porch yesterday while the man read the newspaper, occasionally asking Johnny to read parts aloud to him. He said, "It's healthy for a child to know about the world." But then the man's face had reddened at the sight of one page that he immediately folded and hid beneath a book.

The story's about me, isn't it? Johnny had wondered. *They're looking for me. They're going to find me, and then you are going to go to jail, locked away like you locked me in that room.*

"You understand why I had to secure you in that room for the first few days, don't you?" the man asked as Johnny continued to color. "I need to know that I can trust you—and vice versa. I'm taking good care of you, right?"

"Yes, sir."

"Okay, then, so now you know: as long as you behave, everything's going to be okay. The more I know I can trust you, Danny, the more privileges I can give you."

This morning's "reward" had been this table, which the man had brought down from upstairs and set up in the living room. It was like the art table Johnny had at home, but it was tilted and had a lip on the bottom edge so the artwork wouldn't fall off while you worked on it. The man had also given him a big set of colored pencils and a coloring book. It didn't seem like a normal kids' coloring book. It was called *Historic Buildings of America*, but it was better than nothing. As Johnny filled in the grass in front of the Alamo with his green pencil, he let his gaze wander through the living room window. He had yet to see another house within view—not even from the back patio.

"How long have you lived here?" Johnny asked, trying not to sound scared. It was the first time he had ever asked the man a question about himself.

"Depends on what you mean by here, but I've been in this house for about three years."

"What about before that? I've only ever lived in one house—until this one, I mean."

The man became silent, and Johnny wondered if the man could see that Johnny was only pretending to be his friend now. When he finally spoke, the man sounded sad. "I came out here to get a fresh start after I had some problems in my personal life."

Johnny remembered hearing the man and the woman talk upstairs about some kind of court order and the way the boy was going to change everything. Did it all have something to do with the man's problems? And why hadn't Johnny seen the woman yet? Why was she always upstairs?

Johnny had a sudden idea and said, "I had a bad dream last night. I thought I heard a woman's voice, like maybe it was coming from upstairs."

Silence again.

When Johnny looked behind him, the man was peering at him with flat eyes. "You certainly are a clever boy." Johnny couldn't tell if the man was angry or pleased.

"I—" He didn't know what to say.

The man's face relaxed, and he tousled Johnny's hair once again. "You'll get more answers in due course. Trust is a two-way street, Danny."

My name is Johnny, Jonathan Alexander Buckley. My parents are Andrew and Marcy Buckley. My sisters are Chloe and Emily. We live on Massachusetts Avenue in Washington, D.C.

Yesterday, Johnny found himself answering to that stupid name, Danny, without thinking twice about it. He wasn't going to let the man force him to be someone he wasn't. Even if it took ten years to escape from this house, Johnny would remember who he was and where he came from.

"Thanks again for the pencils and the coloring book." He beamed up at the man with an appreciative smile and then added, "And for this cool table. I never had an art table like this one."

Before Johnny's mommy was a mommy, she was an actress. Sometimes, she would help Johnny write short plays for him and his sisters to perform when Daddy got home. *This is just like a play, Mama. I will act the way I need to, as long as I need to . . . until I come home.*

Chapter 41

That night at seven-thirty, Alex greeted Laurie at the door to his apartment with a gentle kiss on the lips. She picked up the hint of a taste of brine from the dirty martini he was holding.

"Laurie, you really don't need to knock. That's why you have a key." After they got engaged, Alex had made duplicates of her keys and his, along with the keys to their new apartment.

"Old habits."

Leo had bought tickets to tonight's Yankee game for him and Timmy, assuming that Laurie and Alex would be on their honeymoon. She had convinced them to attend despite the changed circumstances, promising to call Leo in the event of a breakthrough in Johnny's case. They were both trying desperately to give Timmy some semblance of a normal life right now.

Alex, knowing she hadn't been able to eat much all week, convinced her to stop by so they could each make sure the other ate a little something for dinner.

"My apologies for starting without you," he said, holding up his glass. Usually, they'd both enjoy a pre-dinner cocktail as they caught up on each other's day, but there was nothing joyful about a drink these days.

"I'm the one who's sorry for being late. I kept waiting for Summer Carver to call me back, but for all I know, that moment will never come. I guess that's why cell phones were invented." She reached into the pocket of her blazer to make sure she hadn't missed a call in the elevator.

As she set her purse on the round table in the foyer, she took in the view across the East River. Instead of feeling excited about their move into a new home, she thought how much she would miss this view. She also missed the time when all her thoughts weren't so negative. Each day that Johnny hadn't been found pulled all of them further into the darkness.

"You spoke to Marcy and Andrew?" she asked.

"Yes, right after they got an update from Detective Langland. They're scared, but they're hanging in there. They wanted me to thank you for everything you're doing."

"Kara called me again today, wanting to know if she could help." Timmy's babysitter had contacted Laurie almost every day since Johnny disappeared. "On top of everything else, I'm worried about the long-term toll this guilt might take on her and Ashley."

He stroked her hair, tucked a loose strand behind her ear, and tilted her chin up to look her directly in the eyes. "Well, you feeling guilty about *her* guilt isn't going to help anyone. One day at a time. Once Johnny's back, we'll call Kara and Ashley and make sure they have some adults to talk to about their anxieties."

She nodded, wanting to believe that day would come.

Alex led the way to his kitchen, where two place settings were already waiting on the kitchen island.

"It smells so good in here," she said. "Much better than the take-out I've been feeding poor Timmy all week."

Seeing that the oven was on warm, she peeked inside to find a seared and fileted trout waiting in a pan, with separate casserole dishes of sautéed spinach and roasted sweet potatoes.

"Leave it to Ramon to make a fish smell like pure butter," she said.

"Can I pour you some wine? Or a martini?"

She declined. "I want to have a clear head if Summer calls. She made it sound like she was going to call me right back. I got the impression from her mom that she might be a little spacey, but now I'm worried that she's up to something. She could have a way of calling Gunther directly behind bars." The easy availability of burner phones inside prisons was well known. "Or maybe she's getting advice from Tracy Mahoney."

"Ryan really thinks that Tracy would be involved in a kidnapping?" Alex asked. Laurie had talked to Alex about Ryan's concerns regarding Gunther's attorney. "I can't picture it."

"Not that she'd aid and abet expressly. But he thinks she stretches the boundaries of ethics in the interests of her clients. She could be turning a blind eye to their plan, or giving them advice with a nod and a wink."

She jumped at the sound of her cell phone ringing in her hand. Laurie pulled the compact recorder from her other pocket and quickly connected it. New York was a "one-party consent" state, meaning that it was lawful to record a conversation as long as one party to the conversation consented.

"This is Laurie," she said.

"It's Summer Carver. I was thinking more about our conversation earlier. Do you believe in karma?"

"The idea that fate has a way of balancing the scales?" Laurie asked. For five years, the man who'd killed Greg walked free, plotting to kill her and Timmy when the time was right. He had eventually paid a price, but only after she had lived in fear for much of her son's childhood. But for now, she needed to say what Summer wanted to hear. "Sure, I believe in karma."

"It means that someone's actions, words, and deeds influence the person's future. Your father lied about Darren's so-called confession, and now something terrible has happened to your family."

"And you think that's karma?"

"I think that maybe if he did the right thing—if he admitted that he was wrong about Darren—the universe might find a way to restore justice in other forms, as well. And that might be a good thing for little Johnny."

Laurie felt like she was getting close, but Summer was never going to admit that she and her brother had Johnny. At best, they would release him after they actually got what they wanted—a confession of wrongdoing from Leo. But Leo had already gamed out the entire scenario with both the NYPD and Detective Langland: Leo couldn't pretend to exonerate Gunther without a guarantee that Johnny would be returned safely. If he did, Gunther would leak any such admission to the media as soon as Leo made it. Gunther would have what he wanted, and they would still be missing Johnny.

In short, they were at a stalemate.

Laurie realized, though, that they still had one advantage over Gunther and the Carvers. Summer had no idea that Laurie knew she was living with her half brother, Toby, in Upstate New York.

"You know what, Summer? We really should meet in person. Just me, you, and my dad. Off the record. We can clear the air. My father can tell you directly what happened in that interrogation room with Darren. I always find that people are more open when they can speak freely." She could almost picture Summer getting reeled in like a fish on a line. "I think we'll be able to give you what you need if we're face-to-face. Wouldn't you like to hear it straight from Leo Farley's mouth?"

Laurie suggested meeting the next day at 10 A.M. Knowing the perfect spot, she suggested a quiet coffee shop in Greenwich Village. With traffic, downtown Manhattan was nearly a two-hour drive from Toby's house in Brewster.

When Laurie hung up, Alex was looking at her expectantly. She broke out into a smile, hopeful that her plan would work. "Now I just have to deal with Toby."

Wednesday, July 22

Day Eight

Chapter 42

The next morning, Laurie and Leo passed a flower delivery van as they walked into a coffee shop called Mocha Mike's at precisely 10:00. Summer Carver was already waiting for them at the tiny table in the back corner, past the barista's pickup station, making a face after taking a sip from a lidded paper coffee cup.

Laurie had chosen this place for a reason, and it wasn't the quality of its beverages. She had popped in here once with Jerry and Grace after a witness interview. The coffee was so bad, and the seating so inhospitable, that Jerry quipped that it must be a cover for a criminal enterprise. *More like Money-Laundering Mike's*, he had joked.

But the dive had suited Laurie's needs this morning to a T because Summer's table was the sole table in the joint. The only other seating options were the barstools lining the countertop along the front window.

In person, Summer appeared younger and more attractive than in the photographs Laurie had seen online, with clear, pale skin, long, black hair, and large blue eyes peering out beneath thick, natural lashes. The result was almost doll-like.

Summer shook Laurie's hand during introductions, but declined Leo's offer of his. "Understood," Leo said, pulling out a chair for Laurie to sit across from Summer, and then taking the seat next to Laurie's.

"I hope you weren't waiting long," Laurie said.

"I was a little early because my ride needed to be somewhere at ten, too," she said. "Do you guys want to order your coffee or something? I got the mocha, given the name, but I wouldn't suggest it."

"We can wait a bit," Laurie said.

Laurie already knew that Summer's ride was her half brother, Toby, who was currently meeting his stepmother at a different coffee shop not far from here, around the corner from the headquarters of God's Love We Deliver. Julie Carver had texted Laurie moments earlier, confirming Toby's arrival at the meeting she had hastily scheduled with him the previous night. Convinced that her daughter was in over her head with Darren Gunther, she had agreed to help Laurie in exchange for Laurie's promise that she would do what she could to help both Summer and Toby if they ended up doing the right thing.

Julie had told her stepson that she had recently learned that her husband had left behind one additional annuity that had not yet been dispersed. It was a modest amount, but Toby was the sole beneficiary. She needed him to sign the paperwork for the funds to be released and suggested that he meet her in the city this morning. While a police officer in an unmarked car watched the Carver siblings as they made their way down to the city, a different officer had installed a tiny recorder beneath the only table at Mocha Mike's. The receiver was inside a decoy flower-delivery van parked at the curb around the corner, and was streamed from there to a feed being monitored in real time by Detective Jennifer Langland, who was stationed outside Toby Carver's house in Brewster.

This needed to work.

"So," Leo said, "my daughter tells me you believe in karma."

Chapter 43

Johnny Buckley sat alone in his bedroom, his stomach still full from breakfast. The man wasn't as good of a cook as either of Johnny's parents, but he sure did like making breakfast. This morning was scrambled eggs, sausage links, and buttermilk pancakes with real maple syrup. His mom always said that if you're going to eat pancakes, you have to get the real stuff.

After he helped the man load the dishwasher, the man had told him to go to his room and not come out until he was asked to do so. "You understand? Do *not* leave that room. No matter what. And remember what I told you about trust being a two-way street. You've been earning privileges. If you defy me, you will lose them. And I can still go find those people you call your parents and sisters. Don't ever forget that, Danny."

Now, alone in his room, Johnny repeated his silent mantra again to himself. *My name is Johnny, Jonathan Alexander Buckley. My parents are Andrew and Marcy Buckley.*

Johnny's entire body stiffened at the sound of an unfamiliar noise. It was the first sound he'd heard for probably a whole hour. At one point, he'd thought he heard a car engine start in the garage. What was this new noise? Footsteps upstairs? Or maybe it was a knock from the front porch.

Johnny stared at the knob of his bedroom door. *Would it even turn?*

He placed his hands over his ears, not wanting to hear the sound again. *Do not leave this room. No matter what. No matter what.*

Chapter 44

Sixty miles north of Greenwich Village, East Hampton police detective Jennifer Langland listened to the audio feed streaming into her wireless headphones as she watched the chief of the Brewster Police Department, Isaac Dawson, bang his fist against the front door of Toby Carver's house one more time. She was here with local police support, but they were letting her call the shots.

"Johnny! Johnny Buckley! Are you in there? We're here to help you, son." Dawson looked back to Langland and shook his head.

She had hoped that if they approached the Brewster house while the Carvers were both gone, Johnny might find a way to make his presence known. So far, Judge Marshall wasn't willing to sign a search warrant authorizing them to force entry onto the property to search for the missing boy. A scream, a cry, even the sound of footsteps would be enough. But this house appeared vacant. Johnny could be locked away where he couldn't be heard, or he might simply be too terrified to respond.

Dawson pointed to one of his own ears, wondering if perhaps the conversation Langland was monitoring might give them the probable cause they needed.

She shook her head. So far, Summer Carver continued to speak in circles, continually appealing to Laurie and Leo's fears for Johnny Buckley as a way to generate sympathy for the "wrongly incarcerated" Darren Gunther. She had not, however, admitted to taking the boy, or that he would be released if only Leo admitted that he had lied at Gunther's trial.

"I don't want to tell you how to do your job," Dawson said, "but the sounds of nature out here can make it hard to tell sometimes what you're actually listening to. Maybe you think you hear a little boy crying, and in retrospect, it turns out to be a bird."

He was suggesting that she fabricate what is known as "exigent circumstances" to justify entering the house without a warrant. For a moment, she was tempted, but Langland wasn't that kind of cop. Besides, a move like that could destroy any chance they had of punishing the Carvers and Gunther. And if they didn't find Johnny inside, it could derail the entire investigation.

There had to be another way.

She texted Laurie Moran. It was time for Plan B.

Chapter 45

Laurie rose from her chair at the back corner of the tiny coffee shop. "I'm going to put in an order. Black coffee, Dad?"

He flashed her an *okay* sign.

"Anything else for you, Summer?"

She declined with a shake of her head. Laurie asked the barista for two large coffees, and then made her way to the ladies' room while he prepared them. Inside, she removed the cell phone that had buzzed inside her pocket while she was still at the table.

It was a new text message from Detective Langland. "No sign of Johnny from outside the house. The judge is on board with Plan B. No other choice at this point. We need that warrant."

When Laurie returned to the table with two coffee cups, she caught Leo's eye and shook her head. There was no good news from upstate. They had to push Summer further.

"Laurie, I have something to tell you—to tell you and Summer—that's going to be very difficult to hear," Leo said somberly. "I want both of you to understand: I have never *lied* to obtain a conviction. But sometimes police have to simplify the evidence. In court, it needs to seem black-and-white, cut-and-dry. Not gray and messy."

Laurie did her best to act shocked, even though they had rehearsed the entire story last night and this morning. The text message from Langland was confirmation that the judge had approved the plan. He would listen in on their conversation in real time and issue a search warrant as soon as he found probable cause.

There was still a risk that Gunther could use Leo's words here to attack his conviction, but at least they had created a record with a court to prove that Leo simply intended to deceive Summer Carver, and his reasons for doing so. Laurie had even gone so far as to notify Lou Finney's daughter in the event Gunther managed to leak the news of Leo's admission before it could be explained.

"When I went back to the station house that night to question Gunther alone, he never admitted to intentionally stabbing Lou Finney. He said what he maintains to this day—that another man intervened with a knife."

Summer's eyes were the size of saucers. She looked at once both horrified and ecstatic. "And you said something totally different. How is that *not* a lie?"

"I'm willing to explain, Summer, but if I'm being totally honest with you, I need you to be completely honest with me."

Her bottom lip quivered, afraid to answer, but she was clearly desperate to hear the rest of Leo's story.

They were so close. Leo nudged again. "You know where Johnny is, don't you?"

She nodded. The microphone beneath the table could not transmit the nod of a head.

"You're nodding," he said, not missing a beat. "But I need you to tell me that little boy's going to be okay."

"He's fine. He's been taken good care of."

"I need your word you'll drop him off somewhere safe—the nearest police station or fire station or hospital—once I give you what you need to help Darren with his case. Okay?"

"I will. I promise."

"All right then," Leo confirmed. "The way I saw it—and still see it, Summer—is that Darren Gunther was in fact responsible for

Lou Finney's death. He's the one who started the fight. If not for the fight, there wouldn't have been a brawl out on the street."

As Leo kept Summer at rapt attention, Laurie snuck a peek at the screen of her phone. A new message from Langland: *That's it! We got our warrant. We're going in NOW. Also got a warrant for Summer's arrest. Backup coming your way.*

Less than a minute later, two uniformed officers from the NYPD entered the coffee shop. Laurie knew their names were Carrie Brennan and Stan Wojcik and that they'd been waiting in the florist delivery van for further instructions from Detective Langland.

"You want to do the honors, Dad?" Leo was still an active member of the department since he'd joined the antiterrorism task force.

"Summer Carver, you're under arrest for the kidnapping of Jonathan Alexander Buckley."

Chapter 46

Chief Dawson flashed a thumbs-up to Detective Langland, signaling for her to take the lead. Once Summer Carver had said the magic words that she would free Johnny in exchange for Leo's supposed confession, Judge Marshall had found probable cause to issue the search warrant they'd been waiting for.

Langland rushed toward Toby Carver's porch, followed by Chief Dawson and a flank of five other uniformed officers. A second team approached the house from the rear.

Boom boom boom! Langland pounded her fist against the front door. "Police! We have a warrant! Open up!"

No response, as expected.

She stepped out of the way and held up her fingers. *One . . . two . . .*

In time with her count, Dawson and one of his sergeants swayed with a battering ram.

Three!

The wooden door broke away from its frame from the weight of their force.

Twelve law enforcement officers swept through the house, weapons drawn, wearing bulletproof vests. A sweep is more science than art, a systematic search to make certain that no one catches the police off guard. Inspect all corners. Cover every blind spot and move on.

"Clear!" Langland yelled as she swept through the kitchen.

"Clear!" a man's voice echoed from the den.

She heard the sounds of kicked doors and footsteps stomping through the house.

Finally, she reached the far end of what appeared to be the master bedroom on the second floor. A set of mirrored sliding glass doors was cracked open by three inches on one side. She approached the closet slowly, keeping her back against the bedroom wall to limit her exposure to a gunshot.

Chief Dawson appeared at the threshold of the bedroom. Catching his eye, she pointed to the closet doors. He extended his weapon, ready to cover her if she drew fire. When she reached the closet, she used her left foot to roll one door to the side and then quickly shifted her body backward to distance herself from whoever might be hiding inside.

But once the door was open, she saw nothing but hanging clothes and an overflowing laundry basket. She moved to the other side of the closet and pushed open the doors in the opposite direction.

"Clear!" she yelled, hearing the distress in her own voice.

She worked her way back to the front door, registering the deflated expressions on the faces of her fellow law enforcement officers.

To be absolutely certain, she walked the property again, inside and out. She inspected every square foot of the four-acre lot, and then walked through each room of Toby Carver's bungalow once more, opening each and every drawer for any clue that a child had been in the house.

Chief Dawson was waiting for her on the front porch, hands on his hips as he watched three departing patrol cars leave a trail of dust on the dirt road to the house.

"I sent the rest of my guys home," he explained. Dawson was probably in his mid-sixties. He had a kind and gentle face.

"Thank you again for everything. I really thought we were going to save Johnny today."

"I only worked one child abduction case in my career, back when I was still NYPD, but I know what you're going through. You wanted to make a different kind of phone call right now."

Once Langland was alone in her car, she fought back tears as she pulled out her cell phone. She pictured Marcy and Andrew Buckley, glued to the phone, waiting for an update. They'd recognize her number on the caller ID. They'd picture their son being rescued, carried to a waiting car where he'd be consoled and comforted.

And then Langland would have to break their hearts all over again: if Johnny Buckley had been in this house in the last week, he wasn't here now.

Chapter 47

Even before Leo Farley had taken his retirement, he was focused more on running the administrative parts of the NYPD than on individual criminal cases. It had been more than a decade since he had personally cuffed a suspect. His interrogation skills were similarly unused. But once he was "in the box," as they said, with Summer Carver, he felt those old muscles fall right into place. Maybe police work was like riding a bicycle.

Because Summer was so clearly obsessed with Darren Gunther, it had been decided that Leo would be the one to handle her interrogation, at least initially. She was more likely to make a misstep in the same room with the man she believed had framed her beloved.

To Leo's surprise, Summer immediately waived her right to a lawyer after receiving Miranda warnings at the coffee shop. Just as quickly, she insisted that she had not kidnapped Johnny. "I only said that to get you to admit what you did to Darren!"

Leo pushed back. "That doesn't make any sense, Summer. What kind of strategy is it to implicate yourself in a serious felony, just to help your boyfriend?"

"Check my phone. I recorded our entire conversation. So it worked, didn't it?"

"Of course it didn't *work*, Summer. You thought you were tricking me with a cell phone recording? We had a judge monitoring that entire conversation. We were the ones playing you, and we did it for a reason. You're the one who kept saying that Johnny was missing because of my bad karma. That justice would balance the scales. Why would you suggest such a thing if you don't actually have possession of this innocent boy?"

"I only pretended to have him. Toby came up with the idea after I talked to Laurie last night. She's the one who compared Darren being locked up with Johnny being kidnapped. I told Toby what she said, and I guess it planted the seed."

"So the two of you decided to interfere in the investigation of a missing child? To waste a full day when police could have been trying to find him?"

"It wasn't even one day," Summer protested. "We set up the meeting last night. I was going to post your confession on the internet as soon as I left that stupid coffee shop, and then tell you I had nothing to do with that boy's disappearance!"

If Summer was telling the truth, she and her brother had highjacked a kidnapping investigation to gain a momentary advantage in their bid to get Darren Gunther out of prison. The more logical explanation was that she was lying. Leo was about to press her again for more details about the abduction when his cell phone buzzed against the table.

It was from Detective Langland.

He left Summer alone in the locked interrogation room to answer the call. *This is it,* he thought. *She's going to tell me they found Johnny. Please.*

Instead, he heard the disappointment in her voice immediately. "The brother's house was a bust, Leo. We didn't find him."

His shoulders heaved forward as if he'd been punched in the stomach. "Were we too late? Did they move him?"

"I don't know. We searched every inch of the property. There's no sign of Johnny anywhere. No indication that he was ever here, in fact."

Despite his follow-up questions, there was nothing more to learn. When he hung up the phone, he forced himself to take five deep breaths. He had been so certain. This was supposed to be the day they brought Johnny home. Had it all been a waste of time?

He re-entered the interrogation room with a new objective in mind. They still had the toll records showing that Toby's car had been used to travel to Long Island and back on the day of the kidnapping. Leo decided that if Summer had an explanation for the travel, she might actually be telling the truth. If she didn't, they might still be on the right track.

"Summer, we can prove you were at the hotel when Johnny disappeared." The evidence didn't actually place her at the hotel, but he wasn't required to explain that to her.

To his surprise, she readily admitted that he was correct. "I went there to find Laurie."

"Why would you try to see my daughter on her vacation?"

"I'm a huge fan of her television show. I thought I could appeal to her sense of justice to help Darren. What better way to expose the truth than to win over the daughter of the investigating detective?"

"How did you know where to find her?"

"Alex Buckley's sister-in-law posted a picture on Facebook, saying the whole family was going to Long Island to celebrate his birthday. The post included a photograph of the hotel. I figured I could have lunch on the deck and find a way to introduce myself to Laurie. But right when I was walking into the hotel, there she was, walking out with Alex and another couple, getting into a black Mercedes with Alex behind the wheel. I rushed back to Toby's car and followed them. Once they got out at the golf course, I figured there was no way for me to talk to her there, so I headed back to the hotel to wait. But when they did return, it was clear something bad had happened. Everyone was running around the beach frantically, and then the police came, so I left."

"Johnny had been kidnapped. *That's* why they were frantic."

"Well, I didn't know that at the time. I just got scared and drove home. You have to believe me: as much as I love Darren and want to help him, I would *never*—never ever ever—take or hurt or even *scare* an innocent little child. Didn't you see how nervous I was when you pushed me to say I'd let him go? Just *pretending* like I had done that, I felt like I was going to get sick."

Leo searched Summer's wide eyes. She looked disgusted with herself.

"Johnny's only seven years old," he said. "He's a sweet boy. He loves to swim and play soccer and baseball. He has twin four-year-old sisters who look up to him, and a mother and father who love him. They really thought we were going to bring their son home today—because you let us believe that."

She hung her head in shame. "I'm so, so sorry."

In that moment, he could see that she was telling the truth, which meant he had been wrong. He had been so consumed by Darren Gunther's false accusations that he had opened himself up to this kind of manipulation. Summer wasn't the only person in this room to feel ashamed.

"You owe it to them, Summer, to come clean with anything you know that might possibly help us find Johnny."

"I told you, I don't know anything. I made the whole thing up."

"But you didn't make up being at the resort when Johnny disappeared."

"I don't know where he went. I think I'd notice if someone snatched a child away right in front of me!"

"A child doesn't have to be carried away to be abducted. The assailant pretends to have been sent by the parents to locate him. Or they claim to be a police officer or other authority figure. You may have seen something that didn't register at the time, but that could break this thing wide open. Put yourself back in your brother's car, sitting in that parking lot. What do you see?"

She closed her eyes and took a deep breath, but shook her head a few seconds later. "It's all a blur. A few cars came and went, but the only one I cared about was Alex's black Mercedes, so I didn't pay any attention."

"Any little detail at all? Nothing is too small. Think, Summer."

She shrugged. "I guess there was the ice cream truck," she said.

"What about it?"

"Nothing. Just that I noticed it. You know how you turn off of 27 and drive down into the parking lot for the resort?"

He nodded, remembering the layout.

"Okay, so most of the cars would either park in the lot or keep going down to the turnabout at the hotel entrance—where the valets check you in. But if you don't turn toward the valet stand, you can keep driving on a separate little road behind the hotel. I saw an ice cream truck go down there."

Leo knew that Detective Langland had interviewed everyone who worked at the ice cream shack, including the ice cream truck driver, who had come back to the shop to refill supplies before hitting the road again.

Summer squinted as if recalling something new.

"What is it, Summer?"

"The ice cream truck. It came in, but then another car went in that same direction, too. But then it returned a couple minutes later. I figured it was a hotel guest who had gone down that service road by accident and then turned around. But then instead of turning down toward the hotel or going to the parking lot, it went back out on 27 again."

Johnny was last seen looking for shells near the ice cream shack. Summer Carver may have seen the car driven by his abductor.

"What kind of car was it?"

She shook her head. "I have no idea. It was white, maybe? Light-colored. Not an SUV or a van or anything."

"A sedan?"

"Yes. Four doors, I think? I'm not sure, though. Oh, but I do re-member one thing! The license plate—it was from Washington. Not the state. Washington, D.C. I noticed because it said something about not paying taxes.

End Taxation Without Representation. It was the motto on li-cense plates from the nation's capital, a reference to the fact that D.C. residents paid federal taxes but had no voting representation in Congress.

Leo left the interrogation room and found Laurie waiting on a bench outside the police station.

"Summer was telling the truth. Gunther had nothing to do with Johnny's disappearance." He hung his head in despair, looking down at the sidewalk. "I wasted our entire week focused on Darren Gunther."

She immediately hugged him and then listened attentively as he brought her up to speed. "It's not your fault, Dad. Gunther and Summer intentionally misled us."

"This whole time, I was wrong, Laurie. But you were right. This was never a case of mistaken identity. Whoever took Johnny wanted him specifically. They came to New York from Washington, D.C. We need to call Marcy and Andrew."

Chapter 48

Marcy Buckley pulled a casserole dish filled with baked macaroni and cheese from the oven. The heat that rose to her face helped hide the tears she had been fighting to control since she received the devastating phone call from Detective Langland: After all that work for a search warrant, the police didn't find Johnny.

Chloe and Emily were blissfully enjoying their dinners when the phone on the kitchen counter rang again. Marcy recognized Laurie's number. She carried the handset into the den, out of earshot of the twins.

Marcy knew there was urgent news when Laurie asked her to bring Andrew into the room on speakerphone. Once Andrew was nestled next to Marcy on the sofa, Laurie began her report. "Summer Carver admitted she was at our hotel the day Johnny vanished. She saw a light-colored sedan drive away from the ice cream shack. The plate was from Washington, D.C."

It only took Marcy a few seconds to process the information. "From the very beginning, you said most crimes aren't random."

"It's no guarantee that the car Summer saw was the kidnapper's," Laurie said, "but the road to the ice cream shack is separate from the main hotel. Plus, you don't see many cars with D.C. plates on Long Island. I don't think it's a coincidence."

Marcy could see from Andrew's face that she and Laurie weren't the only ones who thought they had found a new lead.

"What exactly does this mean?" Andrew asked. "We already racked our brains trying to figure out who might want to take Johnny. You think someone from D.C. followed us to the Hamptons?"

Marcy felt her vision begin to blur. D.C. The Hamptons. The road to the ice cream shack. She imagined hands grabbing Johnny as he bent over to pick up a seashell from the sand. Her son, trembling with fear, in the backseat. No, more likely, the trunk. All alone in the dark, terrified. When she tried to picture the car pulling out of the hotel parking lot, she had a sudden image of a gray sedan—the same one that had been parked at the curb in front of their house only two days earlier.

"Sandra Carpenter came to see us on Monday."

Andrew literally gasped as he processed the possibility.

"I don't know who that is," Laurie said at the other end of the line.

"She's the woman Father Horrigan called about the adoption," Marcy explained. "She's Johnny's biological grandmother."

"And she went to your house?"

"Unannounced," Marcy said. "It was all very strange. She said she couldn't stop worrying about Johnny—that his disappearance had triggered all these feelings she had about her daughter. She wanted to know how she could help us. At the time, I assumed her intentions were good, but now I'm wondering whether she was trying to throw us off track."

"Do you remember her car?" Andrew asked. "I didn't pay it any mind."

"I remember it was a gray sedan," Marcy said. "A Buick. I don't know the different models, but it was a bigger one."

"What shade of gray?" Laurie asked. "Summer said the car was either white or very light-colored."

Marcy searched her visual cortex, trying to pull up the image. "It was a silvery gray, close to white."

Next to her, Andrew had a suggestion. "Leo could pull up the car registration, right, Laurie? It would list the color? Maybe Summer will recognize it if she sees a picture."

"I'll give him a call now."

"Laurie—" Marcy still felt they were all missing the larger point. "We don't actually know what happened to her daughter. When I called Father Horrigan to check on Johnny's birth mother, he had no idea until he called her mother. So everything we thought we knew about that family came directly from Sandra. The drug addiction. The move to Philadelphia. It could all be lies."

Andrew placed a hand over his mouth. "We never even confirmed that Michelle Carpenter is dead."

Marcy suddenly felt light-headed. From the moment when Sister Margaret first placed Johnny in her arms, Marcy had shared an immediate connection to her "miracle baby." But there's no such thing as a miracle.

Her hands shook as she reached for Andrew. "They took him, didn't they? They took our Johnny."

Chapter 49

The open, empty pizza box stared up at Laurie from the living room coffee table, the last remnants of mozzarella stuck on the paper lining. She felt her father watching her as he reclined in his favorite chair.

"It's fine," he said.

"What's fine?"

"The pizza."

"Pizza's better than fine," she said. "Pizza's basically the perfect food."

"Exactly. And did you see how happy Timmy was? It was like you took him to Disney World or something. So stop feeling guilty."

Just as her parents had raised her, Laurie was committed to having meals with Timmy at the dining room table. Granted, Laurie was rarely able to cook the kinds of meals her mother had prepared, but even when it was just the two of them and a bag of carryout, she thought of dinner as the time when she and Timmy put their screens away, turned off all the outside noise, and focused on each other.

But tonight, dinner had been a box of pizza eaten in front of the TV. And because the delivery guy had brought paper plates with the order, they had gone ahead and used them.

The reality was that Laurie was exhausted, physically and emotionally. They all were. For a week, they had been giving themselves and one another pep talks while they continued to put one foot in front of the other, doing all that they could to bring Johnny home.

And today, all those efforts had failed.

While writing off Johnny's adoption as a dead end from the start, they realized now they actually knew nothing about Johnny's biological mother or the grandmother who had shown up uninvited to Marcy and Andrew's home. Leo had put a call in to a friend with the Philadelphia Police Department to inquire about Michelle Carpenter's supposed drug overdose, but he was still waiting for details. Laurie wanted a time machine to go back and start all over again. Or better yet, to stay at the beach with the kids so none of this would have ever happened.

Instead of risking a display of her emotional exhaustion at the dinner table, she had given Timmy his first choice of takeout, along with a proposal that they jump back into their *Bosch* binge. She knew he was still having nightmares, but he was also doing his best to put on a brave face. Now that Timmy had gone to his room to play a video game, she and Leo were free to speak openly again.

"It was sort of nice to just sit and stare at the TV for two hours, huh?"

Her father chuckled. "We should do it more often."

She held up a quick finger, pretending to scold him. "We have rules in this house, mister, and they started with you."

"No, they started with your mother. And trust me, even *she* would have given us dispensation after this miserable day."

Laurie carried the pizza box and paper plates to the kitchen, grateful for the easy cleanup, and returned to the living room. "Hey, at least there was a silver lining to today. We exposed Summer Carver and her brother as liars."

The D.A.'s Office had agreed to charge both of the Carver siblings with felonies. The argument was that even though they did not actually commit kidnapping, they used a threat against Johnny's freedom and safety to coerce Leo into giving them a false admission—the equivalent of blackmail.

Leo didn't seem ready to celebrate. "But we still don't have anything new on Darren Gunther." According to Summer, pretending they had taken Johnny was her brother's idea, and Toby invoked his right to counsel as soon as he was arrested. If Gunther was involved in the plan, they had no way of proving it.

"But their arrests were a top story on the local news tonight," she said, "including their connection to Gunther. Trust me, Dad, I know how media works. The average person hearing the news will think Gunther's a killer who tried to get these two bozos to tamper with the system."

"But the judge hearing Gunther's case isn't your average person hearing the news."

Laurie could tell that she wasn't going to get her father to see the silver lining. Eighteen years ago, he had helped convince a jury that Darren Gunther had murdered Lou Finney. He was determined to prove it all over again.

She was about to offer him a cup of coffee when his cell phone rang on the end table beside him.

"This is Farley."

"*Philadelphia PD*," he whispered.

She was listening to her father's lengthy series of *uh-huhs*, eagerly awaiting any actual information, when her own phone rang. She didn't recognize the number, so she hit the decline button. A minute later, it rang again. This time, she answered, taking the phone to the kitchen so as not to interfere with Leo's call.

"Laurie, oh good, you're there. It's Samantha Finney, Lou Finney's daughter."

"Hi, Samantha. I hope you got my message earlier." Laurie had left a detailed voicemail for Samantha about the Carvers' arrests.

Even though it was only indirectly related to her father's murder, she didn't want Samantha to learn about the development from the news.

"I did, but here's the thing. I saw their pictures on the TV, and I know that guy."

"Which guy?"

"The brother. I think his name was Toby Carver? I know him, Laurie. And so did Clarissa."

Ten minutes later, Laurie hung up the phone and rushed to the living room to find her father.

Before she could get a word out, he told her that he had just spoken to his contact at the Philadelphia Police Department. "Sandra Carpenter was telling the truth. Her daughter Michelle did in fact die of an overdose at her home six months ago. Her neighbor was the one who found the body and called it in."

"So what does that really tell us?" Laurie asked. "That might give Sandra all the more motive to try to take Johnny. She's traumatized by the loss of her daughter, and she told Marcy that she thought of Johnny as the *last living piece of her little girl*. Maybe she wanted another shot at raising him herself."

"There was one thing in the police report for Michelle's overdose that was interesting," Leo said. "When the police asked Michelle's neighbor about the next of kin, she said they shouldn't even bother calling Sandra because if anyone was to blame for Michelle's drug addiction, it was her mother."

"Sounds like there might be more to the story than Sandra's letting on," Laurie said.

Leo handed her a yellow Post-it with a name and number on it. *Lindsay Hart*. "That's the neighbor. Depending on her own connection to drugs, she might be more comfortable talking to you than some crusty old cop."

"Leo Farley? Crusty? I think all those widows who line up to see their favorite silver fox after Mass on Sunday would take issue with that description. But, yes, it makes sense for me to call Lindsay."

"Who were you talking to earlier, by the way? From what I overheard, it sounded important."

"Samantha Finney. She recognized Toby Carver's picture on the news. Did you know that Samantha remained friends with Clarissa DeSanto after Finn's murder?"

Leo nodded. "They were extremely close. At the time of the case, I remember thinking they seemed like a couple of girls who could be part of your friend group. I still can't believe Clarissa died in a car accident."

"Well, that's the thing, Dad. The last time Samantha saw Clarissa was the end of March. They were at an eighties-night dance party organized as a fundraiser for one of the big animal shelters. Samantha's married, but Clarissa tagged along solo. Some guy asked her to dance and they were having a nice enough time—casual and friendly. Toward the end of the night, though, the guy seemed to assume that Clarissa was going to leave with him. *Leave*, as in—" Laurie rotated her hand in lieu of words to complete the sentence.

"I may be your father, but I know what *leave* from a party means."

"Samantha says the guy was really persistent, enough so that they thought about calling over Security. But Samantha's husband exchanged words with him and made it clear that Clarissa wasn't going to wander home with a random stranger. Well, Samantha saw Toby Carver's picture tonight on the news, and she's sure he's the guy who tried getting Clarissa to leave with him. Her husband is certain it's the same man, too. Three days after the eighties party, Clarissa somehow lost control of her car on the Cross County Parkway."

Leo placed his head in his hands. "I said this entire time that Darren Gunther wouldn't fight fair. That's why I immediately thought of him when Johnny went missing."

"But if Toby Carver was in the picture months ago?" Laurie asked. "Dad, what if he killed Clarissa DeSanto because of something she knew?"

That night, after hanging up with Alex, Laurie was docking her phone into its charger when it rang again. She recognized the Philadelphia area code she had used to call Michelle Carpenter's former neighbor earlier that evening.

When she answered, the din of loud voices and music in the background made it difficult to hear.

"Ms. Moran, this is Lindsay Hart, returning your call. I'm sorry to call so late, and it's really loud here, but I want to talk to you about Michelle. Can we meet in person tomorrow?"

"Sure, I can take a train in the morning—"

"No, I'm actually in New York right now."

They agreed to meet at Laurie's office at 9 A.M.

"See you then," Lindsay said. "I don't know how you got interested in Michelle's case, but I never believed that her death was an overdose. She was murdered. I'm certain of it."

Chapter 50

The following morning, Johnny had helped clear the breakfast dishes again and was back to work on his *Historic Buildings of America* coloring book.

"Keep on with your coloring," the man said, inspecting his handiwork. "You show great promise as an artist, Danny."

"What building is this one?" Johnny asked, even though he knew it was the Empire State Building. Uncle Alex had taken him to the top of it when he was in kindergarten. They had taken a picture for Johnny to share with the rest of his class.

Johnny pretended to be wowed as the man explained that the building was considered Art Greco, or something like that, designed by people Johnny had never heard of. Meanwhile, what Johnny really wanted to do was point out that he was only using his blue, green, tan, and gray colored pencils. This was the worst coloring book in the world.

"You sure do know a lot," Johnny gushed. *A play. I am an actor in a play.*

The man appeared to space out for a few seconds before speaking. "I used to be an architect, in fact. That table you're using?"

Johnny thanked him once again for it. "It sure is cool. I like this ledge at the bottom so nothing falls off and you can tilt the book on it."

"Exactly," the man said, apparently pleased by the observation. "That was my drafting table for years. I never made something as grand as the Empire State Building, mind you, but I created some spectacular homes—and a fairly large shopping mall and one office tower of some significance. If I'd kept working, I might have been the next I. M. Pei."

Johnny smiled.

"That's okay. Of course you don't know who that is. He designed the glass pyramid at the entrance of the Louvre. Oh—and part of the National Gallery of Art."

"That one I've been to!" Johnny announced gleefully. Mommy had taken him there last year while Daddy took the twins to the doctor when they both ran temperatures. He had complained about being bored. *I'm sorry, Mama. I wasn't being a good boy that day. I'll never act like that again.* Seeing that the man was pleased with his response, Johnny decided to ask a question. "So you don't make buildings anymore?"

"No. A lot has changed in my life since then." The man gazed into the distance again, and Johnny could tell he was sad.

Johnny flipped to the next page of his coloring book, even though he still needed to pencil in the blue sky over Manhattan. "Which building is this one?"

As the man talked about an architect named Frank Lloyd Wright, Johnny nodded along with interest. *Trust is a two-way street, mister?* Johnny's plan was to earn enough trust to give him a chance to leave this creepy house.

"Can I ask you one more question, sir?"

"Certainly."

"You call me Danny, but what should I call you? Other than sir, I mean."

"What would you like to call me?"

Johnny shrugged. "Your name, I guess."

The man's smile sent a chill up Johnny's spine. "Well, let's see: What did you call the man who gave you meals and put a roof over your head at the place where you used to live?"

Johnny felt like he'd been given a riddle without an answer. Looking down at his coloring book, he muttered. "I called him Daddy."

"Fine then. Why don't we try that then?"

Johnny pressed his eyes shut to stop tears from coming out. The man's hand on his shoulder was surprisingly gentle.

"They didn't tell you, did they?" he asked.

Johnny could not see how wide and innocent his own eyes were when he looked up at the man.

"Andrew and Marcy Buckley aren't your parents. Not really. You were adopted." The man removed a folded sheet of paper from the back of his pocket and handed it to Johnny.

The name of the website was New York Crime Beat. The man had highlighted one paragraph in yellow marker. Johnny wasn't the fastest reader in his class, but he managed to read all the words, silently to himself, without moving his lips, the way they practiced in school.

> According to a law enforcement source, the missing boy was adopted by the Buckleys as a newborn. When asked whether his disappearance might be connected to the adoption, the source stated that police had quickly eliminated that theory and were working on the assumption of an abduction by a stranger.

"Do you know what that word means, Danny? Adopted?"

Johnny nodded silently. Greta Connors from school was adopted and knew all about the town in Florida where she was born.

"Okay, then," the man said. "You got used to living with the Buckleys once before, and now it seems you're getting used to living here. It's all about fresh starts, right?"

He struggled to find words, but only came up with "yes."

"Yes, what?"

"Yes, I'm getting used to living here. Sir."

The man glared at him momentarily, but then his face softened. "Not to worry. We'll get there eventually."

Johnny managed not to cry until he was alone in his room, locked inside once again.

Thursday, July 23

Day Nine

Chapter 51

The next morning, Leo poured himself a cup of coffee in Laurie's kitchen as she scrambled to get out the door. She wanted plenty of time to get settled in at her office before Lindsay Hart arrived.

"I understand if you need to run, but I was thinking more about Samantha Finney recognizing Toby Carver on TV." According to Lou Finney's daughter, Summer Carver's half brother had been aggressively pursuing Clarissa DeSanto at a party shortly before Clarissa's fatal car crash. "He just happens to hit on a witness from the night of Lou Finney's murder while he's in the middle of trying to help Finney's killer get out of prison? That's too much of a coincidence."

"A hundred percent. We're going to track it down for our show on Darren Gunther, Dad, I promise. Right now, we just need to focus on Johnny, which means meeting with Michelle Carpenter's neighbor. I'm hoping she can tell us more about Michelle's mom."

"Understood. But just so you know, I was up all night again, so I circled back to Toby Carver's E-ZPass records."

Toby's toll charges had been their first indication that Summer had driven to Long Island on the day of Johnny's disappearance. Laurie recalled that his toll usage was relatively sparse. She could tell from the gleam in her father's eye that he had found something of interest.

"I looked for eighties dance party fundraisers for New York City animal shelters and found the listing right away," Leo said.

"Look at you, turning into a cybersleuth," Laurie teased. Her father tended to shut down in the face of technology beyond basic emails.

"Credit your son. He's a very patient teacher. Anyway, the event in question was the last Friday in March. Sure enough, Toby Carver's E-ZPass shows a round-trip in and out of Manhattan that night, the first toll activity in weeks. But here's the kicker: he then went in and out of Manhattan every single day after that, ending three nights later. Then no toll charges until Summer went looking for you on Long Island."

Laurie gasped when she saw the connection. "Clarissa's car crash." Samantha Finney had told Laurie that Clarissa died three nights after the eighties party.

Leo pointed a finger in her direction. "Bingo!"

If they were right, Toby Carver had been stalking Clarissa DeSanto, looking for his chance to kill her. It was dark out with heavy rain on an isolated road when Clarissa's car crashed. Toby could have caused the crash by running her off the road.

"What about the license plate readers?" Laurie said. All of the city's bridges and tunnels were equipped with automated cameras that captured dozens of license plates per minute, adding them to a searchable database. "Can you check those?"

"Already on it," Leo confirmed. "An analyst is searching for both Clarissa's plates and Toby's. Hopefully we'll find a connection."

"But what's the motive for killing Clarissa?" Laurie asked. "She told you what she knew about that night eighteen years ago."

"I've got a theory I'm working on. I just need to nail a few things down to prove it. Got a bunch of documents I asked for yesterday to sift through." She could tell that her father was on the hunt and would follow the trail wherever it led. "Now, I believe you have an important meeting at your office."

Laurie hadn't even noticed that he had gathered together her cell phone, briefcase, and house keys while they were talking. "Amazing. Oh, and would you mind—"

"Taking a video of Timmy when he's batting today. I've got it." Leo was going to drop Timmy off at Chelsea Piers for his half-day golf camp, then practice in the batting cages with him before heading home.

She had no idea how she and her son would have gotten through the last seven years without her father.

Chapter 52

Lindsay Hart arrived exactly two minutes before her scheduled appointment. She wore an impeccably tailored white dress with sleek, nude pumps. Her vibrant red hair bounced in loose waves as she walked into Laurie's office. She had the kind of look that made Laurie wonder if perhaps she herself should put in a bit more effort in the glamour department.

"Lindsay Hart," her guest announced with a confident handshake. "Thank you so much for meeting me, Ms. Moran."

Laurie insisted on first names as she escorted Lindsay to the sofa, and then positioned herself in the adjacent gray swivel chair.

"Your office is beautiful. If I'd known that a career in media might lead to a sleek suite sitting above the Rock Center ice skating rink, I might have skipped law school altogether."

"So you're a lawyer?" After everything she had heard about Michelle Carpenter from her mother, this was not what she had been expecting of Michelle's friend and neighbor.

"Oh, I'm sorry. I assumed you knew. I know your fiancé, Alex! Oh, and congratulations, by the way. Your engagement was quite the buzz on the legal gossip circuit when it was announced. We all thought he'd remain a bachelor for life. I was so sorry to hear about his nephew. That poor little boy. I hope they bring him home safely."

Laurie thanked her for her thoughts. She'd had no reason to

mention Lindsay's name when she told Alex about her meeting this morning. The sound of her fiancé's name from this alluring lawyer's lips immediately evoked memories of Alex's former reputation as a man about town, spotted on Page Six and the society pages at various high-profile functions, in the company of similarly well-known women. She reminded herself, though, that she was the one he had fallen in love with. He had chased her, not the other way around.

"How do you and Alex know each other?"

"I'm a white-collar defense lawyer in Philadelphia, but my firm has an office here. We've had a couple of cases that overlapped."

"And you were Michelle Carpenter's neighbor?" Laurie asked. "I apologize, but I got the impression from her mother that Michelle was living in . . . difficult circumstances."

Lindsay barely disguised a roll of her perfectly mascaraed eyes. "Of course you did. Michelle's mother didn't even *know* her own daughter anymore. She probably pictured a rat-infested tenement. Michelle wasn't rich by any means, but she rented a very well-appointed garage apartment behind the house next to mine. The homeowners are an older couple, snowbirds who spend most of the year in Florida. Michelle and I became fast friends when she moved in. She was one of the best-hearted people I ever met, but she told me her mother was convinced she was a failure and a loser."

"And why was that?"

She shrugged. "Because Michelle didn't live up to the big dreams she had as a younger woman. Life threw her a curveball with an unplanned pregnancy, and she made the painful decision to place that baby with a loving family. She said it was the hardest thing she ever did, but also the act that made her most proud. But to her mother, it was like Michelle was marked by a scarlet A for the rest of time."

"But did Michelle ever suggest her mother could be violent . . . or erratic? Or if she ever indicated any resentment over her grandson's adoption?" It was becoming clear that Sandra hadn't been the most supportive mother, but Laurie was trying to figure out if the woman was capable of kidnapping Johnny.

Lindsay shook her head. "As judgmental as her mother was, I got the impression the adoption was the one decision of Michelle's that Sandra actually supported."

"My understanding is that Sandra believed that drugs killed Michelle long before she actually died."

Lindsay's eyes sparked with anger. "That's so unfair. Michelle had been clean for nearly two years. That was the whole reason she moved to Philly. She wanted to get away from old influences and bad habits. Sandra refused to believe she'd turned her life around. Too much disappointment after so many failed attempts in the past, I suppose. So, of course, when the police told her that Michelle died of an overdose, she immediately believed them. The case was open and shut without a second glance."

"But not for you. You think she was murdered."

"The night I found her, we were supposed to do takeout and TV at my house. We'd get together every couple of weeks to keep up with shows we both liked, but mostly to gab. I texted a couple of times when she was unusually late. I could see her car parked in the driveway, so I finally went over to see what was going on. I knocked at first, but then opened the door to check on her."

"It was unlocked?"

Lindsay nodded. "That was her usual, though, at least at that hour. We live—*lived*, I suppose—in a very safe neighborhood. I knew immediately something was wrong. Her apartment was usually so tidy, but not that day. The place was a wreck."

"Like someone had ransacked it?"

She shook her head. "No, more just . . . really messy. There was an open bottle of vodka on the nightstand with a glass tipped over. A bag of chips was left out on the coffee table. Dirty dishes scattered around. Little odds and ends she would normally have tucked away were sprawled all over the place. It just wasn't like her at all. I found her in the bedroom. The needle was still next to her on the bed, a thick rubber band around her arm."

Laurie could tell that Lindsay was still haunted by the discovery. "When was the last time you had seen her?"

"Only three days earlier. I had run next door to borrow some red pepper. And I'm telling you, she was clean and healthy, and her apartment was spick-and-span, just like normal. I told the police that I thought someone had staged the scene to make her seem like a drug addict or something, but they didn't want to listen. It was easier to write her off as yet another junkie."

"According to Sandra, Michelle struggled for years after her pregnancy. Isn't it possible she had another relapse and hid the warning signs from you?" Laurie knew that the chances of an overdose were often highest when addicts relapsed after a period of abstinence, because of a decrease in their tolerance for the drug.

"I don't buy it, not for a second. Michelle was on such a good track. She was actually starting to make a decent living selling her jewelry online. She was trying to sell her designs to one of the big department stores. One of my law partners helped her draw up business plans."

"Sandra made the jewelry sound like a pipe dream."

"Of course she did. Michelle had a real talent. She made this bracelet, in fact." Lindsay held up her right wrist to display a cuff bracelet made of hammered metal. "She was totally committed to her new life. She practiced yoga almost every day, kept a healthy diet, the works. She was trying to make amends, going so far as to track down people from her past to apologize for any grief she caused them. At one point, she was even thinking about apologizing to that jerk who got her pregnant. I told her she didn't owe him a single thing, but, like I said, she was hell-bent on atoning for every possible sin."

"Wait a second. Sandra said—"

"Ugh. Enough with *Sandra said*!" Lindsay recomposed herself after a flash of impatience. "Sorry, she's not exactly a reliable narrator when it comes to Michelle."

"Okay, but apparently Michelle told her that she didn't even know the identity of the baby's biological father. It was a one-night stand."

Lindsay scoffed. "Michelle? A one-night stand—with a stranger? Um . . . no. That would never happen."

"Then why would she tell her mother that?"

"Because the guy turned out to be married with a kid of his own. When Michelle realized they weren't going to be raising the baby together, she decided to go through with an adoption. To avoid any complications, she said she didn't know who the father was."

"She couldn't tell her own mother the truth?"

Lindsay shrugged. "Michelle was worried that her mom would cause a major scene with the married man who sullied her daughter. All Michelle wanted was to do the right thing and move on. She managed to avoid the public drama she feared, but didn't realize her mom would put all the blame on her instead. To be clear, Michelle had no idea the guy was married. They met at yoga, where he'd look for any opportunity to strike up a conversation with her. She was reluctant to date him at first. I think he was a little older? Maybe he was thirty, and she was twenty-two? When he finally convinced her to go out for one dinner, it became a whirlwind romance. She said he was smart and sophisticated and had a good sense of humor. Even all these years later, I could see her eyes light up when she recounted their time together. They were only together one summer, but they were already talking about getting married and having children once Michelle went back to school and graduated from college. The pregnancy was unplanned, but initially she was excited about it. Thrilled, in fact."

"Was he?"

"She never even told him. She went to his office to surprise him with the good news, and there he was, walking out with a family of his own. He was wearing a wedding band she'd never seen before. She watched him strap their kid into her safety seat and kiss his wife before she took the wheel. When the wife left, Michelle did, too. She simply drove away."

"And then what?"

"Nothing. She stopped all contact with him. Found a different yoga studio. She saw no reason to blow up another woman's family, so she removed herself from the picture. It was simply over. So you can understand why I told Michelle she didn't owe him an apology. She felt so much guilt for never telling him about the baby, but he was the one who lied about being married. I was probably a little too vocal with my opinion, because she changed the subject and never raised it again."

"Do you know whether she ever contacted the guy?"

"I have no idea. Oh my goodness, do you think he might be the one who killed her? Why would he do that?"

"Alex's nephew, Johnny . . . the one who is missing? He's Michelle's baby." Lindsay's eyes widened as she realized the implications. "Did Michelle ever tell you the father's name?"

Her brow furrowed, Lindsay shook her head. "No, but the weird thing is that she actually recognized his wife when he was kissing her in the parking lot. She was in charge of the marketing campaign for the restaurant Michelle was managing in Rehoboth Beach and had become good friends with the owners. In hindsight, Michelle realized it should have been a red flag that her boyfriend never dropped in on her at work. Once she saw him with his wife, she understood why."

Laurie was deep in thought, wishing they had looked further into Michelle's death when Johnny first disappeared. Sandra would surely remember the name of Michelle's former employer. Hopefully, the restaurant owners could link them to their marketing consultant. From there, they could locate Johnny's biological father, and hopefully find Johnny.

"Oh wait!" Lindsay exclaimed. "She also told me that he was an architect."

Laurie thanked her for her time and walked her to the elevator.

As soon as Laurie was alone again in her office, she called Marcy and Andrew. Andrew answered and quickly brought in Marcy on the speakerphone.

"Do you have Sandra's contact information?" Laurie asked.

"She left us a phone number and email," Andrew said.

"Do you think she's the one who took Johnny?" Marcy asked. "I assume the police can pull up her address. I'll go there myself right now if I have to. Beg her—mother to mother."

Laurie laid out what she had learned from Lindsay Hart. Even over the phone, she could tell it was a lot for Marcy and Andrew to digest. From the very beginning, Michelle had known the identity of Johnny's biological father but never told him about the child they had conceived. Now it looked like a belated change of heart may have led to both her murder and Johnny's abduction.

Marcy's voice cracked on the other end of the line. "My god. That poor woman. It was already so heartbreaking to learn she'd fallen on hard times and a drug overdose, but murder? Because she told that man about Johnny's birth? But bless that neighbor for getting at the truth. I think this is finally the breakthrough we've been praying for. I feel it in my bones."

"Me too," Andrew said. "It all clicks. We'll call Sandra right now, Laurie, and get the name of that restaurant."

Chapter 53

Nearly three thousand miles from the nation's capital, in Portland, Oregon, a woman who now went by the name of Alicia Nelson wiggled into a pair of body-hugging Spanx as she called out to her nine-year-old daughter in the next room. "Bella, I hope you're brushing your teeth and getting dressed. I can't be late for this presentation today."

She managed to tug the zipper at the back of her dress to the very top on her own, and then inspected herself in the mirror. *Ah, the magic of shapewear.* She considered this peacock-colored sheath dress her lucky charm when it came to landing new clients. Two weeks ago, she could have slipped it on effortlessly, but that getaway to San Francisco with Ben the previous weekend had been a nonstop culinary adventure. A few pounds were a small price to pay for the first trip she had taken with a man since her divorce from Daniel.

She noticed that she was smiling involuntarily as she thought about Ben. Daniel was her college sweetheart, the love of her life, the father of her sweet, beautiful daughter. They were supposed to have spent their entire lives together.

She still woke up in the middle of the night, anxious from the guilt about leaving him. She told herself again and again that he'd given her no choice. She had to leave, not only for her safety, but for Bella's. At the same time, though, she had come to accept that loneliness would be her punishment for the divorce. If she didn't spend the rest of her days with Daniel, she would have to spend them without romantic love.

But then she met Ben. It was serious now. He knew Bella and adored her. Of course he adored her. Who didn't? And last weekend, in San Francisco, she finally told him the truth about her past. The irony? Ben's last name was Robinson, just like hers used to be when she was Roseanne Robinson, or Ro-Ro as her friends all called her. Oh, how she still missed that nickname, but she'd left it in the past, along with Daniel.

She found Bella slapping butter onto a hot Pop-Tart on the kitchen counter.

"Can you at least use a plate or a paper towel or something?"

She tapped her face with an index finger, and Bella planted a good morning kiss on her cheek.

As her daughter perched on her tiptoes to reach for a plate, she said, "Mom, shouldn't you care more about me eating junk food and not a few crumbs?"

Bella was nine, going on thirty. In some ways, it felt like yesterday that she was riding around on her *Frozen*-themed toy Jeep. In others, it was a lifetime ago.

"If buttered toaster pastries are my daughter's only vice, I'd say I'm doing pretty fine in the mothering department."

"Better than fine. The very best. You look nice, by the way. I know that's your favorite dress. Oh, that's right! You have the winery meeting today! You're going to wow them."

Asked to pitch marketing ideas to a small but growing winery, her hope was to convince the owners to launch a high-end weeklong luxury winefest to draw oenophiles from all over the country.

"Thanks, sweetie. My lucky dress and I can't wow them if we're late, though." She needed to drop Bella off at her science camp before making the drive down to Willamette Valley.

"I'll grab my backpack, then I'm ready."

She was wiping a few pre-plate pastry crumbs from the counter when the phone rang. Her heart leapt at the sight of the 302 area code. Rehoboth Beach, Delaware. Her former life. Her nerves settled when she realized she recognized the rest of the number.

"Hello?"

"It's April. Sorry to call so early."

April Meyer, the owner of the Sand Bucket and her favorite former client. What began as a marketing job for a new restaurant in a vacation town had led to a close friendship. The Meyers were one of only three pairs of friends who knew how to reach the woman who used to be Roseanne Robinson.

"I work full-time and have a nine-year-old who acts like a CEO. It's never too early. Nighttime? Now, that's another issue. I'm comatose by nine-thirty."

"Someone called me about you," April said.

This was the message she had been dreading since "Alicia Nelson" moved all the way across the country to the Pacific Northwest. Daniel had found her. He was going to ruin her life again. She braced herself for the news as April continued.

"Her name's Marcy Buckley. She's lives in Washington, D.C."

"I don't know who that is, but, April, you know how careful I've been about protecting my identity here. You're probably the most honest person on the planet, but can you *please* tell a little white lie and say you don't know where I am? For all I know, she's working for Daniel to find me—"

"She's not. Her son is missing. But it *is* related to Daniel. Honey, you might want to sit down."

Chapter 54

Leo was struck by the overpowering smell of disinfectant as he entered the Bleecker Street Boxing Gym.

A man laced up his boxing shoes from a bench inside the door. Noticing Leo's wrinkled nose, he said, "Trust me, bud, it's better than the alternative. You'll get used to it. Haven't seen you here before. Are you looking for a sparring partner? My dad still likes to get in the ring, even though he's turning seventy next month. You might be a good match for him."

"You want me to fight a septuagenarian? Friend, I'm only forty-seven years old."

The man immediately began to apologize, stumbling to explain that he could never guess a person's age accurately, until he noticed the broad smile break out across Leo's face.

"You got me, man. Good one."

"I'm not actually here to box. I'm looking for a guy named Mason Rollins."

Leo had gone first to the NYU campus, where Rollins worked in the janitorial department. A co-worker said that Rollins was a regular at this boxing gym and could probably be found here before his shift.

The man rose from the bench and did a quick visual scan. Two fighters practiced in the ring at the center of the space while a few men looked on, but most of the gym's customers were working out with weights or punching bags. "There's Mason. Past the ring, along that brick wall. You see that row of speed bags? The guy in the back corner. Bright blue trunks."

Leo thanked the man for his help and headed toward Rollins. Rollins's hands flew in high and fast circles as he bounced the speed bag. Right, right, left, left. Leo was only ten feet away and Rollins still hadn't shifted his gaze from the bag. But as Leo was about to speak, Rollins came to a sudden halt, grabbing the bag with both hands to stop it.

"Pleased to meet you, Leo Farley." Rollins's dark hair was shaved nearly to his scalp, and he sported a short goatee that had not appeared in any of his booking photos. He was trim, but his loose-fitting Brooklyn Nets tank top exposed arms that reflected hours at the gym.

"You recognize me," Leo said.

"When some convict accuses you of killing a man you never heard of, you tend to pay attention to the details. You're the one who put Darren Gunther behind bars. If I had to guess, you might be the one person who's certain I'm innocent."

"Innocent on that particular day, at least."

"Touché, Deputy Commissioner. I made some mistakes as a younger man, but I did not stab Lou Finney."

"No, but Darren Gunther's not just 'some convict,' is he? You were at Finn's Bar that night, before the fight broke out. You were celebrating Gunther's twenty-first birthday with him, because the two of you were friends. Close enough friends that he was the one who posted bail after your first arrest."

Mason flashed a knowing smile, revealing a missing tooth on the right side of his mouth. "I was wondering when someone would figure it out."

Leo had had all of the police reports on both Gunther and Rollins for weeks. But the connection between the two men couldn't be found in the NYPD's records. Realizing that they had located Summer Carver through the prison visitation records, Leo had instead done a search of both men's corrections histories. Among the documents he received were the archived records from the jail when Mason Rollins was bailed out for his first arrest, an assault at the age of nineteen. The person who posted his $250 bail was Darren Gunther.

"How'd the two of you know each other?" Leo asked.

"Our mothers were housekeepers for the same service. They'd help each other out—switch shifts as needed, or one would cook meals for the both of us while the other worked. So Darren and I got pretty tight in the process. He got the big scholarship to prep school and Vassar. I didn't, but we stayed in touch—until you arrested him, of course."

"Was the knife yours?" Leo asked.

Rollins shook his head. "Used to be, though, until that day. It was my birthday gift to him. He'd always admired it."

"You were talented with a knife," Leo said. "You could throw one in the air and catch it by the blade between your fingers."

Smile again. "You surely did your research."

Rollins's first assault arrest stemmed from an argument after he was performing his knife tricks at a party and another guest complained and asked him to stop.

"I'm surprised you're being so forthcoming," Leo said.

"I told Darren from the very beginning I wasn't going to lie for him. That stint I did upstate? I know it's a cliché, but it actually changed me. I got my high school equivalence degree, even a couple of college credits. Got off drugs. Gave myself up to a higher power. I'm no saint, but I steer clear of trouble."

"But you knew Gunther was accusing you of a crime that *he* committed."

"He read an article about new DNA testing. High-speed magician stuff, where the lab could get my DNA off this speed bag years from now." Rollins gave the bag a quick jab for emphasis.

"It's called touch DNA," Leo said.

"When I gave him the knife for his birthday, he wanted me to show him my knife tricks, so he knew I'd been handling the blade between my fingers that night. He said he managed to wipe down the handle of the knife with his shirt in the chaos after that bar owner went down, but didn't touch the blade because it would seem too obvious if it were clean. When he read that article, he got a light-bulb over that big brain of his, wondering if I might have left some DNA behind on the blade."

"And that's why he filed the petition for new DNA testing?" Leo asked.

A corner of Rollins's mouth lifted. "Can you believe it? The whole thing was a Hail Mary pass. He figured that another person's DNA on the blade might be enough to get his conviction thrown out. Turns out they found it at the top edge of the handle, so he must have missed a spot. He actually didn't realize there'd be a sample of my DNA in a database for comparison. I'm not entirely sure I believe him, but he at least says he didn't mean for my name to get dragged into it."

"You make it sound like you've been speaking to him on a regular basis. Was this on the prison phones? I'm surprised he'd be so risky."

"Darren's much too smart to make that kind of mistake. He sent someone else to deliver his messages."

Leo was fairly certain he knew who that person was. "Toby Carver?" he asked, holding up his phone to display a photograph of Summer's half brother.

"You know your stuff, Farley."

"The district attorney's investigator tried to interview you. You declined. Why not defend yourself then?"

Rollins held his gaze for several seconds before speaking. "I didn't feel the need to talk to that man, because he didn't know the connection between me and Darren. You did, so the jig is up, as they say. I meant it when I said I don't want to get on the wrong side of the law again. Declining an interview's not a crime. Lying to a cop, on the other hand, might be, as I understand it."

"My guess is Darren also promised to share his court settlement with you if you kept quiet."

Mason said nothing.

"Do you remember the waitress who was working at the bar that night?" Leo scrolled on his phone to an old photo of Clarissa De-Santo that he had gotten from Samantha Finney. "This is Clarissa DeSanto. She saw the two of you together, didn't she?"

"I think I'm done talking to you, Deputy Commissioner."

"Then I guess I'll add your name to the charge of conspiracy to commit murder."

"Whoa, whoa—I told you, I was long gone by the time that man was killed."

"I'm not talking about Lou Finney, Rollins. Clarissa DeSanto was killed three months ago. Toby Carver ran her car off the side of the road in a fatal rollover crash. But you already knew that, didn't you? Because you helped him and Darren Gunther plan it, to make sure she wasn't around to tell other people that the two of you were friends."

Mason's face contorted with fear. When he spoke again, his cool demeanor was replaced by genuine panic. "She's . . . *dead*? I swear, I had no idea. I just assumed she was getting paid off, too."

"Right now, it looks like you, Toby, and your friend Darren killed her to spring your buddy from prison, set me up as a liar, and split the big paycheck he'd be getting from the state. So you better explain."

"I didn't know any of this in advance. One day, some dude from the DA's Office shows up, asking me about the night that Darren got arrested. When he told me my DNA was on that knife, I freaked out. I had no idea about touch DNA or whatever. Then the next day, that guy Toby tracked me down at my apartment. He said I'd get twenty percent of whatever money Darren hustled out of the state for locking him up. All I had to do was stay mum. Not tell anyone about my connection to Darren."

"What about Toby's half sister, Summer? Was she involved?"

Rollins shook his head. "At least, I don't think so. Toby said she was a flake, but she really believed Darren was innocent. I got the impression she's, like, in love with him or something. Toby was the one with the street smarts."

"And what about Clarissa?"

"I told Toby there was a problem with their plan, because the waitress on duty that night had seen us together. I could tell we were getting on her nerves. Once my name got into the press as the big bad felon whose DNA was found on the knife, she'd probably recognize me and make the connection. Toby said it wouldn't be a problem, though."

"You got that woman killed, Mason."

The color drained from his face. "No! Please don't say that. I thought he meant she'd be getting a cut of the money, too. I got the impression Toby would be, as well. It seemed like they were doling out lottery money. I can't believe Darren got me pulled into this."

"Maybe the two of you can talk about it when you join him in Dannemora."

"Please, no. You've got to believe me, I didn't know they were going to hurt that girl. Let me help you. I'll do anything."

"*Anything?*" Leo had a plan.

Chapter 55

Marcy Buckley paced in circles around her kitchen island, waiting for the phone to ring.

From the moment Laurie had called this morning, all the links in the chain had connected. Marcy's first call was to Sandra Carpenter, who easily recalled the name of the Rehoboth Beach restaurant where her daughter worked—the Sand Bucket. *We used to call it the Sandra Bucket because I spent so much time there when I visited.*

From there, Marcy left a voicemail message for the restaurant, assuming they wouldn't get back to her until the late afternoon. Instead, she received a return call within the hour from one of the owners, April Meyer. April was initially overjoyed to learn that Marcy and her husband were the ones who had adopted Michelle's baby. *That's all she really wanted, was for her child to have a loving family.*

April remembered Michelle fondly and recalled counseling her during her unplanned pregnancy. *That poor girl was so terrified to tell her mother what was happening. She was certain her mother would disown her.*

April was clearly floored when Marcy explained that the biological father was married to the woman who was responsible for marketing the restaurant's opening launch. And then Marcy had moved on to the real bombshell: Johnny's kidnapping.

"We have reason to believe that Michelle reached out to this man and told him for the first time about the child they conceived. We think he's extremely dangerous. If we're right, he killed Michelle and has Johnny."

For the first time, the other end of the line had fallen silent. She thought the call had disconnected until April finally spoke. "I'll have to get back to you."

If Marcy had to guess, April was in the process of contacting the woman who had been in charge of their marketing. Somewhere, a woman was learning that her husband had been unfaithful. That he had cheated with a young waitress that the woman had known and trusted. That a child had been born from the union. Her heart would probably be broken.

Marcy prayed that whoever the woman was, she'd be able to see that Johnny was the person who mattered most right now. He was an innocent child.

The ringtone of her phone sent her heart racing. It was an unknown caller. "Hello?"

"Mrs. Buckley? My name is Roseanne Robinson. My ex-husband's the man you're looking for. His name is Daniel Turner."

Marcy did her best to spell out what she knew about Michelle Carpenter's life after Johnny's birth. "It was a downward spiral. She became addicted to drugs, floating around for a few years. But she eventually recovered and was staying clean. She moved to Philadelphia and was making a living selling handmade jewelry online. She was attending meetings. She thought the drugs were her way of punishing herself for the affair she had, albeit unwittingly, with a married man."

Marcy saw no need to mention that Daniel had led Michelle to believe that they would be getting married and having children together.

To Marcy's surprise, Roseanne sounded genuine. "That poor girl. I can't imagine what she was going through. I was in that restaurant at least once a week. I would talk to her all the time about her pregnancy. To think, she knew the whole time that I was married to the father. It must have been gut-wrenching for her."

"You had no idea he was having an affair?"

"Danny and I went through a rough patch that one summer when I didn't think we'd make it. He was always working, or on his phone, or running off to yoga. I thought he might be bored with our marriage. Sometimes I even wondered if there might be another woman in the picture, but I never confronted him about it. That must have been when he was with Michelle."

"Is that why you separated?" Marcy asked.

"No. At some point, things just seemed to get better. He was home more. Less distracted. He bought himself a motorcycle, and I thought, *Okay, I guess it was some kind of early midlife crisis, and this stupid Harley's what he needed for some excitement.* But that must have been after she saw us together and ended the affair. The timing lines up. We were good again for the next few years. But then a truck hit him when he was riding that ridiculous death-machine. I'll never forget the day I was called to the hospital. I sat in the emergency room, convinced I'd never see my husband again. Then I got the news that he'd be okay. He had a traumatic brain injury, but he would survive. I truly believed I'd gotten a restart on my life. That we'd go right back to the way we were."

"How terrifying," Marcy said. "When was this?"

"Five years ago."

"Johnny was already two years old," Marcy said. She had no idea at the time that another woman was out there, a stranger, her life playing out in parallel with Marcy's, leading them both here. Their children were half siblings.

"I was absolutely devoted to taking care of him," Roseanne

said. "We found a fantastic personal injury lawyer. He got a settlement that left us financially comfortable for life. But the TBI completely altered his personality. He became paranoid, irrational, and hot-tempered."

Her explanation of her ex-husband's condition was clearly the product of years spent trying to understand it. According to what she had been told by doctors, a rare but real subset of patients with traumatic brain injuries develop what resembles a psychotic disorder within the first two years of their injury. Symptoms such as hallucinations, paranoia, and delusions often lead to a misdiagnosis of schizophrenia. Even more common among patients are smaller but noticeable personality changes, such as impatience, outbursts of anger, and a lack of both empathy and impulse control.

"I was miserable as a result," she said, "but initially I felt too guilty to leave because his conduct wasn't his fault."

"Yet you eventually left," Marcy noted.

"One night, he was hallucinating. He was absolutely convinced that I was fighting him with an army of soldiers. He was yelling at people who weren't even there, and then he physically attacked me. I realized I had to leave him for my own safety and for Bella's. After that incident, I got a restraining order to prevent him from contacting either of us. I didn't think things could get worse, until he violated the court order. He broke into the house I had rented, armed with a knife, and accused me of brainwashing Bella against him. Bella was trembling with fear. I threw myself in front of Bella to protect her, certain that he was going to kill both of us. He raised the knife, and I begged him, sobbing, to take my life if he had to, but to spare hers. He suddenly turned around and ran from the house. After that, I finally got permission from the court to change my name and relocate with our daughter. I literally have not spoken to anyone from my former life beyond a few trusted friends until now. I want to help you, Mrs. Buckley, but I can't let Danny find me."

"I don't want Danny to find you either, Roseanne, but *I* need to find *him*. He has my son, and what you've told me about your ex-husband makes me fear even more for his life."

"I haven't spoken to him for nearly four years," Roseanne said. "We had our apartment in Washington, D.C. It's in an old historic building that Danny absolutely cherished. He would never sell it. But, if I had to guess, he's in Delaware, not the city. We used to have a little townhouse a quarter mile from the beach. But after the motorcycle accident, he grew more and more paranoid. He wanted more land, more privacy. He bought a place north of the main beach community, outside of Cape Henlopen State Park."

As Roseanne recited the address, Marcy was texting the incoming information as fast as she could to Laurie, who would know how to use it.

"This is amazing, Roseanne. Thank you so much. I know it can't be easy to realize that Daniel might be involved in all of this."

"Okay, there's one more thing I need to tell you. If you're thinking about calling the local police there in Delaware? Don't do that."

Marcy's brow knitted, wondering why Roseanne would advise her against calling the police. "Luckily, my husband's family has close contacts with law enforcement. I'm sure they'll be able to get cooperation."

Roseanne sighed on the other end of the line. "Danny's older brother, Charlie, is the chief of the Rehoboth police. He's in total denial about Danny's condition, and abused his power trying to keep me from getting the court orders I needed to protect me and Bella. If it weren't for him, Danny would have ended up in prison for breaking into my home and attacking me with a knife in front of my child. I'm so sorry, Mrs. Buckley, but I just have to warn you: if you call Charlie, he's going to tell Danny that cops are looking for him, and if he feels cornered, I'm terrified of what Danny might do to your boy."

Chapter 56

A half mile outside Cape Henlopen State Park, a hundred and twenty miles from his family's home, Johnny Buckley sat at the foot of the bed inside his assigned room.

He unfolded the piece of paper that the man had given him the previous night. He read it for what must have been the twentieth time. He didn't even need to sound out the syllables anymore. A detective named Jennifer Langland confirmed that "police are operating on the assumption that Johnny Buckley was abducted by a stranger." But there was one sentence he could not forget: *According to a law enforcement source, the missing boy was adopted by the Buckleys as a newborn.*

The top of the page said it was from something called New York Crime Beat, but Johnny decided that the whole thing was a lie. This wasn't a real newspaper or anything, just a sheet of paper from the man's printer. Anyone who knew how to use a computer could write whatever they wanted and claim they found it on the internet. Obviously, the man had made up this fake article to be mean to Johnny.

Because that's what the man was: *mean.* A mean bully who said things and did things just to hurt people.

My name is Johnny, Jonathan Alexander Buckley, he whispered to himself quietly. *My parents—my real parents—are Andrew and Marcy Buckley. My name is definitely not Danny!*

He fell silent as the sound of footsteps echoed down the stairs. The man's voice. "I think I am going to tell him the truth tomorrow about who I actually am."

It was followed by the woman's voice. "What about me? How should I introduce myself?" This was the first time that Johnny had ever heard the woman come downstairs. He had started to wonder if perhaps she was a prisoner, like him, being kept in a separate room upstairs.

"As my wife, of course. My beautiful, loving, and loyal wife. He's a wonderful boy, Roseanne. You'll come to love him just as much as we love Bella."

"I'm sorry again that I took Bella away from you." To Johnny, there was something funny about the lady's voice. She sounded sort of like a cartoon character. Ever since he first heard her voice, he had thought of her as the one person who might be willing to save him. Now that he could hear her more clearly, he thought she sounded nice. She definitely didn't seem as scary as the man.

"But then you came back," the man said. "And we're a family again. And now we have Danny Jr., too."

If the woman had left this awful house once before, maybe she wanted to leave now, just like him. Maybe she, too, had been pretending to like the man, because *The more I know I can trust you, the more privileges I can give you.* Maybe they could team up together and help each other escape.

But to do that, he needed to see her.

Johnny folded up the sheet of paper, stashed it beneath his mattress, and stepped quietly to the bedroom door. His hand shook as he reached for the knob. He would take one quick peek at the woman and see if she looked like someone he could trust.

If the man spotted him, Johnny would say he needed to go to the bathroom. The man would believe him, Johnny assured himself, because Johnny had been on perfect behavior for days.

With a growing sense of terror, Johnny left his room and crept down the hallway toward the bathroom. Two more steps, and he'd be able to see around the corner into the living room, where the voices were coming from.

He craned his neck and scanned the room for the woman. For a second, he let himself hope that she might spot him and give him a reassuring wink or a smile. Instead, he saw the man sitting alone on the sofa, his back to Johnny.

And then he heard the cartoon voice, even though no one else was in the room: *I love you to the moon and back, Daniel.*

Johnny's gasp of astonishment brought the man immediately to his feet. "Why are you out of your room?" he thundered. "Were you trying to leave this house?"

Johnny's voice quivered as he forced himself to answer. "I . . . I have to go to the bathroom. I can't hold it anymore."

The man stared at him for five full seconds before sighing. "Next time, yell for me to come get you. I need to know where you are at all times. You know the rules."

"Yes, sir."

"We talked about this, Danny. Yes, *who*?"

"Yes . . . Daddy."

"See? That wasn't so hard, was it?"

Inside his head, Johnny was screaming, but he could see the man was delighted. He decided to take one more chance. "I thought I heard someone else out here. I got scared something was wrong."

The man's face went blank with sudden confusion, as if he had awoken from a daze. "No, just the TV is all."

Once the bathroom door was closed, Johnny fell to the floor and sobbed in silence. The television wasn't on. There was no woman.

No one is going to save me.

Chapter 57

Leo sat with Mason Rollins in a conference room at the District Attorney's Office as the lawyers finalized the details of his cooperation agreement with the police. In exchange for the DA's promise not to file charges, Rollins would wear a wire and contact Toby Carver. Once Carver incriminated himself for witness tampering and the murder of Clarissa DeSanto, the next step would be to convince Toby to testify against Darren Gunther.

Leo felt his cell phone buzz at his waist. It was Laurie. He signaled that he was excusing himself from the room and navigated to the hallway.

"Laurie, you always have a reporter's instinct when something important is happening. Wait until you hear what I learned from Mason Rollins. And still, all in time to pick up Timmy from golf camp—"

"Dad, we found Johnny. Or, at least, I think we did. His name's Daniel Turner. He's Johnny's biological father." Laurie delivered the facts at a rapid-fire pace. A motorcycle accident. Head injury. Personality changes. Hallucinations and paranoia. "Marcy spoke to his ex-wife and got a last known address for him, near the Delaware Coast, in Rehoboth Beach. We just have to figure out the best way to get Johnny out of that house."

"I can call the local police right now. Connect them to Detective

Langland. If they're a small-town force without full SWAT-level resources, they can probably pull in state police. Outlying communi-
ties like that usually have cooperation agreements with the state for
major crime responses."

"There's a problem though, Dad. Daniel Turner's brother is the
local police chief down there." She relayed everything they had
learned from Turner's ex-wife about the police chief's enablement
of his brother.

"I can tell you this for certain: Detective Langland won't be able
to go to Delaware without local authority. Same goes for me as far as
the NYPD is concerned. And we can't try to retrieve Johnny on our
own as private citizens. It's too dangerous."

"Well, we can't call this guy's brother, either. According to his
ex-wife, the brother would give Turner advance warning that the police were looking for him. If that feeds into his paranoia, who knows
what he might do to Johnny."

"The other option is the FBI," Leo said. So far, the local field office had been leaving the investigation to Detective Langland, offering federal resources as appropriate. "One of the agents here should
be able to contact the Delaware office and hopefully skip some of
the red tape. I'll call Detective Langland now."

"Okay, but call her from the car. Brett just told me that the studio
belongs to a private jet concierge service—a little secret he never
bothered sharing with the rest of us. He's booking us a charter to the
regional airport closest to the beach."

"What about Timmy?"

"Alex said he can leave the courthouse to meet him at Chelsea
Piers. Batting cages and all." She had finally convinced Alex that he
would be most helpful taking care of Timmy rather than joining her
in Delaware. "Hurry, Dad. We need to go now!"

Chapter 58

Marcy slowed her minivan to a steady roll as she made her way through the E-ZPass toll for the Chesapeake Bay Bridge. On a normal day, she would take a moment to appreciate the white light shimmering up from the sun's reflection on the bright blue water, but instead, she revved the engine as soon as she saw the all-clear that her toll had been processed.

According to the GPS, she still had ninety-two miles and an hour and fifty-two minutes to go before her destination. She had raced into the car as soon as she could after getting Daniel Turner's address from his ex-wife. Fortunately, her neighbor had been home and agreed to watch the twins.

Hold on, Johnny. Mama's on her way.

Her cell phone rang through the car speakers. The screen in the dash identified the caller as Andrew. She hit a button on the steering wheel to answer. "Oh, thank God. I've been calling constantly, but your phone was off."

"I'm so sorry, babe. I was in court, and Judge Dickinson has a zero-tolerance policy. He had a lawyer jailed for contempt once when a phone rang during closing arguments. I got your messages. I'm on my way back to the firm now. I'll go straight to my car and meet you in Delaware."

"Okay, and Leo and Laurie are on their way, too, in a private plane. Detective Langland is trying to loop in the Delaware FBI to make an end run around Turner's brother. I don't understand what's taking so long. A child's missing, and we likely know where he is. They should drop everything and go get our son right now."

"I'll call Chuck Martin who works at the Department of Justice to see if he might be able to pull some strings, too." Chuck was a law school friend of Andrew's and now worked in the DOJ's Criminal Division. "I'm probably about forty-five minutes behind you. When you get there, find a restaurant or some place to wait nearby and text me the address. Don't go to the house by yourself. We don't know what the layout is, and it's possible he'd recognize the minivan if he's been watching us."

They didn't know yet whether Daniel Turner had followed them to the Hamptons from Washington, D.C., or if he had already known that they were planning to go to New York for vacation. Marcy would never forgive herself for posting their vacation plans on Facebook for the entire world to see. She had never given a second thought to the privacy settings on her account and had put Johnny in danger as a result.

I'll never do something so thoughtless again. Please, God. Just let us have our son back.

Chapter 59

Daniel Turner could feel himself smiling as he watched Danny Jr. work on his new jigsaw puzzle, a map of the United States.

He noticed that if the name of a state was legible on a piece of the puzzle, more often than not, Danny had an idea of where it belonged on the map. He himself had always had a knack for geography as a child, too. Maybe Danny would go on to develop an interest in architecture, as well. He certainly had artistic potential, based on his drawings and coloring.

He was still worried about Danny's earlier comment about having heard a woman's voice in the living room. He thought he had stopped having those episodes after he had finally learned the truth about Danny. He tried describing them to his neurologist last year, but he wasn't as good at explaining things as he used to be. Plus, how do you get someone to understand what it feels like to be absolutely convinced that your ex-wife and daughter are with you, living with you, loving you . . . only to realize in the next moment that you are in the house absolutely alone?

During his most lucid moments, he understood these were the reasons he had lost Roseanne and Bella. The underlying cause may have been the damage to the temporal and frontal areas of his brain, but the end result was the same: he had made his family miserable and afraid. But during the hallucinations, everything was good again. He was in control of his choices, Roseanne loved him, and Bella would let him fly her in the air like an airplane, zooming in circles. The next second, though, they'd be gone, and he would realize how broken he was.

But then he got that shocking phone call from Michelle Carpenter. He rarely even thought of her all these years later. Maybe he had buried the memory of her, trying to bury his shame for having cheated on Roseanne, the love of his life. Until the motorcycle crash changed everything, his relationship with Michelle was the only real mistake he'd made in his marriage—and it was a terrible one. He met her in yoga class two days after Bella said her first full sentence. *Me play, dada.* She was a young toddler by then, but for some reason, those three little words made it real. He was daddy to a little independent person who would need him forever.

Was it the pressures of fatherhood that made him pursue Michelle? A need to prove that he was still attractive to a younger woman? He never meant for it to go on for months, or to lead to talk about a future and marriage and children. He had known he needed to break it off, but then she had been the one to end it. Nowadays, they'd call what she did "ghosting." She simply disappeared. No return calls. No more yoga. And he certainly wasn't going to pop into her workplace, given his wife's regular presence there.

When she called him six months ago, she finally explained why she had cut him out of her life. She described how she had driven to his office to tell him the good news about the pregnancy, only to spot him with Roseanne, Bella, and his wedding band. Nearly eight years later, she contacted him out of the blue, after spending years as a drug addict. She swore up and down that she never told anyone the truth about the baby's paternity—not even Daniel himself, as it turned out. It felt like she'd dropped a nuclear bomb on his world, so she could "find peace," in her words.

Peace? Why did *she* deserve peace? Roseanne at least had a reason for taking his daughter away from him. His brain made him do things that scared her. But what Michelle had done was unforgiveable. His only crime was infidelity. He didn't deserve to lose the right to know his son—to even know *about* his son—as punishment. "I need to see you in person," he had pleaded. "To hear about his birth. You at least owe me that."

Oh, in the end, she had found her peace all right. Thanks to the sedative he had slipped into her cranberry juice and club soda, she was sloppy and slurring as she rambled on about the nice Irish priest who found the perfect couple to steal his son. And then she flew high as a kite after he placed that needle in her arm. It hadn't taken him long to make a mess out of her apartment. He knew from his brother that the cops would put two and two together: A former junkie, dead of an overdose. Case closed.

He hadn't pumped the fatal dose of heroin into her vein until he had the information he needed. Even after he pulled out his gun and threatened to shoot her in the head, Michelle refused to tell him where the baby was. Instead, she had begged him to leave the child—*his* child—alone. "I swear to you, I would not have given him up unless I knew he was going to a good home. He's a happy little boy. I see pictures on the mom's Facebook page. He has two adorable little sisters—twins. His father's a successful lawyer—his uncle just got named a federal judge. He'll have every opportunity. *Please*, just let him have his life without the two of us to mess it up."

She died trying to protect her son, but ended up giving Daniel what he knew would be enough information to identify the family. How many new federal judges could there be?

Now he patted Danny Junior on the top of his head. "Good job on the puzzle, buddy. Do you know what this place right here is?" He pointed to the District of Columbia.

"That's Washington, D.C.," Danny said.

"Is that where you live?"

He searched his son's eyes as he mulled over the right answer.

"No, Daddy. That's where that other family lives. I live here with you. Are we in New York?"

Daniel's heart soared with happiness. This was his second chance at fatherhood, and it was working. That's why those hallucinations of Roseanne and Bella had stopped after he killed Michelle, or at least, he had thought so until today.

"No, Danny. Our house is right here," he said, dropping a finger a couple inches to the right. "In a state called Delaware."

His mind raced with a blend of triumph and hope. He had finally won his boy over.

He was also proud. His plan had required a level of patience and planning that he had wondered if he still possessed. He waited a full five months after Michelle's death, wanting to be certain that no one connected the boy's eventual disappearance with his biological mother's tragic demise. Then, a month ago, he tucked a miniature GPS tracker beneath the bumper of the Buckley family's minivan after following Danny's fake mother to a Costco parking lot. He watched the car's movements for patterns, hoping to find the perfect opportunity to bring Danny back home where he belonged. In the end, he hadn't needed the tracker at all. He made his move after seeing the woman's Facebook post about going to the Hamptons for a family vacation, assuming an abduction outside the D.C. area would deflect any possible suspicion from him.

An alert sounded from his cell phone. It was the latest update from the GPS tracker. He had decided to leave the tracker in place rather than risk being seen retrieving it. According to the spy gadget's manufacturer, the device was untraceable, but out of caution, Daniel had routed the alerts through three different layers of forwarded, anonymous accounts.

Daniel began to blink rapidly as he felt a vein pulse against his right temple. According to the tracker, the minivan was moving south on Coastal Highway, only eleven miles from his house.

He placed his fingertips against the side of his head, trying to stop the throbbing. "Go to your room, Danny. Daddy needs to think."

Chapter 60

Marcy flinched at the sound of her cell phone. According to the screen, it was Andrew. "Hey, are you close?" she asked.

"Still forty minutes out. Any word from Laurie and Leo?"

"No. And not from the FBI or Detective Langland yet, either. I'm jumping out of my skin, knowing that Johnny might be a few miles from here."

"Did you find a good meet-up place?"

"Remember that outlet mall on Highway 1 as you're coming into town?" It had been a couple of years since they had visited Rehoboth Beach, but Andrew had a good memory.

"Right side of the street?"

"Exactly. It's a crowded lot, and I'm parked at the back. Seemed like a safe enough place to wait for now."

"Sounds perfect. I'll meet you there. Make sure you're sharing your location with me, so I can find you in the actual parking lot once I arrive."

"Good idea." A beep sounded in her ear as another call came into her phone. The screen said it was a blocked caller. "There's another call. I better get it in case it's the FBI."

"Okay, hang in there, babe. This is going to be over soon. I can feel it. Love you."

"Love you, too." She hit a button on her phone to accept the new call. "Hello?"

"Mrs. Buckley?"

"Yes."

"This is Detective Eddie Miller calling from Long Island about your son, Johnny. My colleague Detective Langland wanted me to check in since she's got her hands full right now with Johnny's case."

"Did she get hold of the FBI yet in Delaware? I'm at the edge of town now. Are they coming?"

"Yes, they have a couple of agents on-site now, in fact."

"Already? I got the impression she was wading through a maze of red tape."

"She was, but once she got the right person on the phone, the pieces fell into place quickly."

"So they're at Turner's house? Now?"

"No, no. Not yet. They're nearby, though, making plans for your son's extraction. Where exactly are you? They want to make sure you're there when it goes down. It'll be a comfort for little Johnny to see his mother immediately."

Her eyes watered at the thought of holding her son again. "I'm at the outlet mall on Highway 1."

"Okay, if I give you an address, can you find it?"

"Yes, as long as my phone GPS can pull it up." She foraged in her purse for a piece of scrap paper and jotted down the address.

"You'll actually need to go north away from Rehoboth Beach. The town name is Lewes: L-E-W-E-S."

"That's where Daniel Turner lives. What if he sees them coming?"

"We had the same operational concerns here, but the FBI assured us they know what they're doing. The lots out there are several acres, and they say the area is wooded, near the state park. I'm told the address you're looking for is an adjacent property, marked by a mailbox out front, then you turn left down a long dirt road. But hurry, Mrs. Buckley. They're getting everything in place to move in. If everything goes smoothly, you're going to have your son back real soon."

Chapter 61

After hanging up the phone, Daniel Turner unlocked the wall safe that was hidden behind a painting of the Jefferson Memorial. He pulled out all of the bills inside — close to a quarter million dollars, his emergency cash in addition to the four million dollars he had from his lawsuit settlement, stocked away in an offshore account. Once the cash was loaded, he placed his handgun on top, zipped the duffel bag, and made his way downstairs.

He found Danny perched on the edge of his bed, pretending to be at ease, but Daniel could see the boy was nervous.

Why wouldn't he be? He had finally gotten adjusted to his new home — with his real father — when Daniel had to ask the boy for his fake mother's telephone number. "I just want to tell her that you're safe and happy here, Danny, so she won't be worried about you anymore. You want her to be able to sleep at night, don't you?"

The boy had nodded and recited Marcy Buckley's cell phone number from memory.

Daniel knew the name of the lead detective from the news reports covering Danny's disappearance, so had claimed to be Detective Langland's colleague. From there, Marcy had confirmed his worst fears. They knew he had the boy. Even worse, the police in New York were bringing in the FBI, which meant his brother, Charlie, couldn't be the one to save him from jail like he did after that unfortunate incident with Roseanne.

"Did you call . . . Marcy?" Danny asked.

"I did. She was relieved to know you're here and doing well. She has her two other children—her *actual* daughters—so I wouldn't worry anymore about the Buckleys. They'll be fine."

Danny's face scrunched up as he began to sniffle, and Daniel wondered if perhaps he had gone too far.

"Hey, remember how I told you that the more I trusted you, the more privileges you'd earn?"

Danny nodded, his eyes laced with a mix of hope and wariness.

"How do you feel about going for a car ride? The beaches here are beautiful."

"Really?" His eyes widened, and Daniel's heart swelled. It was the first time the child had seemed genuinely happy in his presence.

He still couldn't figure out how the police had narrowed in on him. When he drove to New York, he had swapped his license plates for a set he stole off a car in D.C. And Michelle had been adamant that she never told anyone the identity of Danny's real father.

He shook off his lingering curiosity. What mattered now was that they were looking for him, and he had no desire to be found.

Maybe he would even let Danny hug Marcy one final time to say good-bye. When the FBI arrived, they would find her body on the empty lot that Daniel owned behind this one. The discovery of a homicide would trigger a wide-scale police response that would include local and state police in addition to the FBI agents who were already on their way. The ensuing chaos would give him extra time to get out of the area. And he and his son would find another place to live under new names, never to be seen again. Roseanne had disappeared with Bella. There was no reason he and his son, Danny, couldn't do the same.

Chapter 62

As Marcy Buckley took the right turn off Route 9, her GPS system advised that she was only three minutes from her destination.

Based on the map, she was fairly certain that the address she'd received from Detective Miller was about a quarter mile from the entrance to Daniel Turner's property, which was located around the next turn, and before the state park. The FBI had been correct that the area felt more like the woods than the outskirts of a crowded beach vacation community.

She had just gotten off the phone with Andrew, who was still half an hour away. She pulled up Laurie's number on her phone and hit the call button. As she listened to the unanswered rings, she passed a woman around her age working on a fence at the side of the road. Behind her, two miniature goats frolicked in the open field. Her heart hurt, imagining Johnny crying out from the passenger seat: "Mama, look at the baby goats. Can we stop and say hello? Please, please?"

Laurie's outgoing message pulled her back to reality.

"Hey, Laurie. I've called a few times, and it kept going straight to voicemail. It's ringing now, at least. Hopefully that means your plane has landed. A Detective Eddie Miller called me from East Hampton. He works with Detective Langland and told me where to meet the FBI. I assume you and Leo have the same info. I don't want to jinx it, but it feels like this is actually going to work. Say a little prayer, okay?"

Marcy pulled her car to a stop at the sight of a rickety green mailbox with peeling paint, the house number she was looking for barely legible on the side of the box. Beyond the four-by-four holding up the mailbox, she made out tire tracks of dirt imprinted in what was otherwise an untended lot of overgrown grass and weeds.

She saw no sign of the FBI or other law enforcement, but recalled the assurances of Detective Miller: *The lots out there are several acres, and they say the area is wooded, near the state park. I'm told the address you're looking for is an adjacent lot, marked by a mailbox out front, then you turn left down a long dirt road.*

This was no time to hesitate. Johnny had spent nine days in captivity. The least she could do was drive through unfamiliar land to be there for him, waiting, once he was free.

She took a deep breath as she made the turn, feeling truly hopeful for the first time since Johnny disappeared.

Chapter 63

Daniel Turner drove the quarter mile from his driveway to a dirt road leading into the seven-acre corner lot behind his own property. The main entrance, to which he had directed Marcy Buckley, corresponded to the street address on the town's survey. He was taking the back road in, but eventually, he and Mrs. Buckley's paths would intersect.

He had bought this parcel three years earlier from the Garney family, who had eight sons, only four of whom moved out of the family home after becoming adults. The remaining sons hosted parties four nights out of the week and raced dirt bikes around the property by day—the louder the better from all indications. Even when Daniel had been a Harley fan, he had never approved of bikers who intentionally made as much noise as possible. And after the settlement from the accident, his first priority had been to find a remote and quiet respite from society. When it became clear that the Garney boys were going to interfere with those plans, he struck a deal that the parents could not refuse, buying the property only to tear down the house and add to his vacant land.

He cut the engine next to a small pond on the property, before a cluster of trees he'd need to hike through to reach the cleared land where the ramshackle house had once stood. Next to him in the passenger seat, Johnny reached for the clasp of his seatbelt.

"You should stay here," Daniel said.

"By myself?"

He sensed fear in his son's voice. He never wanted his son to be afraid again. "Not to worry. This is an extra property I own. I just need to check on something real quick before we head for the beach." He had decided that keeping Danny in the car was the safest plan. He had no idea how long it would be before the FBI arrived.

Still, after he retrieved his gun from the duffel bag in the trunk, he made a point to be sure that Danny saw him holding it, just in case. "It's for my safety while I check out the property," he added.

He noticed that Danny slumped lower into his seat. He was such a good boy. And Danny had been compliant to a T. He trusted him not to run away while he was gone.

He walked away with a satisfied smile. They'd be off to a fresh start in no time.

Chapter 64

The clerk at the rental car counter at the Salisbury Regional Airport handed Laurie a form in triplicate with a ballpoint pen. "I just need you to cross the t's and dot the i's," she reported cheerfully, as a chime sounded from Laurie's briefcase.

Next to her, Leo was on his own phone, still trying to navigate the bureaucracy of the FBI.

They had no time to spare. She took the pen from the clerk. The sooner they could hit the road, the better. Her phone stopped ringing.

Chapter 65

Marcy had driven about a quarter of a mile onto the property, searching for any sign of the FBI agents, when the path of flattened grass came to an end. If she drove any farther, she'd have to trample over growth that was nearly four feet high.

She turned off the engine of the minivan, expecting the FBI to suddenly announce its presence. Greeted with silence, she stepped from the minivan and walked toward the one patch of land that had been cleared, presumably for a new house to be built.

Still, no one came.

She had turned back toward her car when a man emerged from the woods behind the clearing.

"Mrs. Buckley?" he called out.

"Oh, hi. I was starting to wonder if I went to the wrong place."

"Absolutely not. I'm Special Agent Gregory Jenson. The rest of my team is set up about fifty yards into the woods here. We're being cautious about anyone spotting our activity." He must have noticed her eyeing his polo shirt and khakis warily. "Sorry, I was off duty when we got the call out. I came straightaway."

He pulled a wallet from his back pocket and flashed what looked from this distance like a badge. As he replaced his wallet, she noticed the firearm tucked into the side of his waistband.

"Just follow me this way," he assured her.

Marcy was three steps from entering the woods when a chill ran up her spine. For the second time in a week, she thought about the words of her former acting coach: *Pay attention to what you know, because every experience you ever had might be important right now.*

First it was Detective Langland asking a colleague that Marcy didn't know to call her with this address. Until then, Langland had always been the one to contact Marcy and Andrew directly. Now she was greeted by a single FBI agent, rushing her into the woods. Her son had been missing for eight days, and suddenly she was being asked to hurry to his suspected kidnapper's neighborhood, alone. None of it made sense.

"I'm going to wait in the car until my husband gets here. He's only two minutes away," she lied, turning back toward her van.

"This can't wait, Mrs. Buckley."

She picked up her pace, knowing that a real FBI agent would not sound so panicked.

She was reaching for the car door when she felt the impact of a pistol whip across the back of her head. She fell to the ground and heard the man's voice behind her. "Get on your knees. Now."

As she pushed her palms into the dirt, trying to regain her balance, she tipped her head down and caught a glimpse of the man, raising his pistol. His jaw was set, his mouth pinched. She had no doubt that he was going to execute her.

Instead of raising her body, she dropped immediately to the ground and rolled beneath the minivan. She crawled as fast as she could to the other side and let out a small scream as a crack rang out. The minivan lurched. He had shot out one of the rear tires. Driving out of here was no longer an option.

She clambered to her feet and searched, breathlessly, for an escape route. She ran into the woods just as she heard the gun fire again behind her.

• • •

Johnny Buckley was crouched low in the passenger seat of the man's car, wondering what the man was up to. He had pretended to be excited at the idea of visiting the local beaches, but his real excitement had been about the prospect of leaving the creepy house that had become his prison.

Now that the man had left him on his own, Johnny finally had his opportunity. The car wasn't locked. He had seen the man walk into the woods. He could finally escape.

What are you waiting for? he asked himself. *No one else is going to rescue you. You have to move.*

But, instead, Johnny sat absolutely still, ducking his head to make sure no one could possibly see him. The distant sound of waves was the only noise beyond a faint breeze whispering across the treetops.

And then a loud blast pierced the stillness like a cannonball.

And then two other shots rang out. A gun. It had to be the man's gun.

Johnny unlatched his seatbelt, opened the car door, and ran.

Chapter 66

Aside from her time in nursing school, Gretchen Harper had lived in Lewes, Delaware, all forty-three years of her life, born and raised on this same ten acres of land, only two miles away from Cape Henlopen State Park, where her father had been a beloved park ranger.

Since she had moved back into the family home alone, she had even come to enjoy the property chores that had once fallen to her father. She pulled another zip tie through the chicken wire and snapped it tight around the metal pole she had just replaced. She gave the fencing a good tug and it stayed intact. "That should do the trick, you two." Her miniature goats, Ernie and Bert, bounced around in the grass together near her feet. They wouldn't be running out to the road again anytime soon, but she'd add a few more zip ties to be safe.

She was securing her last loop when a green minivan made its way past her house. She threw up a wave to be friendly, but wondered where the car was headed. The only other lot on the street was the Garney property. She wondered if that oddball Daniel Turner was finally going to sell it, which would mean months if not a year of construction on a new house. Even so, the new neighbors would have to be better than those Garney brothers.

She had gathered up her supplies and was tucking them back

into place in the barn when she heard the sudden crack of an explosion. She hadn't heard a sound like that since she'd had to call the sheriff on the Garneys for shooting targets on their land.

She was replaying the sound in her head, wondering if it was a gunshot, when she heard two more blasts. *Boom! Boom!*

She ducked low, scurried to the house, and grabbed the kitchen phone.

9-1-1.

"This is Gretchen Harper on Bonner Road. I just heard at least three shots fired nearby. Tell Chief Turner that it sounds like they came from his brother's empty lot!"

Chapter 67

Laurie pressed the rental car key and heard a *chirp chirp* from the next row of cars in the lot. A small gray SUV waited in the spot they were looking for.

She hesitated a few steps from the car and looked to her father.

"Want me to drive?" Leo asked, a small grin on his face.

She broke into a smile. "Yes, please."

"I was wondering when you were going to remember that you barely know how."

Growing up in New York City had many advantages, but comfort behind the wheel was not one of them. "Well, I'm an excellent naviga-tor." She entered the town of Lewes, Delaware, where Daniel Turner lived, into her phone's GPS system and then propped the screen on the dash where her father could see it. "Or at least, my phone is."

They were halfway there when Laurie reached for her phone again. "Marcy was going to find a good spot for us to meet up. Let me get an update." When she clicked on the telephone icon, she saw she had a new message from Marcy. She hit the speaker button on her phone so Leo could hear.

"Hey, Laurie. I've called a few times, and it kept going straight to voicemail. It's ringing now, at least. Hopefully that means your plane has landed. A Detective Eddie Miller called me from East Hampton. He works with Detective Langland and told me where to meet the FBI. I assume you and Leo have the same info. I don't want to jinx it, but it feels like this is actually going to work. Say a little prayer, okay?"

Laurie hit a button to return Marcy's call, but after four rings, they heard her outgoing message.

"Eddie Miller?" Laurie asked as she hung up.

"Never heard of him. Let me call Langland."

Detective Langland didn't bother with a greeting when she answered. "Leo, I'm pulling every string I can find. The problem is there's no FBI field office in Delaware. It's covered by the Baltimore office. Two agents who'd normally run any kidnapping investigation were going to head out to Daniel Turner's house, but they decided to pull in the local satellite office instead. It's in Dover, about forty miles away, so I think we're almost there."

The news would explain Marcy's excitement.

"And you had a colleague named Miller reach out to Marcy?" Leo asked. "We're trying to figure out where to meet her."

"Miller? Who's that?"

Laurie knew from her father's grimace that he shared her sudden panic. "A Detective Eddie Miller apparently called Marcy, said he worked with you, and told her where to meet the FBI."

"No, that wasn't us," Langland said. "There's no Eddie Miller in our department."

Laurie called Andrew as quickly as she could.

"Hey, Laurie. You and Leo landed, I assume?"

"We're almost to Lewes. We were planning to meet Marcy, but she's not picking up." She kept her voice calm, not wanting to alarm Andrew until they were certain. "Someone called her and gave her an address to meet the FBI."

"Yeah, she called from there."

"So you know for sure she arrived? She's with the FBI?" Laurie's fears began to subside.

"She was still a few minutes away when she called. I tried her a couple of minutes ago for an update, but she didn't answer. I assume she's talking to the FBI agents."

Next to her, Leo was shaking his head, obviously worried.

"But you have the address?" Laurie asked.

"I couldn't write it down while I was driving, but she shares her location with me, so I can find her that way."

"That's great. Can you check now?"

"I'm only about five miles from the turnoff. I'll call you back—"

"Andrew, this is Leo. Can you pull over to the side of the road safely?"

"Right now?" Andrew asked, his voice suddenly filled with fear.

"Yes," Leo said calmly.

"Okay, hold on. . . . Yeah, okay, I'm pulled over now. What's wrong?"

"Whoever gave Marcy that address wasn't law enforcement," Leo said. "We think it was Daniel Turner. We need to find her right now."

Chapter 68

Marcy winced from the sting of a thorn branch slicing the side of her ankle as she traversed the unlevel wooded terrain. She reached toward the pain on instinct and lost her balance, catching herself before her face hit a nearby tree.

She leaned against the tree for support as she checked the cut on her leg. She was bleeding, but she was more worried about her head. She had no way of inspecting the wound, but when she reached back and touched the tender spot at the base of her skull, the blood on her palm looked fresh. She took the time to pull off her cotton sweater and use it to apply pressure. The tank top layered beneath it would do little to protect her from thorns and tree branches, but she needed to stop the bleeding.

Her capri pants and ballet flats were yet another disadvantage against Daniel Turner, who was armed with a gun and presumably knew his way around these woods. She had run so blindly and frantically that she had lost any sense of direction. She felt an urgency to keep moving to get away from him, but was terrified that she might end up running toward him instead of furthering the distance between them.

She sucked in her breath as a loud, deep shriek broke the silence. It was short and staccato. She replayed it in her head and decided it was only a bird. As she took another step, she heard the chirp again—but this one was slightly higher pitched. Then she heard both sounds at once. Not birds, and not a chirp. More of a bray. Sheep. No . . . goats. The miniature goats she had seen by the side of the road. The woman by the fence.

She closed her eyes, trying to internalize the direction of the sounds, and then began to move toward them. Focused now, she allowed herself to continue moving, but forced herself to slow her pace. Fast steps were louder. And every time she lost her footing, she was certain that the resulting noise would give her location away.

This time, she wouldn't let herself get turned around.

She felt herself getting closer to the ongoing braying, when she heard the unmistakable sound of footsteps in the leaves to her right. Searching for the largest nearby tree, she ducked behind it and turned sideways, trying to make herself as small as possible. It was never going to work. If Daniel Turner stepped within six feet of this tree, he would see her for sure.

The crinkling of the leaves continued. Spotting a softball-sized rock on the ground, she slowly crouched and reached for it with her right hand.

The footsteps moved closer.

She'd only have one shot at surprising him. She would need all of her strength and a lot of luck. Knowing it would probably be her final decision before she was killed, she sprang into a standing position and pulled the rock back over her shoulder. If she could, she would aim for his head.

But when she looked at the spot where she'd expected to find her target, she saw no one. Only when her gaze moved lower did she see the person who belonged to the footsteps.

"Johnny!" She dropped the rock and placed both hands over her mouth—from the shock of seeing her son, and to keep herself from crying out loud with happiness.

His eyes widened as his mouth went agape. "Mama?" He rubbed his eyes as if he were waking up from a dream.

She fell to her knees and pulled him into a tight hug. "Shhh, sweetie. I'm here. Mama's got you. But we have to be very, very quiet. And we need to find our way out of these woods."

"The man's house is that way," he whispered, pointing behind him. "And when he walked into the trees, I think he went *that* way," pointing about eighty degrees in the other direction. "I didn't want to go either of those places, and I ended up here."

She felt herself smiling. He was such a smart boy.

Marcy was right that Daniel Turner must have known the property well. They heard his voice before they heard his footsteps. And even through the dense growth of woods, they had no trouble seeing the gun aimed in their direction.

"Danny! I told you to stay in the car." The man's face was beet-red and the cords in his neck bulged from rage. "You were fooling me, weren't you? You were *never* going to stay with me. You were going to leave, just like *them*."

"Please," Marcy pleaded. "He's a seven-year-old boy. He heard gunshots. He got scared. He was out here looking for *you*. Weren't you?" She looked down into Johnny's eyes and could see his fear, but could also see that he understood what she was saying.

Johnny nodded slowly. "I wanted to make sure you were okay," he said quietly. "You told me you were taking the gun for protection. I thought something happened to you."

The man pinched the bridge of his nose with one hand, but kept the weapon aimed at them.

"I need to think. Come on. We're going for a car ride."

Chapter 69

According to the GPS, Leo and Laurie had nearly reached the location Andrew obtained when he searched for Marcy's phone. "Dad, look," Laurie cried out. "There's the minivan!"

Laurie's optimism was short-lived. As he stopped the car, she could see that something was wrong with the minivan. It looked off-kilter.

"Stay here," Leo said, getting his gun from the console. "And keep an eye out for the FBI. They're supposed to be on their way."

He approached the van in a low hunch, pulled open the driver's-side door, and then closed it, shaking his head. He was walking away when he stopped and crouched, examining something near his feet. Climbing back into the car, he reported the news. "One tire's shot out, and her cell phone was in the driver's seat. And Laurie, there's drops of blood on the ground by her car door."

"I don't think we can wait for the FBI, Dad."

"Pull up Daniel Turner's address."

Leo stopped on the road in front of Turner's house. "It's too big a risk to drive right onto his property. He's probably got cameras or motion sensors if he's as paranoid as his ex-wife said."

"So what are we going to do?"

"You wait here, and I'll find the house through the woods."

"Dad, no. You can't walk up there on your own."

They heard the sound of tires on the dirt road behind them. Laurie turned and spotted overhead lights on top of the approaching vehicle. "Look, the FBI, just in time," she said.

He checked out the rearview mirror. "That's local police," he said, rolling down the window.

The car's only occupant was probably in his mid-forties. He had dark hair and a well-groomed beard. Laurie knew that the stars sewn on his uniform's sleeves indicated that he was high in the department's leadership, but it was his nameplate that resolved any uncertainties. *C. Turner.* The passenger-side window of his vehicle was already down.

"We got a report of some gunfire out here. Can I ask what the two of you are doing by the side of the road? This area's designated 'no hunting' in case you're wondering."

Leo looked at Laurie. One glance was enough to reach an agreement. They had no choice. Charlie Turner was the only help they had right now. He was Daniel's brother, but he was also the police chief.

"I'm Leo Farley, still on the job at NYPD. If it's all right with you, Chief, I'm going to reach for my wallet to show you my ID." Chief Turner nodded, and Leo presented his badge to the chief's satisfaction. As Leo laid out the events that had brought them to this dirt road, the chief's face fell further, each piece of evidence an emotional punch to the stomach.

He suddenly put his car into gear.

"Chief," Leo said, "I'm not a crackpot. This is serious."

"I know," the chief said. "That's why you're going to wait at the police station while I call for backup."

"With all due respect, Chief, we don't have time to wait. My daughter and I will go to the house by ourselves if we have to. And if you try to stop us, the lives of a little boy and his mother could be on your hands."

"Are you carrying?" the chief asked.

Leo raised the side of his shirt to display the gun holstered at his waist.

The chief clenched his jaw and held Leo's gaze. "Fine. Follow me. There's a side road a ways up. We'll stash the cars and cut through the woods to the house. Daniel's got the main drive alarmed like Fort Knox."

After they parked, they let Chief Turner lead the way on foot, followed by Leo, and then Laurie. As they were about to enter the woods, the chief turned. His face was somber. "I was thinking about your evidence. Some of it must have come from my former sister-in-law, Roseanne."

They did not respond.

"Back then, I couldn't see the full extent of my brother's problems. After she left—for good—I realized I didn't do Daniel any favors taking his side like that. He would have been better off getting some help. Anyway, I won't ask where she is, but if you happen to talk to her, please let her know I'm sorry."

"Let's see if we can get your brother the help he needs now," Laurie said.

They followed him into the woods.

Marcy Buckley tried to keep her attention focused on the rocky and narrow dirt road leading to Daniel Turner's house, but she could not stop seeing the gun pointed at her in her periphery from the passenger seat, or Johnny's terrified expression in the rearview mirror.

She flinched as Turner reached his left hand across her and hit a garage door opener clipped to the flip-down sun visor.

As they waited in silence for the garage door to roll open, none of them saw the three people emerge from the woods just in time to spot them drive inside.

Chapter 70

Laurie could see a switch flip in Charlie Turner at the sight of Johnny and Marcy Buckley inside the white Chrysler sedan. Until that moment, she sensed that Charlie believed there would be some rational explanation for whatever misunderstanding had made his younger brother the leading suspect in the disappearance of a missing child. But once he saw the kidnapping in progress with his own two eyes, he had immediately shifted modes. He was no longer acting like a helpful family member. He was a police chief on an urgent call out, and he was speaking to Leo as a fellow law enforcement officer.

"We've got exigent circumstances to enter," Charlie whispered, even as the garage door was still moving. He used the radio handset mounted on his shoulder to call for backup. "I've got a house key. You and I can cut around back. But my brother's paranoid. He could have installed cameras around the entire perimeter of the house for all I know. If he sees us coming, we'd be putting that boy and his mother in serious jeopardy."

Laurie thought about those drops of blood that Leo had seen near Marcy's car. They were already in jeopardy. "You said you got a report of shots fired in the area. What if you knock on your brother's door, just to see if he heard anything and make sure he's okay? You could keep him occupied while the two of us enter the house from the back and find Johnny and Marcy."

He looked up at the sky, thinking through her plan. "Yeah, that might work. Once the FBI and backup arrive, I can probably convince him to come out for the arrest. And if he tries to drive away, he'd have to wait for that garage door to open. I could shoot out a tire and then run for cover." He pulled a set of keys from his pocket, slid one from the ring, and handed it to her. "There's a deck around back and a set of French doors that'll lead you to the kitchen. I'll try to get him outside to talk to me, but no guarantees."

Under cover of the woods, Laurie and Leo positioned themselves out of view of the front porch, then watched as Charlie walked toward the house. They heard a knock, followed by silence, followed by another set of knocks. "You home, Dan?" he yelled. "Got a call of some hunters shooting out here. Figured I'd stop by and say hi."

A moment later, they heard his voice again, at a lower volume. Laurie couldn't make out the words, but took it as a sign that Daniel Turner had opened his front door. Leo led the way to a wooden deck at the back of the house, his gun held at the ready.

Curtains were drawn inside the French doors that Charlie had described, so they could not see the home's interior. As Leo stepped on a mat in front of the doors, the mat suddenly gave way, and Laurie's father lurched sideways, one foot sinking beneath the decking. He grunted in pain and then bit his lower lip, fighting back a scream. She looked down to see the bottom of his calf locked in the steel jaws of a bear trap.

He tried to lift his ankle, but the metal trap was larger than the width of the deck boards that had been removed. Whether the booby trap had been intended for unwanted visitors or for Johnny if he tried to escape, it was now keeping her father from entering the house.

She reached down to see if she could figure out how to open the jaws. "Nothing's budging."

"He must have monkeyed with the release," Leo whispered. "It's the only way this makes sense as a trap."

She reached for the door, but he grabbed her hand. "Not alone."

"Dad, we don't have time. We need to find them."

He extended his right hand, offering her his gun. It had been a while since she'd gone to the range with him, but she knew how to fire this weapon if it came down to it.

"Don't worry about me, Laurie. Just go!"

Laurie slipped the key in the French door and turned it slowly, leaving the key in the lock as she stepped inside.

The French door opened into a breakfast nook off the adjacent kitchen. The nook provided a clear view of the home's dining area. Past the dining room, she saw a man standing at the open front door. A handgun was visible at the back of his waistband.

"Really, Charlie. I've got to go. I've been under the weather. Don't want to get you sick by having you in."

Daniel Turner didn't even wait for his brother to say good-bye before closing the front door and bolting it shut. Seeing a door ajar on the opposite side of the kitchen, Laurie dashed toward it and stepped inside to hide. From her vantage point of what turned out to be a large pantry, she now had a partial view of the living room, where Marcy and Johnny were huddled together on the sofa.

Turner entered the room, his gun now in his hand. "You didn't make a peep, but I better not find out you hatched some kind of plan while I was gone, or it will be the last decision you'll ever make."

Tears rolled down Johnny's face, and Marcy's eyes darted wildly between her son and the heavyset man pointing a gun in their direction. Blood was smeared across the right side of Marcy's neck, and the yellow sweater balled in her hands was streaked brick-red.

"Please don't hurt my mama," Johnny wailed. "I'll be good. I'll stay with you."

"But she's *not* your mother, Danny. I told you that. Don't you understand that yet? *I'm* your real father. *I'm* the one who was supposed to raise you, and she stole you from me."

"That's not true," Johnny yelled. "You're a liar. And you talk to yourself because you're crazy."

"You shut your mouth, little boy!"

When Johnny began to sob uncontrollably, Marcy jumped to her feet and stood defiantly in front of him, guarding him from the shots that could be fired at any second. Laurie thought she heard the sound of a door opening to her left, but she could not see far enough into the kitchen to know whether someone else had entered the house.

"He didn't mean that," Marcy said. "He's seven years old, and he's scared. Please, I am *begging* you . . . with my *life*. Do whatever you want to me, but please don't hurt him. I'm the one you're mad at. I'm the one who took your baby away from you. I had no idea, I promise."

"Because Michelle lied—to me, to you, to everyone. How many lives did she ruin? I didn't want to do what I did to her, but it was the only way I could get my son back. I had to make sure that no one would come looking for me when Danny disappeared. So we could get a fresh start . . . together."

"And you still can. I lied when I said my husband was on his way here. No one else knows about you. It was supposed to be a closed adoption, but Michelle told me your name in complete confidence. I never told another person. Do you understand? Please. Just send Johnny upstairs, and you can do what you need to do. You don't need to hurt this sweet little boy."

"Mama, no!"

Johnny tried to push his mother out of the way. They were each trying to save the other from harm. Laurie knew she couldn't wait here much longer. The situation was escalating too quickly.

She was about to crack the pantry door open farther when Charlie Turner stepped from a narrow hallway into the living room, his weapon drawn.

"Dan. You don't want to do this."

Laurie dropped to a crouch, pushed open the pantry door slowly, and got into position behind the kitchen island, where she'd have a direct shot at Daniel Turner if it came to that.

Dan. You don't want to do this.

Daniel Turner blinked his eyes three times, wondering if he was having another hallucination. When did Charlie come inside the house? Hadn't he been out on the porch?

"Is that really you?" He could hear the confusion in his own voice.

"Dan, you don't want to hurt anyone else. I know you."

"You *don't* know me. Not anymore. You don't know the things I've done."

"I helped you after that trouble with Roseanne, and I'll help you again," Charlie promised.

"This is a lot worse," Daniel said. "The two of them here. And Michelle. You don't even know about Michelle."

His head darted toward the sound of a voice from the kitchen. "Drop it!" A woman sprang upright from behind the kitchen island, pointing a gun directly at him.

Daniel had done his homework on the Buckleys and their entire family. He recognized the woman as Laurie Moran, the future sister-in-law with the TV show. Charlie apparently had not come here alone.

"We know about Michelle, too," the woman said. "It's over."

"We'll get you a good lawyer," Charlie said pleadingly. That was his brother, always trying to help him. "You're not responsible in the eyes of the law, Dan. It's the head injury. The frontal lobe damage.

You don't have control over your own actions, don't you see? The doctors will lay it all out. We'll get you help."

Charlie loved him, but Daniel knew that their relationship had changed ever since that incident with Roseanne. Charlie now treated him less like a brother and more like a child who needed to be watched over or pitied.

You don't have control over your own actions. He simply wasn't the same man he used to be. He had days when he couldn't tell the difference between fantasy and reality. And now it was clear he couldn't even control his impulses. He certainly couldn't take care of a child, but was he even a full human being anymore? What had he become?

Even though he had two guns pointed at him, Daniel could not take his eyes from Marcy Buckley. It was as if she had found a way to grow three sizes larger, trying to place herself between him and little Danny. And everything she had said about being the only one to know his identity was obviously a lie, but what a strange kind of lie it was. She had been trying to convince him to kill her and spare this boy who wasn't even hers.

He thought about the last time he ever saw Roseanne, when he found out where she was living after the divorce and broke into the house to beg her to come home. The determination in her eyes and the desperation in her voice as she pleaded with him not to hurt Bella—Marcy Buckley, right now, was just the same.

He also thought about Michelle Carpenter's expression when she realized that he was set on finding the baby she had given up. She had begged him not to go looking for him. Like Roseanne four years ago. Like Marcy Buckley now.

These were mothers willing to die for the children they loved.

She might not be related to him by blood, but this woman loved his son as much as any child could hope to be loved.

"Get up, Danny!" he ordered.

"No, no, no, no." Marcy threw herself frantically across the boy's body on the sofa. "Please, no!"

"Move!" he yelled. "Go outside. Right now."

Both Marcy and the boy froze in confusion. "I'm talking to Johnny," he said calmly, forcing himself to use the name given to his son by the Buckleys. "Stand up and go outside and wait. I promise you that your mother will be fine."

Marcy rose to her feet and pulled Johnny to his feet, giving him a tight hug. "Do what he says, Johnny. For me. You're so brave. I love you so much."

"Listen to your mom," Daniel said. "And remember one thing, Johnny. No matter what you hear, or what you learn, I wasn't always like this. Something happened that changed me, which means you'll never be like me, okay?"

Daniel could tell that the words only confused the boy, but he hoped that one day, he would understand. At least he wouldn't be scarred by the sight of what was about to happen here.

"You're going outside first, Johnny," Charlie said. "And your mom and Auntie Laurie are going to join you real soon. I promise."

His eyes full of worry, Johnny finally let go of his mother and began to walk backward slowly. Daniel felt his heart break once again as he watched his son walk out the door to begin the rest of his life.

Leo had not heard anything since Charlie had followed Laurie inside. And then just as he heard the unmistakable sound of Laurie's voice yelling "Drop it!" he finally managed to spring the trap open, freeing his leg.

He reached for the knob of Daniel Turner's back door but then stopped himself, wincing from the pain shooting through his ankle. He tried to place weight on his injured leg, but couldn't do it. He didn't have a gun, and he could barely walk. He suspected a broken bone. As desperately as he wanted to run to Laurie, he was terrified that his sudden appearance would make matters worse. He'd never forgive himself if he got Laurie killed by acting too rashly.

He was about to open the door when he heard another voice. "Help! Somebody . . . help!! Is anyone here?"

It was Johnny, and he was outside. Limping, Leo made his way to the side of the house, following the sound of Johnny's voice. Spotting Johnny in the driveway, running toward the street, he let out a loud whistle. Johnny jumped in response to the sound. When his head turned in Leo's direction, Leo waved for him to move toward the wood line.

When their paths finally met, Leo felt his eyes moisten as the boy grabbed him in the tightest hug imaginable.

"My mom." His words were frantic, his breath warm against Leo's face. "She's in there with the bad man. And Aunt Laurie, too. And another policeman."

"Shhh. We're not going to let anything happen to your mom, okay? And your daddy got here, too. Let's go find him." Laurie had shared their exact location with Andrew via her cell phone when they parked the car, and Andrew was convinced his years as a Boy Scout would help him navigate his way through the woods from there. "He's going to be so happy to see you."

Leo took Johnny's hand to lead him away from the house. Just as he spotted Andrew heading toward them, they heard the sound of a single gunshot boom across the treetops.

The last nine days had felt like years, but the nightmare ended quickly. There would be no Day Ten of their terror.

Marcy ran out the front door within seconds of the gunshot. Charlie Turner yelled at Laurie to follow her. "Go!" he ordered.

Marcy's voice sounded almost primal as she called out for her son.

"Johnny!! Where are you? Johnny! Mama's here now. It's safe to come out—I promise!"

"We're here!" Johnny's voice echoed across the treetops.

Laurie watched as Johnny and his father emerged from the woods moments later. Marcy fell to her knees on the dirt path, pulling her son tightly against her. Andrew stroked Johnny's hair, reassuring him that they were all going to be okay. Laurie felt a knot in her throat as she watched tears of joy stream down their faces. She was about to head for the back of the house to check on her father when he, too, stepped into the clearing. He was limping, but his face was overcome with relief when he made eye contact with Laurie. She nodded in his direction, reassuring him that the family was finally out of danger.

The Turner family's nightmare had a very different ending. Once he had ordered Johnny to leave the house, Daniel Turner had raised his gun toward Marcy and announced he was going to pull the trigger, giving the chief of police no choice. When the FBI arrived, they found Charlie cradling his younger brother's body, praying that he would finally have peace.

Chapter 71

Five Weeks Later

Laurie heard a knock at the door. "Come on in!"

Even though today's gathering was a small one, she'd had what felt like a constant parade of visitors. She smiled at the sight of her father behind her in the mirror.

"You look happy," she said. The limp he'd had for weeks was unnoticeable today. His injuries from Daniel Turner's bear trap had led to swelling and bruising, but no broken bones.

"Of course I do. Today's the happiest day of all."

"Yes, but I suspect it has something to do with that phone call you had to take."

"Work talk can wait," he said.

"Come on. Tell me."

"Fine, you dragged it out of me. The plan worked. Gunther admitted everything." As planned, Mason Rollins's cooperation had been enough to persuade Toby Carver to do the same. He had made a surprise visit to Gunther's prison that morning and gotten him to implicate himself in the murders of both Lou Finney and Clarissa DeSanto. "They captured the entire conversation on tape at the prison."

"I'm so happy your name got cleared, Dad."

"More important, Gunther will be in prison for the rest of his life.

The DA is going to reduce the charges against Summer because of the help she provided in the investigation."

The door opened again, and Grace and Charlotte tumbled in, champagne glasses in hand.

"Leo, what are you doing in here?" Charlotte asked.

"No boys allowed!" Grace teased.

"That only applies to the groom, not the father of the bride. My daughter and I were discussing my very important job of walking her down the aisle."

"Speaking of which, it's officially time, Laurie," Charlotte said. "You ready?"

"I've never been more ready for anything."

They had rescheduled the wedding only after Marcy and Andrew assured them that their entire family was ready. Johnny now had a basic understanding of the lives of his biological parents and how they had ended. Roseanne Robinson and Sandra Carpenter had even volunteered to meet with him when he was older so he could learn more about Michelle and Daniel before things had gone wrong for them.

Marcy and Andrew knew he'd have other questions and concerns as he grew and matured, but for the time being, he was their happy boy again.

Today, Johnny was also the ring bearer, leading his sisters, the flower girls, down the aisle to where Alex waited, with Andrew by his side. On the other side of the priest stood Timmy, ready to serve as Laurie's untraditional best man.

Also bucking tradition, the string quartet played "At Last" by Etta James for their small procession. Ramon, Grace, Jerry, and Charlotte were the only guests besides family. Grace fanned her eyes with perfectly manicured hands, trying not to cry.

As Laurie took her place at the altar, she gazed up and smiled at Alex. He looked perfect. Everything was perfect.

"You okay?" he whispered. She had never seen him so content.

She nodded. Perfect, except she knew she would never make it through the vows without shedding some tears of her own.

As she turned to make sure her father had taken his seat, she had an image of Greg sitting next to him. He was smiling. He was happy for her.

"Let's do this," she said.

At last.

Acknowledgments

It has been our joy to complete another Under Suspicion novel together. Laurie Moran and her crew provide more than enough material to fill the imaginations of two storytellers.

Once again, our biggest champion on this adventure has been Marysue Rucci, vice president and editor in chief of Simon & Schuster. Thank you, as well, to her right-hand assistant, Hana Park.

We are also grateful to the advice of Professor Barry Scheck, co-director of the Innocence Project, whose expertise regarding the use of DNA evidence in wrongful conviction claims is unrivaled. Though he generously shared his scientific knowledge with us, this book and the lawyers in it are works of fiction. We suspect the story would have unfolded quite differently had Professor Scheck been on the case.

Last, but never least, we thank you, dear readers. Words on a page do not become a story until you read them. This book is dedicated to you.

Enjoyed *Piece of My Heart?*
Discover more from the *Under Suspicion* series . . .

The Cinderella Murder

Television producer Laurie Moran is elated when the pilot for
her reality drama, *Under Suspicion*, is a success. Each episode
revisits a cold case, and the very first episode helped
to solve an infamous murder.

Now Laurie has the ideal case to feature in the next instalment of
Under Suspicion: the Cinderella Murder. When Susan Dempsey,
a beautiful and multi-talented UCLA student, was found dead,
her murder left numerous questions. Had she ever shown up for
the acting audition she was due to attend at the home of an up-
and-coming director? Why does Susan's boyfriend want to avoid
questions about their relationship? And why was Susan missing
one of her shoes when her body was discovered?

AVAILABLE NOW IN PAPERBACK AND EBOOK

SIMON &
SCHUSTER

All Dressed in White

Five years ago Amanda Pierce was excitedly preparing to marry
her college sweetheart. Then Amanda disappeared the
night of her bachelorette party.

In present-day New York City, Laurie Moran realizes a missing
bride is the perfect cold case for her *Under Suspicion* television
series to investigate. By recreating the night of the disappearance
at the wedding's Florida resort with Amanda's friends and family,
Laurie hopes to find the same success solving the cases
featured in the series' first episodes.

But Laurie and *Under Suspicion* host Alex Buckley quickly
discover everyone has their own theory about why
Amanda disappeared into thin air . . .

AVAILABLE NOW IN PAPERBACK AND EBOOK

**SIMON &
SCHUSTER**

The Sleeping Beauty Killer

Casey Carter was convicted of murdering her fiancé
fifteen years ago. But Casey claims – has always claimed – she's
innocent. And although she was charged and served out her
sentence in prison, she is still living 'under suspicion'.

Her story attracts the attention of Laurie Moran and the
Under Suspicion news team – it's Casey's last chance to finally
clear her name, and Laurie pledges to exonerate her.

Now Laurie must face an egomaniacal new co-host, a relentless
gossip columnist who seems to have all the dirt and Casey's
longstanding bad reputation to once and for all prove
Casey's innocence – that is, if she's innocent . . .

AVAILABLE NOW IN PAPERBACK AND EBOOK

**SIMON &
SCHUSTER**

Every Breath You Take

The Met Gala ball: the world's most glamorous fundraising party.
People would kill for an invitation.

Three years ago, Virginia Wakeling, a member of the Met's board of
trustees and one of the museum's most generous donors, was found
dead in the snow outside the building. Police soon discovered that
she'd been thrown from the roof during the Met Gala, but
no one has ever been arrested for her murder.

Although suspicion has always hovered around Virginia's much
younger boyfriend, there are a bevy of suspects. Laurie Moran
decides to investigate Virginia's death for her television show, *Under
Suspicion*. But the more she pries into Virginia's murder, the
closer Laurie comes to discovering just how dangerous an
invitation to the Met Gala can be . . .

AVAILABLE NOW IN PAPERBACK AND EBOOK

**SIMON &
SCHUSTER**

You Don't Own Me

Martin and Kendra Bell have the perfect life. But cracks have started to appear on the surface of their marriage. Kendra suspects that Martin isn't the kind and generous man she fell in love with. And Martin believes that Kendra is hiding a drinking habit – what else could explain her rapid personality change?

And then someone guns Martin down in front of his own house. Despite Kendra's rock-solid alibi, suspicion falls on her shoulders. Five years later, Martin's killer remains at large, and Kendra remains a suspect.

Now, with Martin's parents threatening to take her children from her, Kendra will have to get help from the only people who believe she's innocent: Laurie and the *Under Suspicion* team. And what they uncover will change everything.

AVAILABLE NOW IN PAPERBACK AND EBOOK

SIMON &
SCHUSTER